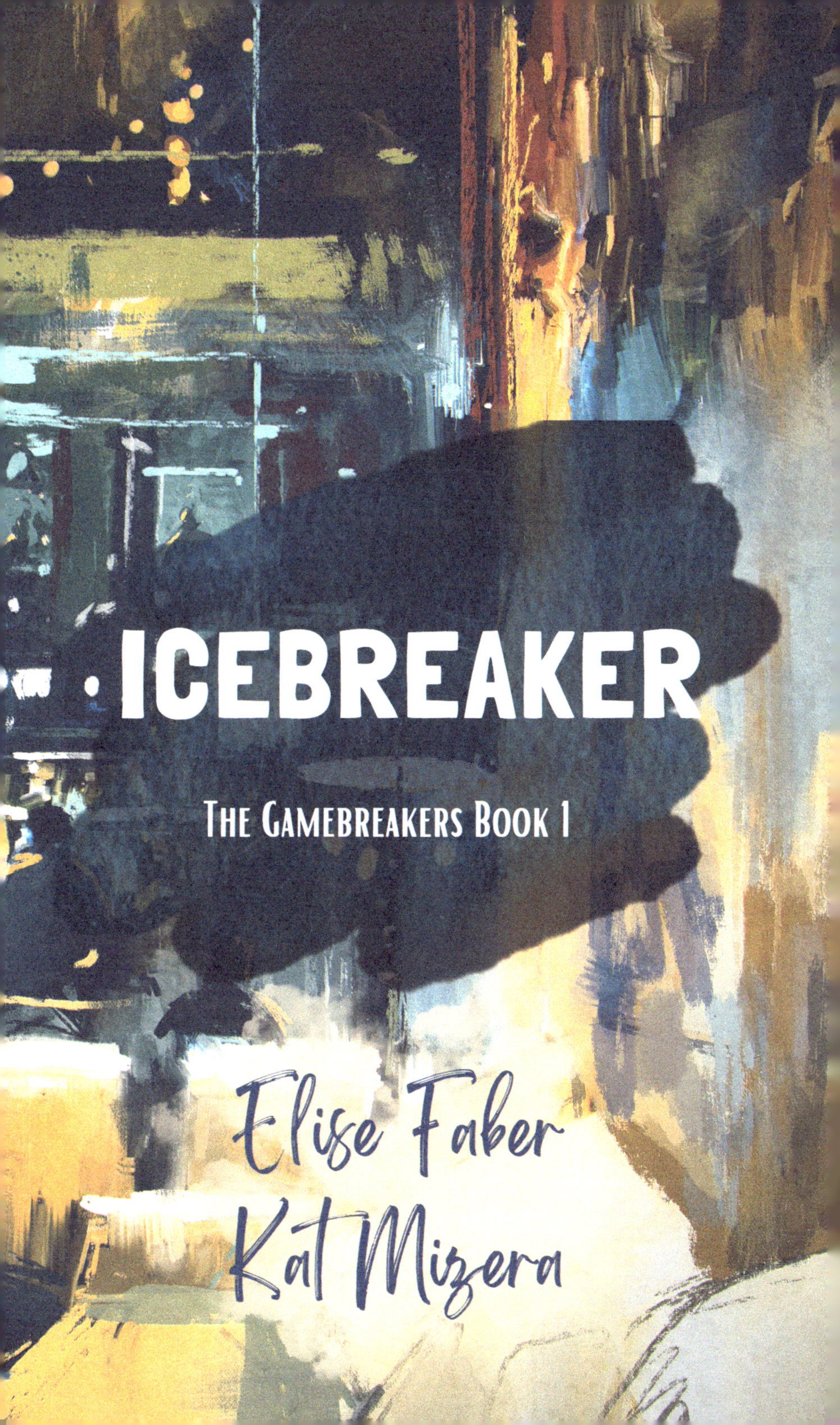
ICEBREAKER
The Gamebreakers Book 1
Elise Faber
Kat Mizera

GAMEBREAKERS

CHAPTER ONE

Aspen

"You missed a spot."

I grind my teeth together at the sound of my supervisor's voice, biting back the sharp response I want to allow out.

Boss.

She's my *boss*.

Exhaling, I search the area for the spot I've supposedly missed and try to ignore the fact that my hands are cramping and the smell of disinfectant is burning my nose.

Oh, and my back aches.

And my knees are throbbing from having spent the last hours scrubbing the cupholders and plastic undersides of the rows and rows of chairs that fill this section of the arena.

If I've learned anything about people doing this job—

It's that they're disgusting.

Sticky fingerprints and spilled beer. Crunched up popcorn and dried nacho cheese. Sprinkles of salt from pretzels and half-chewed gum stuck to the bottom sides of these seats I'm cleaning.

Trash.

Just like the woman standing over me.

Cheryl—manager of the environmental services company I work for—smirks.

Because this is her favorite game.

Playing whack-a-mole with invisible specks of dirt and grime.

"Tut-tut," she tsks when I've finished another three-sixty sweep, wiping down the seat bottoms and cupholders and even the concrete floor in my vicinity.

I grind my teeth together.

This job isn't *all* bad.

The pay is shit and the hours are worse.

But it's safe and quiet and if I just ignore the fact that Cheryl is a freaking troll then it might be pretty close to perfect.

Minus the half-chewed gum.

Digging deep for patience, I give an even closer inspection to the area I've been cleaning.

There's a single kernel of unpopped popcorn trapped way back beneath a nearby seat and I use my brush to unstick it, snag it with my gloved hands, tuck it into the plastic trash bag I've been schlepping around my section of the arena.

"Tut-tut."

Christ.

I keep looking, unhook my towel and reach toward one of the seats in the most fucked-up version of Hot and Cold I've ever come across before.

Unfortunately, this isn't the first time I've played it.

Cheryl is the fucking worst.

"Tut."

I change directions.

"Tut!"

Again.

"Tut-tut!"

If I spray bleach in her eyes, the authorities will know that it's an accident, right?

Then again, the authorities investigating an unfortunate bleach accident will bring attention.

And if there's anything I'm desperate to avoid, it's attention from the authorities.

One final stretch, and I see it.

A single sticky fingerprint that I've missed, almost impossible to see unless I'm right on top of it—or over it, I suppose, considering where Cheryl's standing.

I swipe with my cloth, disappear that fingerprint like I'm a goddamned magician, and then I turn to finish—

"Tut!"

Fuck. My. Life.

"I don't see anything else," I say, careful to ensure that each of my words is evenly spoken, that not a single thread of the derision I have for this woman slides into my tone. "Can you show me?"

Silence.

Long enough that I tune into the rest of the sounds in the largely empty arena—the rustle of the trash bag belonging to Lonnie, who works the next section over, the soft humming that Desiree makes as she sweeps down a long flight of concrete stairs, the thud of a door closing, the murmured conversation from somewhere nearby.

And Cheryl's heavy sigh.

"Start over." A sniff. "None of these are nearly up to standard."

My mouth opens, my angry retort nearly dancing right off the tip of my tongue—

I clamp my teeth together so fiercely that pain shoots through my jaw.

But I manage to catch the reply, to stop the words, to bite back my own beleaguered sigh.

And instead, I nod.

I grab my supplies and make the long trek to the top of my section.

And then…

I start over.

———

MY BODY IS A RAGING collection of aches and pains when I finally dump my trash into the receptacle and go gather my stuff from my locker.

Exhaustion pulls at my mind, making the edges fuzzy, and I know that I'll sleep well tonight—even if my neighbors in the apartment next-door decide to have their usual screamfest.

Hoodie on—despite being sweaty—because I'll regret not having it the moment I step out the door, the cool bite of the predawn air hitting harder than the chilled crispness that creeps off the ice from the rink that the Southern California Vipers call their home.

The arena—fondly referred to as the Snake Pit—will be busy tonight, the sold-out game against one of the team's biggest rivals, the L.A. Phantoms.

A fact that means I'm very happy to not be on cleanup duty tomorrow.

The stands will be packed. The mess they leave behind overwhelming.

Thankfully, that won't be my problem.

Backpack on my shoulders.

Beanie pulled low over my forehead.

Glasses pushed up my nose.

Keys out and each of the tiny metal weapons tucked between my fingers, ready to use as needed.

Because I'm practically alone in the arena.

The one security guard, Josh, who would offer to walk me to my car, is out sick.

And the others?

Well, fuck if I know.

Probably finding a way to get laid in an empty office.

Shaking my head, I close my locker, hit the hallway, and it's not that much later that I'm pushing through the exterior door, that bite of cool air sinking right through my layers to nibble at my skin.

I shiver, turn toward my car—

And promptly lift my key-filled hand in the direction of the man hurrying up to me. "Back off!" I snap, hopefully wielding them like an Amazonian goddess (though, more likely I look like a rabid raccoon after someone's trash, especially since I spent the last hours sweating through my makeup as I scrubbed and swept).

"Easy there, sweetheart," the man says silkily.

Here's the thing.

I don't trust silken words. I don't trust the men allowing them to slide off their tongue like they expect me to melt into a puddle of goo.

And I sure as shit don't trust a man dressed all in black, loose sweatpants and a hoodie that hides most of the major features of his body, who's snuck up on me, who's approached when I told him to back off, and who's trying to smolder at me like he expects me to go back with him to his car so he can chop me up into tiny bits.

He steps closer.

I move back, wishing that one of those sleeping security guards might wake up…oh right about freaking *now*.

The door had been swinging shut behind me and it collides with my side, sending pain radiating through my already aching body.

Ignoring that, I snag the metal panel, gripping it tightly, inching back toward the arena.

I'll slam it shut and—

The man comes even closer. "Baby girl, I just—"

I lift my hand with the keys, bare my teeth, going for rabid raccoon now without compunction. "I don't have the energy to pretend to like you today, so go away and bother someone else."

He stills, leans back, brows lifting in surprise.

Like he's shocked I'm not just giving in.

I brace, inching further inside, ready for the rage to come out.

It *always* comes out.

Instead, he lifts both hands, palms out, as though in surrender.

I don't buy it, not even for a second.

Why? Circle back to the rage always coming out, even if at first it seems like it'll be tempered with a smile.

"Look, honey—" he begins.

"I'm not your sweetheart or honey or baby." I shuffle in farther, bringing the door with me.

"Baby girl," he says.

I frown. "Seriously?"

"You're not my *baby girl*," he says by way of explanation. "And I'm not going to hurt you—"

It's all I can do not to sniff in derision.

Because I've heard that before.

As though he seems to pluck that thought from my mind, he freezes again, hands still up, palms still out, expression evening out, maybe softening the tiniest bit.

Ugh. Can this day get any worse?

I narrow my eyes. "If you actually mean that," I say icily, "then just go."

"I can't."

Irritation blooms in my middle. "Why?"

"Because I need to get inside."

Security? Anyone from fucking security want to do their job?

"No," I snap, stepping fully inside, closing the door behind me.

Or trying to, anyway.

He catches it with a big, broad hand, stops it from closing with barely an inch to spare. "I need to get inside."

"I don't care—"

"I don't have my badge, and—"

I yank at the door.

He holds it fast. "Wait!"

I jab at his hand with my keys. "Back. Off!"

"Ow! Fuck!"

A blip of guilt, but I push it aside.

Especially, when he shoves his foot into the opening and wrenches the door wide.

I snarl at him and lift my key-loaded hand again.

Fuck jabbing. I'll escalate to stabbing.

Which will risk bringing attention, but I can't really worry about that right now, can I?

"Wait," he says as he keeps the door open, not trying to shove past me. "Please. Jesus, just take a breath. I work here—"

I snort.

He eyes me but continues, "I work here and forgot my badge. I just need to get inside and—"

I snort again.

His eyes, deep pools of emerald, flare with annoyance, but he keeps talking. "My name is Banks Christianson. I'm the captain for the Vipers, as you probably know, and I have a session this morning—"

This man is a hockey player?

He's thin, not slender, but definitely not the huge six-feet-plus bulk of what I'd expect from a hockey player.

And he's not all *that* tall—barely six inches above my five and a half feet.

Plus, I can't help noticing as he smiles at me that he has all his teeth.

And yeah, he's pretty, but like *that's* going to convince me he's telling the truth.

"—with my skating coach and I need to get ready—"

My bullshit meter is blaring. "Yeah, right."

"Okay," he mutters, that smile dropping away. "What's going to convince you to let me inside?"

"Nothing," I say, lifting my chin. "Now go away before I call security."

And hope they come.

His eyes light up. "Yes," he says. "Call security."

I frown.

"Or better yet"—he drops one hand toward his pocket and I snarl at him, full rabid raccoon again—"*I* will." Those green eyes on mine again, mouth tipping up at the edges. "Easy, trouble. I'm just grabbing this." He pulls out his phone.

I blink, a sinking sensation beginning to bloom in my belly.

This man might be telling the truth.

Or he's a bigger bullshitter than I am.

He jabs at his cell's screen, and I watch, the worry in my stomach growing.

But that settles after a moment when he pulls his phone from his ear and scowls at the screen.

"What?" I can't help but ask.

He sighs. "No answer."

That tracks.

Still…he could be lying.

His gaze comes back to mine. "You're not going to let me in, are you?"

There's something in his words that has that pesky guilt coming back, but I ignore it, keep my chin lifted. "No," I say. "Now, go away."

His shoulders slump, and he starts to retreat.

Relief pours through me—

"Wait!" he suddenly exclaims, making me jump, the door

halfway closed. He jabs at his screen again then shows it to me, and I see that he's pulled up Instagram.

Pulled up the team's Instagram account—with the millions of followers and blue check mark and…

The picture of *him* as the top post.

Wearing a jersey with a C emblazoned on his chest.

I flick my eyes from the photograph up to his face.

That worry becomes an inferno eating at my insides.

Because it *is* Banks Christianson standing in front of me.

Fuck.

I'm so getting fired.

Then I do the only thing I can.

I step aside and finally let the captain of the Vipers walk into the arena.

CHAPTER TWO

Banks

THE SMELL of cigar smoke and whisky hits my nostrils the moment I step inside The Sapphire Room. I see my buddy Atlas hanging at the bar talking to one of the bartenders, and I head in that direction. The bass reverberating through the speakers makes everything shake, and Atlas grins as I clap him on the shoulder.

"Hey, man." He reaches out for a one-armed hug.

"Place is hoppin'," I note.

"It's Colt's birthday." His eyes meet mine. "This is what he would've wanted."

"Yup." I look to the bartender. "Gamebreaker, please. And keep them coming." It's the club's—and our—signature drink.

Bourbon, Amaretto, honey, a cherry or two, and a twist of orange with a sprig of rosemary.

A twist on a traditional Old Fashioned.

Because Colt had come up with it in college.

"Bro, I need some food first," Atlas says, shaking his head.

"Oh, believe me. There will be food." I've planned an extravagant dinner for this celebration of our dead buddy's birthday. We've done it every year since his passing and this year I'm in charge of the meal.

Filet mignon, lobster, caviar, twice baked potatoes, roasted asparagus, and a baked Alaska that would hopefully set the place on fire.

Figuratively, of course.

We—Atlas, our buddies Royal and Dash, and me—own The Sapphire Room.

It's a joint business venture, a private gentleman's club where we can come to relax, unwind, and let loose once in a while without the prying eyes that often invade our privacy. We aren't all in town at the same time very often, but we always make it work on Colt's birthday.

Four years of celebrating without him seems like both an eternity and the blink of an eye.

Has it really been that long since he was killed in action?

I push the morbid thoughts away.

We agreed early on that we wouldn't mourn or mope on his birthday.

Instead, we celebrate the way he would have wanted: wild, with reckless abandon, and

fun.

So that's what we do.

I take a sip of my drink and hold it out to Atlas. "Cheers."

He clinks his glass of water against mine. "Cheers."

"Where the fuck are Royal and Dash?"

He makes a face. "Dash is either picking him up and dragging him out of the house or arguing with him about why he doesn't want to come."

"Goddammit." My thoughts go dark again.

First we lost Colt.

Then Royal was in a car accident last year that cost him the use of his right hand. A rock and roll guitar legend who can no longer play.

It's devastated him.

And there isn't a damn thing we can do to make it better.

"There they are." Atlas motions with his head and I raise my glass in their direction.

"About fucking time!" I yell out.

Hudson—or Dash as we've called him since our college hockey days, because he was as fast on the ice as his last name dictates—laughs while Royal flips me the bird. Dash in his typical jeans and tee while Royal's wearing a suit tailored to perfection tonight, and if you don't look for the lifeless hand on the right side, you'd never know anything is amiss.

"Where are the strippers?" Dash demands, shaking my hand and then pulling me in for a hug.

"It's early, man," Atlas says. "Chill. Dinner first. Then the ladies."

"It's the only reason I came," Royal mutters.

I give him a sour look. "Thanks, man. Good to know our friendship means something to you."

He doesn't respond, his gaze traveling to a woman walking across the room.

She's average height, with long dark hair and a smokin' hot body.

There's something familiar about her but I don't know who the hell she is or why she's going behind the bar.

I turn to Atlas, who's more involved with the day-to-day management of the club. He's become a billionaire in the eight years since we've graduated from college, so we tend to let him run things. "Who's that?"

"New bartender. Her name's Aspen."

"Interesting." I watch the sway of her ass as she comes around the outside of the bar and starts wiping it down. Her movements are easy, practiced, as if cleaning is second nature.

I'm enjoying watching her and the way her soft curves look in the standard uniform all female employees wear. Black tuxedo-style vest, a short black skirt, and low black heels.

An elbow to my ribs brings me out of my lust-addled haze.

"Easy, champ." Dash follows my gaze. "She works for us."

"I won't fire her if she sucks in bed," I say with a chuckle.

Atlas narrows his gaze at me. "Don't fuck with the help, man. We don't give most of them enough hours to keep them loyal, so we have a lot of turnover. I'd like to not have to hire an entire new crew every couple of months. The paperwork alone is a pain in the ass."

"Isn't that Leo's job?" Royal asks, referring to the club's manager.

"He doesn't do anything without running it past me," Atlas responds. "And this place isn't some tax write-off. It's personal. I keep my finger on the pulse and—"

"Can we eat?" Royal interrupts. "I'm fucking hungry."

"More like *hangry*," Dash mutters.

"The caterer just got here," I say. "Let's go sit down."

We wander over to the dining area and settle at a table in the back.

It's our usual place.

No one sits here the rest of the year, no matter how busy it gets.

A little placard on the table reads "Reserved for Colton Blackwood and company."

Twenty-four-seven / three-sixty-five.

There's *always* a table reserved for Colt.

The caterers I hired come out and start serving the meal, which puts everyone in a better mood. Even Royal is a tiny bit less grumpy, despite me arranging to have all of our steaks pre-cut. It irks him to have to ask for help, so I do my best to take that out of the equation whenever possible. Yeah, he needs to figure it out since this is his life now, but we can afford the best of everything, so why not eliminate one tiny stressor?

An unnatural silence settles around us as we eat.

Normally, we're loud and boisterous on Colt's birthday, but there's something different tonight. A somberness that isn't like us. I don't know how to fix it, so I let my gaze drift back to the bar.

Aspen is laughing as she talks to a customer, throwing back her head and letting that glorious hair fan out like a halo around her shoulders.

Damn, she's hot.

I can picture that hair wrapped in my fist as I fuck her, my mouth feasting on hers and that perfect body beneath me.

"You need to get off the Aspen train," Atlas says, as if he knows exactly what I'm thinking.

"Fuck off. She's into me." I say the words even though I have no way of knowing that.

"She's not," Atlas says. "I can see it in her body language."

"A hundred bucks says she shoots you down." Royal pulls a bill out of his wallet and puts it on the table.

"I'm in." Dash digs some cash out of his wallet and puts it with Royal's.

"Well, I'm not missing out on seeing you get shot down." Atlas adds to the pile.

"Fuckers." I get out a final hundred-dollar bill and put it with theirs.

"If you sleep with her, money's yours," Dash says.

"If she sends your sorry ass packing," Atlas says. "And she will—you owe each of us a hundred bucks."

I roll my eyes.

Money's not an issue.

It's the principle of the thing.

"Can I eat my dinner first?" I pop a bite of steak into my mouth.

"She's so gonna shoot you down," Royal says, laughing.

It's good to hear him laugh, even if it's at my expense.

It so rarely happens since the accident.

The mood lightens a bit and talk switches to the Vipers' current season. They come to games whenever they're in town and I know they follow my career, which is both nice and sometimes annoying. We played college hockey together back at Massachusetts Southern University, which was where we met, so they know the game well enough to give me shit about it when we suck. Especially when I suck.

"Last game was a shit show," Dash says. "And you weren't getting much ice time. What's up with that?"

Great.

Last thing I need is to talk about my career.

Not tonight.

"I'm getting a drink," I say, getting up and heading for the bar even though we have a waitress taking care of us.

Aspen looks up with a friendly smile as I approach. "What can I get you?" she asks.

"Gamebreaker, please."

"Coming right up." She pulls out a tumbler and pauses to stare at something on the counter. I look down and see a small neon pink Post-it note with writing on it.

"Are those the ingredients?" I ask, leaning on the bar curiously.

"It's my first night here," she acknowledges. "I memorized how to make it but haven't actually made one for a customer yet."

"I'm happy to pop your Gamebreaker cherry," I tell her.

She nods, focusing on the drink as if I'm not even here.

She's going to be a tough cookie to crack.

"A little heavier on the amaretto," I say. "We want it strong but flavorful."

"Sure thing." She adds a little more and reaches for the bottle of house bourbon.

"Use house bourbon for regular customers," I tell her, "but I prefer the Blanton's. Gold Edition. It's on the top shelf."

She eyes me. "That's a premium whisky and requires an upcharge. Is that okay?"

I smile. She doesn't realize I'm one of the owners. "Believe me, sweetheart. I can afford it. Just put it on my tab."

She frowns but obligingly climbs up on the stool provided for when the bartenders need to get something from the top shelves, which is where we keep the good stuff.

She has long, toned legs and a curvy little ass I wouldn't mind taking a bite of.

There's something familiar about her too, as if we've met before.

But I would have remembered her.

She's just my type, with dark hair, big, dark eyes, and round, perky tits.

Between her ass and her boobs, I can already picture her naked, on her knees, ready to suck my—

"Single or double shot?" she asks, startling me out of my reverie.

"Double."

What the hell.

The drunker I get, the less I'll miss Colt.

Or worry about the fact that I haven't scored a goal yet this season.

"Here you go." Aspen puts the drink in front of me and I give her a slow, lazy grin, along with an obvious once over.

"Thanks." I put a twenty on the bar. "That's for you."

"Thank you." She drops it in the tip jar.

"Where did you bartend before this?" I ask, taking a tentative sip.

Damn. It's perfect.

"Pinelli's."

That's a well-known national chain of Italian restaurants.

"Why'd you leave?"

A look of annoyance flashes across her face but it disappears quickly, replaced by a polite mask of nothingness. "Long story."

She picks up a rag and wipes down the area where she made my drink.

"I have time."

"But I have other customers." She moves away, talking to a couple of guys who'd just come in.

Why does she seem familiar?

"You need anything else?" she asks me as she makes drinks for the two guys she was talking to.

"Your phone number?" I suggest.

She almost rolls her eyes.

I can practically see the effort it costs her not to do it and I bite back a laugh.

She's something.

"This is my job," she says in a polite tone. "I'm here to work, not find dates."

"Fair enough." The smile I flash gets me laid regularly. "But we don't have to *date*."

I let the insinuation hang in the air.

This time she doesn't hold back, shaking her head as her eyes lift heavenward. "Thanks but no thanks."

"You'll change your mind," I say confidently. "Girls like me."

"Maybe, but I'm a woman, and I'm busy, so I don't have the energy to pretend to like you." With that, she flounces off toward the other end of the bar, making it more than obvious she's turned me down.

And even from here, I can hear my friends roaring with laughter.

CHAPTER THREE

Aspen

IGNORING the slickly put together male whom I turned down isn't easy.

Especially when I can feel his gaze fixed on me from across the room as I make up my next round of drinks—some beers, a glass of wine, and several Gamebreakers, which is The Sapphire Room's signature drink. It's based on an Old Fashioned but has a dash of honey and Amaretto to go along with the usual flavors, and is topped with cherries, an orange peel, and a sprig of rosemary. It's insanely popular—I've made at least a dozen since tall, blond, and not-easily-dissuaded popped my Gamebreaker cherry then finally got the hint and left my bar—and the club is hopping, packed almost wall-to-wall, so I've been working nonstop.

To round out the tray for the waitress running tables, I open three bottles of beer and set them next to the other cocktails I've already mixed up—these ones not requiring me to look at my cheat sheet taped to the bar because they're the standard drinks every bar has.

Rum and Coke. Three cosmopolitans. One gin and tonic.

And a martini—dry—because some asshole wants to be James Bond.

"It's ready—" I start to say.

Then grind my teeth together.

Because suited and pretty with the overarching confidence and the gorgeous body (yeah, I may not be interested, but I'm also not blind) is back.

I think it's the glasses.

He's giving me Clark Kent vibes—I just want to undo those buttons and reveal the Lycra bodysuit beneath.

It'd do incredible things for his ass, I'm sure.

I glare at him. "Excuse me," I snap, looking beyond him for Marissa, who's waiting on the tray.

"You're excused,"

Annoyance blooms in the pit of my stomach, burns through my veins. "Move," I grit out, planting a hand in his chest and shoving him away from the side of the bar, from where he's blocking the flip top section that keeps the cretins out of my space.

Something that doesn't work for this asshole, apparently.

Marissa, thankfully, comes over then, snagging the tray and lifting it with ease as she expertly navigates through the writhing crowd.

Sighing, I turn back to the man in front of me. "Yes?"

His brow arches up, but he doesn't comment on my snarky tone, just slaps a hundred on the bar.

"What's that for?"

"Four Gamebreakers and your tip."

I don't miss that his words are slightly slurred, but I don't say anything, just nod and get to work.

Glasses on the bartop. Top-shelf whisky and the shot of amaretto. Honey. Twist of orange. Couple of cherries. Rosemary sprig.

Eventually, though, my tongue can't help but loosen. "That's too much for a tip," I say, putting his change in front of him, minus my earned twenty percent, which I hold up for him to see before I slip into the shared tip jar.

I'm not the only one busting my ass.

The rest of the crew needs their share too.

His eyes hit mine, holding for a second.

But then he picks up the change I'd set on the bar and puts that in the jar as well.

Nice.

And yeah, I'm thinking that begrudgingly.

I shrug, start to turn to take my next order.

"You're beautiful."

Christ.

I take that back.

"You should have quit while you were ahead," I mutter, ignoring him as I pick up a new ticket and study the order, committing it to memory before I get going on the first drink, scooping up some ice and filling my shaker with the ingredients for a lemon drop.

His brows flick up. "How so?"

"You were almost nice there for a second," I say, squeezing a lemon into the shaker, the aromatic scent of citrus hitting my nose.

I inhale deeply, allowing it to overtake the hundreds of other scents in the air.

My favorite fragrance in all the world.

Nothing is as clean, as invigorating as the scent of a freshly squeezed lemon.

It reminds me of cooking with my grandma, how she'd have me rub a quarter of the fruit over my hands to neutralize the odor of onions and garlic we often used copious amounts of, to make sure I was clean and presentable for—

"I'm always nice, baby."

Blinking away the past—that's not my life anymore—I cap the shaker, lift it over my shoulder, and roll my eyes. "Sure you are."

He leans an elbow on the bar, moves in close enough for me to see the specks of gray in his emerald eyes. Pretty, pretty eyes. Hair so smoothly styled that I'm almost desperate to muss up the strands. The top button of his crisp, white shirt undone, calling for my lips, for my tongue, for my fingers to get busy and undo the rest.

Get a grip, Aspen.

The thought is sharp, a mental slap, but I'm grateful for it.

Because it snaps me out of my idiocy.

"Don't be like that, baby—"

I take a half step back—half because there's not a lot of room behind the bar and because it's busy as shit with my coworkers moving back and forth in the narrow space—and lift the shaker, sending the ice and liquid rattling around inside it.

Cutting off his words.

I expect irritation to creep into the lines of his face.

Instead, he just stays in place, arm on the counter, body a picture of lazy and carefree, his lips curving upward at the edges.

Fuck, he's got a great smile.

But I accompany that thought with another mental rebuke, realizing that I've shaken the drink for long enough.

I pour, set the filled glass on the counter, get working on the next.

"Why don't you think I'm nice?"

My brows shoot up and I jerk my head toward the trio of men eating and drinking at their table in the back. "Don't you have friends to get back to?"

One shoulder lifts and falls lazily. "I'd rather talk to you."

"Rather win the bet, you mean," I mutter, adding vodka and ice and cranberry juice.

Confusion on that pretty face.

I elaborate. "I didn't miss your friends splitting those hundreds on the table," I tell him. Nor their laughter as he'd returned to their reserved table, drinks in hand, that had filled the bar. Those warm rumbles of masculinity had drifted through the air, stroked phantom fingers over my skin.

I'm not interested in men—I've been burned enough times that my break from the opposite sex is looking permanent—but even *I* can't deny the quad is as intoxicating as those Gamebreakers I've been whipping up all night. Of course, they're not nearly as captivating as this man in front of me, and I haven't even heard him laugh, though I bet that it would make him even hotter.

He's just…

Fucking hot.

Ugh.

Fucking *trouble.*

Especially when he shrugs in that lazy, loose-limbed way, and gives me a million-dollar smile. "There's always double or nothing."

"See?" I snap. "Not nice."

"But *not nice* can be oh so good."

I snort, shake the drink briskly then pour it out the cosmo, before checking the ticket for the next part of the order. "What's the bet this time?" I ask.

"A smile."

I scowl, not missing the burst of laughter that draws from the corner. Assholes, all of them. Even if they are hot. "Are you *trying* to lose even more money?"

Another shrug. "I can afford it."

"And what else?"

"What's that, baby?"

I dump a little too much gin into the glass then decide, fuck it, someone's about to have a great night, as I add the egg white and vermouth, raspberry syrup, and lemon juice, barely noticing the zing of freshness in the air this time.

Because I'm too annoyed with tall, blond, and pesky.

"What else is involved in the bet?" I grind out. Because I know he didn't come back over here for just a smile.

His mouth quirks. "Just one curve of those pretty lips." A beat. "*And* your phone number."

My scowl deepens, the laughter grows, and I clamp on the tin on the shaker, start going to town on mixing the contents of the clover club. It'll be half foam by the time I'm done, but better that than tossing the concoction at this asshole.

I pop the tin off, add ice, start shaking again to finish off the drink.

And all the while, I'm holding tight to my temper.

I need this job.

Men are assholes.

It's not like I don't know that.

By the time I'm done shaking, he's still there, still cocky and smirking and hot as shit, but I don't give him the satisfaction of acknowledging him as I finish the order, as I move a few feet away and whip up some other drinks.

He's watching me the whole time.

Ugh.

And then I run out of things to do.

Something he seems to sense because he closes the distance between us.

"Fucking. *Men*," I mutter, slamming the bottle of booze I'm holding down onto the counter—thankfully not breaking it— and glaring up at him. I arrange my features into my ugliest smile, hoping it'll deter him.

Then I toss my towel on the bar top, meet the eyes of Johnny, the bartender working next to me. "I'm taking my break."

He nods.

I narrow my eyes at tall, blond, and really freaking annoying.

"My number is 555-Fuck-Right-Off."

CHAPTER FOUR

Banks

"REMEMBER that time Colt went into the locker room with that puck bunny and we stole his clothes?" Atlas asks.

The memory makes us laugh.

"Coach was so pissed," I add. "He had to do laps for a week."

"He got us back, though." Dash shakes his head fondly.

"I don't know what the hell he put in our water bottles, but I never shit so much in my life," I groan, shaking my head. "Fuck, my ass was sore."

"Asshole," Royal mutters.

We all chuckle, and then momentarily get somber.

Remembering.

Wishing things had turned out differently.

"To Colt." Dash lifts his glass.

"Happy thirtieth birthday, man." Royal says, clinking his glass to Dash's.

"I hope there's a party in the afterlife," I say, adding my glass to the mix.

"You think you're allowed to party in heaven?" Atlas asks.

"You think they *let* Colt into heaven?" I counter with a grin.

"He didn't believe in all that," Royal says, "but they probably let him in anyway, cause he was the life of the party."

"And the best brother ever. That has to count for something."

"He'd look badass in wings, right?" I ask.

The others give me a look and then we all laugh.

"I fucking miss him," I say, dropping my head for a moment.

Every once in a while, the grief hits hard.

Right in the gut.

And I have to breathe through it.

It's been almost four years, and it still hurts like it was yesterday. I can still picture his face, hear his laughter, feel the sting of one his shoulder punches. He had a hell of a right hook. My jaw still remembers the time he nailed me after I accused him of hitting on my then girlfriend.

"You fucking think I'd do that?" he'd demanded. *"To you? Fuck off with that bullshit."*

Then he'd clocked me.

And I hadn't fought back.

Because he was right.

He wouldn't.

He was a stand-up guy and the five of us were brothers.

Still are.

Even now that he's gone.

"You just left us," Royal says, meeting my gaze as I look up. "Don't do that. Don't go where you just went. Not tonight."

"I was thinking about the night I accused him of fooling around with Lisa."

"Your jaw was sore for a week," Atlas says with a grin. "And you deserved it."

"I thought I was in love." I shudder, remembering the

petite blond I was so crazy about. Until I caught her in the locker room going down on our college team's goalie.

Fucking goalies, man.

"Love is overrated," Royal mutters.

He's the only one of us who's been married, and it was an ugly divorce.

Personally, I'm not anti-relationship—I'm just busy.

Playing pro hockey keeps me on a rigid schedule for eight or nine months of the year. Training, practices, games, and road trips make up ninety percent of my life from mid-September when training camp starts until at least mid-April, which is the end of the regular season. Some years the season goes until June, although that doesn't happen often.

"Guys, my shift is almost over so they're letting me go," Marissa, our waitress, says. "Do you need anything from the kitchen or bar before I head out?"

Atlas slips some bills in her hand—C-notes, if I know him —and whispers something I can't hear, but she smiles, nods, and heads toward the back.

The strippers I hired are supposed to be arriving at one a.m. and it's just after twelve-thirty now.

The Sapphire Room isn't a strip club, but we own the place and can do whatever the fuck we want. Still, it's a lucrative business so we try to keep our once-a-year shenanigans as respectable as possible. The older crowd is mostly gone, leaving the millennials and a handful of guys in their early twenties watching the replay of a game on the TVs over the bar.

The pool tables are empty now, which is good, because that's where the girls are going to dance. At least, that was what I told the person I'd called when I'd scheduled them.

"When are the girls getting here?" Royal asks, reading my mind.

"Soon," I reply.

I glance over at the bar to where Aspen is wiping down the mess a couple of guys made.

She won't like the strippers.

I know that instinctively.

I can just see her pretty face tight with annoyance, mentally chastising us for being misogynistic assholes, even though she won't dare say it aloud—or hell, maybe she will with the verbal lashing she's given me all night.

Part of me thinks it's funny, but another part is suddenly tired of the game.

Tired of the façade that everything is great in my life.

It is but it isn't.

Losing Colt hurt in ways I can't explain, impacting us all differently.

Royal got married and let her fuck him over financially.

Atlas threw himself into his work, not taking time for much of anything else. He's an even bigger workaholic than I am.

And Dash…well, Dash has a hero complex. He runs an incredibly successful security and bodyguard company, protecting the wealthy from threats of all kinds, but he puts himself in harm's way every fucking day and it kind of terrifies me.

He's strong, capable and well-trained, but shit happens.

We know that firsthand.

I don't know what I'll do if something happens to another one of us.

First, Colt.

Then Royal's accident.

It feels like the rest of us are ticking time bombs.

Jesus, am I morbid or what?

I'm about to get up and go back to the bar. Bantering with Aspen is better than the bullshit going on in my head right now.

But the strippers have just walked in and everyone has noticed.

Especially Aspen.

Her eyes narrow, and for some reason, she looks right at me. The accusation in her eyes is impossible to miss and I can't explain why I'm suddenly uncomfortable. I don't know her, not really, and I sure as fuck don't owe her anything, least of all an explanation.

Yet somehow, I feel like I should say or do something.

Anything to get that look of disgust off her face.

What the fuck is happening to me?

I shake it off and flash a smile at the strippers who are talking to Leo, as he shows them where they can change and lock up their stuff.

We are many things, but stupid isn't one of them. Even in a situation like this, where things will inevitably get wild, the girls—and their belongings—will be safe. We pride ourselves on that, both at the club and in life.

"Now *this* is a party." Royal sits up and for the first time all night, there's a gleam of excitement in his eyes. It's nice to see, even though I know it's going to be short-lived. He'll take one of these ladies home tonight and will forget her as soon as he wakes up. But at least he's living, because for a while I thought he might not make it. Not from the injuries, but mentally. Not being able to play guitar nearly destroyed him.

A glutton for punishment, I amble over to the bar to get another round—we'll need them for what's coming—but Aspen has her back to me.

"Hey, there," I say in a casual voice.

"More Gamebreakers?" she asks, her back still turned.

"Yes, please. Four. Doubles."

She whirls. "You know that alcohol and naked women don't mix well, right?"

The censure in her voice is unmistakable.

For a moment, I'm taken aback, but I suddenly understand that she's worried about the girls. That we'll do something inappropriate. Or worse.

And that pisses me off.

"Listen," I say in an even tone. "You can think whatever you like about me—about us—but that shit you just insinuated? Just fucking no. Stop it right there. Have I touched you tonight?"

She blinks.

"Answer me," I continue. "Yes, I've hit on you all night, but you're a bartender. If you tell me I'm the first guy to do it, you're a fucking liar."

She doesn't respond, staring at me with what appear to be hazel-colored eyes. They're more noticeable now that we're up close.

"I repeat—have I touched you?"

"N-no." She seems a little nervous now, which wasn't my intention, but I'm not playing this kind of game with her. Other games? Absolutely. But not this one. Not one that maligns my character.

"Have I said anything over-the-top inappropriate? Have I used crude words or talked about sex? Have I made you feel like I would hurt you?"

She hesitates for a fraction of a second, but then shakes her head. "No."

"And I'll treat *them* exactly like I'm treating you. Except for maybe the lap dances. But they're here willingly, and believe me when I tell you, we're paying them five times what most strippers make for a night like this. So never, ever insinuate that I'm that kind of man. I'm no saint, and I'll absolutely spend the entire night trying to get you to smile so I can win a hundred bucks I don't need, or working on getting your phone number to win another hundred bucks I don't need, but that's as far as it goes unless and until you give me the green light. And if you need me to walk you out to your car at the end of the night, because it's late and someone may be lurking around, you can bet your last dollar that's all that'll happen out there."

For a moment her jaw tightens but the fight seems to drain out of her.

"I'm sorry," she says after a moment. "I didn't mean it… *that* way. I just—"

"You did. And I get it. Rich, single playboys getting shit-faced on what would have been our buddy's thirtieth birthday. Way too much alcohol, decadent food, cigars, dancing, flirting with bartenders, and now strippers. Believe me, I really do get it. But you don't know us. And you don't have any idea what the friend we're celebrating meant to us. So please don't judge. I'm fine with being called an asshole—I probably am—but I wouldn't hurt anyone. Least of all a woman who works for me."

With that, I turn and walk away.

CHAPTER FIVE

Aspen

"Damn," I whisper as I watch him walk away, shoulders tense, each stiff stride radiating with fury.

He didn't even grab his drinks.

And Marissa is off, sitting at the other end of the bar and chatting with Johnny as he gets a head start on the closing duties, so I can't even give her puppy dog eyes and beg her to bring the drinks over.

Plus, I'm not going to make my new coworkers pick up my slack, especially on my first night.

Which means I'm going to have to woman up, finish these fucking drinks, and then bring them over to the men.

And the strippers.

"Damn," I whisper again, but I manage to ignore my inner squirming as I finish the four double Gamebreakers.

"Things are looking a little heated with the boss." I look up, see that Marissa has abandoned Johnny and his cleaning to plunk herself down onto a barstool in front of me.

Least of all a woman who works for me.

I blink, hear his voice again.

Least of all a woman who works for me.

Works. For. Me.

Oh, my god.

He'd said that and I hadn't processed it and—

"Ex-excuse me?" I croak, hoping that I'm spiraling into some sort of delusion, even while knowing that I'm, unfortunately, both sober and completely sane.

Her brows furrow. "You *do* know that while Leo is the one who oversees us all day-to-day, those four"—horror blooms as I follow her nod toward the group where tall, blond, and maybe not completely horrible returned—"actually own The Sapphire Room."

I did not know that.

I fucking *didn't* know that.

How could I have?

It's my first freaking day!

"They *own* it?" I squeak.

"Yup." She jerks her chin toward the men. "That one on the left who fills out that suit to sinful perfection is Atlas—"

I allow my eyes to drift over the clean-shaven man with dark brown hair who is wearing what is, indeed, a gorgeous suit—albeit not as appealing to my misbehaving lady parts as the one tall, blond, and frustrating is sporting.

"—and Royal's next to him—"

Cue sexy, dark long hair that's falling around a handsome face, a suit that is less old money and more rocker chic—but no less appealing than Atlas's—covering his leanly muscled frame.

"Hudson," she says, "or Dash as everyone calls him, is on Royal's left—"

Easily the bulkiest of the four, Hudson—or Dash—is wearing jeans and a black T-shirt that's straining against the broad spread of his chest and shoulders. He also hasn't stopped scanning the space, seemingly taking in all of the comings-and-goings, assessing any potential dangers, and somehow doing it all while appearing completely relaxed.

"And next to him?"

Tall, blond, and pretty's name—

"That's—"

Music blares loud enough to make me wince, completely drowning out Marissa's last words.

But I don't have time to wonder further about tall, blond, and fills-out-a-suit's name—

Because *that's* when the strippers come out.

The worry that was blooming in my belly, tangling with the guilt of misjudging the man, with another statement from his clipped-out words—*what would have been our buddy's thirtieth birthday*—dissipates.

Because if they really are missing their buddy they wouldn't be tugging a quartet of half naked women onto their laps and all but motorboating their ways into oblivion…

Would they?

I grind my teeth together when my gaze is drawn to tall, blond, and Clark Kent.

He looks like he's having the best night of his life.

Like he's completely forgotten that I exist.

Well, if he's the boss and just passing the time…that tracks.

Who *am* I, anyway?

Just another employee, another woman to pay.

I don't like the kernel of jealousy that's sitting in my belly.

Jealousy? Ha. The only jealousy I'm feeling is because she has better boobs than me.

"Want me to take these over?" Marissa shouts over the din, and I start to shake my head.

"You're off the clock," I tell her, the thrumming of the music making my ears hurt. "I can—"

"I'm heading out, anyway," she all but yells before tossing a wink over my shoulder. "Johnny and I have a hot date."

"Yeah," Johnny says, close enough that I don't have to strain to hear him too much, "with our bed."

Another wink and then Marissa is carrying the tray over to the table of troublemakers.

"Last call's done," Johnny tells me, "and the rest of the stragglers will clear out with the loud music—"

My eyes slide around the space, taking in the few remaining patrons packing it in and heading for the door.

"If you can just bus those tables and clean your station, that'll do it for our part of closing." He jerks his chin toward the opposite end of the space. "You need anything else, just signal to Leo."

I follow his stare, see The Sapphire Room's manager sitting at a table, surrounded by paperwork.

"Otherwise, once the cleanup is done, you'll just need to hang out until the boss men are done partying in case they need anything."

Anything more than a boatload of alcohol and titties flying around their faces?

Luckily, I don't say that out loud.

Instead, I nod, forcing a smile at Marissa as she returns the tray, exchanging shouted goodbyes, and then keeping myself busy.

Or attempting to.

Because no matter that I've scrubbed my station until it's gleaming and searched every empty table and alcove for stranded or abandoned glasses, I still can't take my eyes off the men.

No.

The *man*.

Big hands gripping curvy hips, encouraging the rhythmic grinding.

Thick thighs parted enough to give the stripper's gorgeous ass enough space to work, but also a cushion to sit on as she thrusts her tits in his face, as the gleaming blonde strands of her hair fly around in time to her movements.

A sexy, confident smile that says he's enjoying himself, that he's not shy, that he is absolutely a god in the fucking sheets—

I drop a glass.

Thankfully, it bounces off the black mat on the counter and I manage to corral it before it topples to the floor and shatters.

"Get it together, Rockwell," I whisper, deliberately putting it into an empty space in the rack and turning on the industrial dishwasher.

But the longer I stand there, waiting for the powerful men who are apparently my bosses to either wrap it up or need something from me, the harder it is for me to breathe.

The girls are taking a break from dancing—or at least the one who's sitting in my man's lap—

Not *my* man.

Christ.

I *want* to be the one sitting on his lap, want to be the one who so confidently sinks my fingers into those dark blond locks and shoves his gorgeous face into my not-as-nice-as-hers-but-still-fucking-great breasts.

Hot breath on my skin.

A calloused hand skating along my side.

A thick cock pushing home—

My lungs tighten further, spasming so fiercely that black spots appear at the edges of my vision.

I need fresh air.

I need to get the fuck away from the girls and the pulsing music and…

Tall, blond, and—

I need to go.

Tossing my towel on the counter, I signal to Leo, telling him that I need ten.

He nods, but I'm already moving out of the bar, walking

down the hall, pushing through the metal door and stepping out into the night air.

The employee lot is mostly empty, and thankfully, when the door closes behind me, quiet descends, enshrouding me into a stolen moment of peace.

Leaning back against the wall, the rough stucco of the old building biting into my bare arms, I just take this chance to breathe.

What's wrong with me?

I don't know, but I don't have the chance to find out either because the door swings open and I have to jump back so it doesn't slam into me.

"Sorry," the man who's been causing my brain to short-circuit all night mutters, catching the metal panel with a big palm. The action is oddly familiar, but I don't get a chance to process it as he steps out into the cool night air. "I didn't mean to almost hit you."

"It's okay," I manage to push out, shifting to the side so he can move past me.

Only, he doesn't walk by me, doesn't head for one of the cars in the employee lot as I expect. Instead, he stops in front of me, eyes glued to mine. "You okay?"

Okay?

I'm losing my mind and I'm exhausted and I don't know what I'm doing with my life and my vagina has decided to abandon all common sense.

"I'm great," I lie.

Half of his mouth quirks up. "Right," he says, and the disbelief the man manages to cram into five letters is impressive.

"I'm just tired," I find myself saying, and while that's the truth, it's only one small sliver of it.

A lush ass rubbing on this man's lap.

Big hands cupping hips and breasts.

A smirk as he kisses his way down my body, as he parts my legs, flicks out his tongue and—

"I figured," he says softly, jarring me out of the fantasy, but not before my thighs tremble and my pussy convulses with need.

"It *is* after closing," I reply tartly.

The other half of his mouth curves, transforming the half smile into a confident grin that has me ridiculously wet.

I should have just given him my phone number.

Then he would have lost interest and none of this would have happened.

"I know," he says and for a second, I almost panic, thinking I'd spoken out loud. But then he's talking again and I'm scrambling to focus on anything except for my needy pussy. "It *is* late," he tells me. "Which is why I grabbed your stuff and I'm going to walk you to your car."

I blink.

Then again.

But, nope, he's still holding up my backpack and jacket, the latter of which he thrusts at me, and I woodenly shrug on.

I nod toward the door. "Leo—"

"Our party's not going to end any time soon," he says. "Atlas is sending Leo off, and we'll lock the doors and keep going until the sun comes up."

"Celebrating your friend," I whisper.

His grin fades and I hate that my words ruined it, that I made it disappear. "Yeah," he says softly. "Celebrating Colt."

My heart squeezes at the grief in his words, but I don't lean into it or apologize. Some part of me senses that will make him sadder.

And I don't want him sad.

I want him cocky and smirking and full of swagger.

"If you guys tear the place apart," I say icily, lifting my chin and fixing him with my best glare, "I expect you to pick up after yourselves."

Silence between us for a heartbeat too long.

Then he grins. "Fucking beautiful, but so much fucking trouble."

"So says the man who spent all night drinking expensive whisky and pawing strippers."

He starts walking toward the lot, and since he's still holding my purse, I find I have no choice but to follow him. "I resent the term pawing," he says. "It's more like appreciative petting, and it's only been the last hour."

I roll my eyes. "If you say so, Mr. Pawtastic."

A snort, but he passes me my purse. "I don't need an escort," I tell him.

One broad shoulder lifts, drops. "I'm going to give you one anyway."

"My car's right there—" I nod toward the black, older model Mercedes. It's about a decade beyond being luxurious, but it gets me where I need to go.

Most of the time.

"Good," he says. "We're almost there."

Stubborn.

Annoying.

But I still can't stop the tiny flicker of warmth blooming to life in my belly.

Just like I can't stop this man from walking me right to my driver's side door, or checking the back seat for interlopers, or waiting until I sit inside, lock up, and start the engine.

Just like I can't stop my eyes from drifting up to the rearview mirror as I pull out of the lot…

And seeing him standing there.

Watching me as I drive away.

CHAPTER SIX

Banks

THE MORNING after Colt's birthday celebration is always hard, but never more so than today. I left the club around four-thirty, went home to shower and take a cat nap before practice, and now I've stumbled into the locker room two minutes before we're supposed to be on the ice. I rip open my locker, shove in my personal items, and immediately start yanking on my gear.

"Someone's going to be skating laps," our team's starting goalie, Vinnie Lacroix, says with a laugh.

"Yeah, yeah." There's no doubt that might happen if I don't get out there on time, but sometimes Coach Wilkes is cool.

Sometimes.

Other times he's a beast with no fucks to give—you screw up, you pay for it.

I was traded to the Vipers from Pittsburgh three weeks before Colt's death, and it was excruciating trying to navigate that pain and the subsequent grief surrounded by guys who didn't know me, had never heard of Colt, and basically didn't give a shit.

Your buddy died.

Sorry, man.

Move on, that's life.

They didn't understand. How could they?

But Coach was great about it, giving me time to work through my grief and find my footing with the team.

My friend, West, understood as well.

He kept the rest of the team at bay as I sobbed in the shower after the first game, protecting my privacy, my reputation, and my ego, even though I didn't give a fuck about that—or anything, really—at the time. But it helped me get over the initial hump. I took a couple of days for the funeral, and then I came back to SoCal ready to play and move past the worst of it.

Of course, I'm not sure I'll ever truly get past losing one of my best friends, because I'm still working on it.

"Colt's birthday," West says, standing next to me as I pull on equipment at warp speed.

"Don't," I warn.

"Hey." He holds up a hand. "Just looking out for you. Coach is in a mood. Fontana got his ass chewed for having the wrong practice jersey on. Just a head's up."

Great.

Just what I need—Coach Wilkes ready to chew someone's ass and me running on sixty minutes of sleep.

Thank God it's not a game day.

"I'm good," I mumble.

"You sleep at all?"

I shake my head. "I'll be okay."

"I've gotta go, but let me know if you need anything." He clomps off toward the tunnel as I'm lacing up my skates, wondering how bad Coach is going to ream me when I'm the last one out there.

Luckily, there's an issue with the ice that requires maintenance, so everyone is just milling around shooting the shit when I approach the rink.

Thank fuck.

I stay toward the back of the crowd that's gathered in the tunnel and on the bench, waiting, filled with restless energy.

Personally, there isn't enough coffee in the state of California for how tired and hungover I am, but there's no help for it. I popped a Sudafed before leaving the house in the hopes it would give me a jolt of energy, and it seems to be working since my eyes are open and I'm standing upright.

I can party with the best of them, but I'm a professional athlete who needs to be in top form every time I hit the ice.

And I haven't scored a goal yet this season, which isn't like me.

Yeah, it's only mid-October—so we're just two weeks into the regular season with half a dozen games under our belts— but I'm considered one of the elite scorers in the league.

Well, I used to be.

Last year wasn't my best, and I'm already frustrated even though we're barely underway this year. I'm on the first line, a winger that both scores and sets up plays. So far, I haven't been doing either this season.

Which means I need to step up.

I don't know what I'll do if they trade me.

It's part of being a professional athlete, but my life is here. I worked hard to make this trade happen, spent time building connections here.

And it's not just where I live, but where Atlas and Dash and Royal live. Where Dash's little sister, Briar, and her daughter—my goddaughter, Frankie—live. Where The Sapphire Club is. So much of my life is here, I can't imagine trying to navigate everything from Toronto or Tampa or any other city.

"Boys, it looks like today might be a bust," one of the coaches yells out. "An issue with the ice. I want to see half of you in the conditioning room and the other half in the lounge watching video. Cash—Coach Wilkes wants to see you in his office."

Fuck.

The guys started calling me Cash because hockey is awash with nicknames. Cash is to Banks what Chubbs is to Asher— our rookie with plenty of baby fat. And frankly, Chubbs versus Cash? I'll take Cash any day of the week.

Bonus is that I didn't end up with something like Lock or Vault or Dumbass.

A chorus of "ooohs" follows me down the tunnel, my team- mates giving me shit like we're in fucking high school and I steel myself for what might be coming.

Please don't trade me.

I'm not the praying kind, but the thought of leaving Southern California makes me want to be as I walk through the door of Coach Wilkes' office.

"Sit down, Banks," he says, and I can't help but notice he looks tired, which isn't like him.

I sink into the chair across from him warily then find myself blurting, "Are you trading me?"

He meets my gaze. "Do you *want* to be traded?"

"Fuck no." I pause. "Sir."

Silence for long enough that I start to squirm.

"Talk to me," he finally says. "What's going on? Woman trouble? Money problems? Gambling?" He squints. "Drugs? Whatever it is, I can help if you'll let me."

"None of the above," I respond.

He lifts a brow in that quintessential *coach* way.

"I don't know what it is," I admit, "I just can't seem to get anything going when I'm out there."

He pauses for an inordinately long time, thinking so hard I can practically see the wheels turning. "I'm going to switch up the lines," he says finally. "Not as a punishment. But maybe moving things around will help you find your footing. I'm putting you on the third line with Fontana and Holloway."

The *third* line.

Jesus fucking Christ.

The sports pundits are going to have a field day with this, and there isn't a damn thing I can do about it.

———

THE NEXT TWO weeks are filled with much of the same bullshit as far as hockey goes. A road trip to northern California, Portland, and Seattle is no help to my game, but at least I get an assist on the first home game when we get back. However, I'm determined to figure out what the hell is going on, so I'm back to coming in early to work with our skating coach.

I'm on a strict low-carb, high protein diet, focusing on trimming off the rest of the weight I put on over the summer, and skating, shooting, and grinding my way back to the first line. Even if it kills me.

And these early ice times just might.

I'm not a morning person even on the best of days, and driving to work for an extra practice before our actual practice feels like self-inflicted torture, but what choice do I have? I have to push myself to get back to top form if I want to stay in SoCal—and I really do.

I grab my bag and walk toward the general employees' entrance. There's no one at the player entrance at six a.m. so I have to go in through a different door, which was how I'd run into that woman who didn't know me a couple of weeks ago.

A total ball buster.

Just thinking of her spunky attitude makes me chuckle.

I pull out my badge and am just about to swipe it when the door swings open, almost hitting me in the face.

"Jesus!" she hisses, clamping a hand to her chest. "You scared the shit out of me!"

And there she is, my little spitfire.

Except…

I stare.

She stares back.

"What are you doing here?" we demand in unison.

"Aspen?" I'm confused. I hadn't recognized her at the club —between the bartender outfit and the makeup she wore, she looked like a completely different woman. Today, she's wearing another ratty beanie, has glasses that are sliding down her nose, and her hair is tied back in a messy ponytail instead of tumbling down her back in curls I want to see spread out on my pillow.

Not to mention that her baggy sweats and giant hoodie aren't exactly *flattering* to all the curves I know she's hiding beneath that loose fabric.

She's still adorable, but it's a completely different look than how she'd been at the club.

"M-Mr. Christianson?" she sputters, shock written into the lines of her face. But barely a heartbeat later, I watch that fiery attitude emerge with her snapped-out question, "Are you following me?"

I roll my eyes. "Seriously? The question is more like, are you following *me*?"

She scowls. "Why would I be following you? I work here!"

"So do I. Which is what I told you the last time we did this little dance."

She stares again.

I continue to stare back.

"Wait—that was you?" Now she seems even more annoyed.

And frankly, so am I.

"A couple of weeks ago," I grit out. "You weren't going to let me in. Remember?"

"I remember but…" A shake of her head, her voice softening. "It's just…you looked different at the club."

"So did you," I point out, deliberately glancing down at her oversized hoodie and baggy sweats.

Her eyes narrow. "You own a nightclub *and* you play pro hockey?"

I narrow mine right back. "And you work here overnight in addition to bartending?"

"Obviously."

The word is sharp, but I don't bite back. Probably because something inside me clenches at the idea of her working two physically demanding jobs just to survive. "That's a lot of hours."

"I only get three shifts a week at The Sapphire Room. And I have bills to pay."

"Understood." I pause, wishing I had time to talk to her some more, but Coach Mercier is waiting for me. "Well, I have to get to practice."

"At six in the morning?" she asks dubiously.

I shrug. "We put in extra time on the ice sometimes."

Our eyes meet and for a moment I'm not sure what's happening.

It's like the moon and stars have aligned for us to keep running into each other, and despite her fiery attitude as she does her best to keep me at arm's length, there is no mistaking the spark between us.

She wants me.

Even if she won't admit it.

Or give me her phone number.

"I'll see you soon, Aspen," I say, breaking the spell and slipping inside.

I can feel her eyes on me as I make my way toward the elevators, but I don't look back.

She's already skittish, and the last thing I want is to scare her off.

I'm going to ask Dash to find out more about her for me. I can't seem to help myself.

I'm intrigued by her.

Aroused.

Fuck.

I need to get that little spitfire out of my head and focus on hockey.

"About time," Coach Mercier calls out when I join him on the ice.

"Good morning to you too," I reply.

He smirks. "Nothing good about this morning. Not for you, anyway. Start skating."

I sigh. "Laps? Really?"

"You said you wanted me to be brutal. It starts with cardio. Moves to stick handling. Ends with weights."

"And then practice?" The question is rhetorical since I already know the answer.

But I asked for this, so I can't complain.

Much.

I use the first lap to get my feet under me and warm up my body, and then I take off, imagining a pack of rabid dogs on my ass.

My legs burn and my lungs feel like they'll never get enough air, but eventually Coach blows the whistle and I glide to a stop, resting my hands on my thighs.

"I like the times on those last few laps," he says, even though I didn't realize he was timing me. "If you can find that speed during games, you'll keep everyone on their toes."

I'm breathing too hard to respond, but I lift my head to nod.

As I do, I notice movement in the stands.

A beanie covering a messy ponytail, lush curves hidden beneath miles of fabric. Adorable black glasses sliding down a pert nose.

Aspen.

She stayed to watch?

My throat goes dry, and my dick twitches.

And I can't lie. I would totally skate those laps all over again if I thought it would impress her.

It won't. Not my little spitfire.

She's pretty far away but our eyes meet for a moment anyway.

I freeze, not knowing what this pull between us is and why it feels like a strike of lightning whenever we're in the same room together.

I just know I need more of her.

My thoughts are interrupted as Coach Mercier hands me a stick and starts setting up cones.

Jesus. He's going back to the most basic of basics.

I've been stick and puck handling since I was five years old, growing up in South Dakota. I've come a long way since then, but today I feel like a little kid again, my dad urging me to skate faster, shoot harder, focus.

The next hour is easier, since I can handle the puck all day long.

But I'm going to be wiped at practice.

I need a protein drink and ten gallons of water.

Maybe Aspen has time to go to breakfast with me.

I look up, suddenly excited, but the spot where she was sitting is now empty.

As I scan the arena, I realize she's gone.

And I'm a lot more disappointed than I should be.

CHAPTER SEVEN

Aspen

"Tut-tut."

Please God, no.

I'm barely hanging on because I'm completely exhausted after my shift at The Sapphire Room last night—Johnny called out sick and Leo asked me to cover.

I'm too new to turn down shifts, especially when I want more of them so I can get out from beneath Tut-Tut Bitch Boss From Hell's purview, and I'm sure as shit too *broke* to turn them down, especially ones that pay as well as they do at the club.

My tips alone are a game changer.

I don't have to fight to stop management from taking a cut —something that's illegal, but something I've shut up and tolerated plenty of times in the past.

Keep the job and lose some tips.

Or lose the job *and* my ability to pay my electric bill.

There's not even a question—

"Tut-tut."

I close my eyes, reach for my patience.

It's slippery, my grip flimsy, but I manage to find it…for the moment.

"Good morning, Cheryl," I say, continuing to swipe at the bottom of the seat, determined to not play Hot and Cold today.

Unfortunately, she doesn't want to let the game go.

"Tut-tut," she tsks again as I slide forward and start cleaning the next seat.

My temple starts to throb as I debate the shortest path that'll get me to starting over—because that's where this is going to end up anyway—and I need to do it without losing my temper…or my job.

Because I like having electricity.

And food in my fridge.

"Tut—"

I snag my carry-all of cleaning products, my trash bag, and I stand up.

Cheryl's eyes go wide, her Karen-style comb-over bob shimmying as she glowers at me. "What do you *think* you're doing?"

"My cleaning is clearly not up to standard," I say through gritted teeth, trying my best to keep my tone neutral, to not go with the nuclear option—

And there's no doubt that spraying my bleach into her eyes would be the nuclear option.

If I'm arrested, and I'm certain that Cheryl would make sure of it, my family might find me.

There's a reason I've moved to this coast, and it's so I don't have to deal with their bullshit, not ever again. They made it abundantly clear that they don't want to accept me as me, so…

Three thousand miles and starting over without them in my life.

"I'll just"—I nod up to the highest row in the section—"go to the top and begin again."

I have the imminent pleasure of watching Cheryl sputter.

But only for a second.

Because then Bitch Boss comes out.

"Excuse me?" she says icily.

And, goddammit, but I can't help it, can't keep the snark contained. "You're excused," I mutter, slipping by her.

"How dare you talk to me like that?" She lifts her chin, straightening her spine completely so she rises to her full, bitchy height. "You only have this job because of me, and you'll treat me with the due respect that my position requires of you."

Boomer implosion incoming.

I brace, hold tight to my temper.

You need electricity. You need food. You need more shifts at The Sapphire Room before you can commence with the bleaching of Bitch Boss.

"She *has* this job because you love being in a position to Lord what little power you have over the people who work for you."

I freeze, fingers clenching on the bag, my stomach twisting.

Because I've thought those words a hundred, a thousand times.

But it's not me saying them out loud.

It's Banks Christianson—the man who moves like liquid lightning on the ice, the man who cleaned up to model gorgeousness at the club, the man who's standing next to Cheryl, hair in a messy tumble, stubble on his jaw, and fury flaring in the deep green of his eyes.

Oh, God.

He's going to blow.

I widen my eyes at him in warning, silently telling him to cool it.

A warning, of course, that he doesn't heed.

"And Aspen isn't some underling you can just order around—"

I drop my trash bag, grip his arm. "One second, please,

Cheryl," I say calmly as I haul him away. My heart is pounding, throwing itself against my ribcage, as I drag him down enough stairs that I can berate him properly without Bitch Boss listening in.

Although maybe if I do it within earshot she'll stop being such a twat.

Unlikely, but a woman can hope.

I draw to a stop, stare up into emerald eyes filled with fire and my heart starts to beat in double time, dancing along with the butterflies in my stomach. Banks Christianson is hot when he's pissed, and some small, insane part of myself wants to push him down into one of these seats and lick him all over.

Or suck on a very specific body part.

He jerks against my hold, and I focus, digging my nail into his hard bicep in order to keep him in place.

"Stop," I hiss.

"She's a fucking bitch," he snaps, expression ragey, body so fucking taut I'm shocked it doesn't snap like an overstretched rubber band.

"Yes, she is."

That, at least, has him stopping, those angry eyes fixing on mine.

"She *is* a bitch," I continue, and somehow, despite my traitor of a heart and those butterflies creating a tornado in my belly, I'm able to keep my words calm. "But I need this job."

"Why?" he snaps. "You can just pick up more shifts at the club. I fucking know it pays better."

"So spoken like a man who's never actually worked a real job," I grind out. "It's not that simple."

The Sapphire Room isn't open to the public, so there are less shifts available than a normal bar. Yeah, they pay better, but that means competition for full-time positions is high and there aren't enough hours to go around.

"Explain it to me."

I snort. "Okay, Cap," I say sardonically. "Normal people

don't have million-dollar contracts. I have bills to pay, and I like to—I don't know—*eat* occasionally."

Sparks of fury dance in his eyes. "I know—"

"Do you?" I snap, dropping his hand and using my now free one to jab at his chest. "Do you really?" I jab again. "I don't actually think so. Because if you did, you'd realize how close you are to fucking things up for me at a job I *need*."

His expression sobers. "Little spitfire, I didn't mean—"

I glare, using all my self-control to keep the bleach holstered. "This is my job. If you get me fired, I'll kill you. Now go away and play with your stick or something."

Spinning on my heel, I don't bother to look back as I make a pitstop to pick up my trash and tell Cheryl in my most professional voice possible that "I'll start at the top."

Then I'm climbing to the top of the stairs, getting on my hands and knees.

And I get back to cleaning.

Though, thankfully, I'm able to finish this time around without the side of interruptions.

———

MY BODY PROTESTS as I heft my trash bag into the dumpster, but I ignore it.

Mostly because I'm so tired that it's taking every bit of my concentration to keep one foot moving in front of the other.

Trash thrown.

Supplies away.

Belongings gathered.

Now to go home and sleep for a million hours—and that's only the slightest amount of hyperbole.

I slam my locker shut, tug down my beanie, push up my glasses.

And then I'm shoving out into the cool morning air, feeling the breeze on my cheeks, struck by the beauty of the sky and its oranges and pinks and blues. Sunrise is a beautiful thing, and it's a beautiful thing that pulls me out of my fatigue for long enough to suck in another breath, to appreciate the wispy clouds dancing along the horizon.

To appreciate that I can stand here, free to…well, *appreciate* them.

But it doesn't take long for my exhaustion to rear its head and I start moving again.

I need to sleep for the aforementioned one million hours.

I make the long walk to my car, bleep the locks, and wrestle with the handle that hates these cold early mornings as much as I do.

Eventually, I get it working and climb into the driver's seat, jabbing my keys in the ignition and turning it—

Then frowning as I hear a click.

And not the soft rumble of the engine turning over.

I turn again.

Click.

"Fuck my life," I whisper, resting my head against the steering wheel, and then doing it again for good measure.

Harder and with rhythm.

Okay, fine. I'm banging my head against the steering wheel.

But it's either that or scream and—

Well, I haven't completely ruled out screaming yet.

Tap. Tap. Tap.

My yelp fills the interior of my car when someone knocks on my window.

No. Not *someone,* I realize as I turn my head.

It's Banks, looking tall and handsome and with concern in those pretty green eyes.

Fuck. My. Life.

CHAPTER EIGHT

Banks

I'D WAITED for her to get off because I was determined to buy her breakfast.

I didn't anticipate her car not starting.

She's currently staring at me in wide-eyed horror, and I can't tell if it's because I scared her or because she doesn't want me to get involved. It's probably a frustrating combination of the two, but I'm nothing if not persistent.

"Open up, Aspen," I call out, tapping lightly once more. "Let me help."

Her forehead drops to the steering wheel again, as if she's so frustrated she can't function, but after a few more seconds, I hear the lock disengage and I open the passenger side door. I slide in beside her, taking in the expensive but slightly worn leather seats and a dashboard that was probably beautiful when the car was new.

"Rough morning, huh?" I ask.

"You have no idea," she murmurs, her forehead still resting on the steering wheel.

"Can you turn it over one more time? Let me hear what's happening."

She doesn't lift her head, merely turns the key in the ignition, and the annoying little *click-click-click* tells me it's probably the alternator. It's possible it's the battery, but my gut tells me it's not.

"It's bad, right?" she asks glumly.

"We can't know for sure until we get it to a mechanic, but it might just be the battery."

"Don't bullshit a bullshitter," she responds. "Tell me the truth."

"I think it's the alternator but—"

Another thunk against the steering wheel. "Fuck my life."

I grimace at the sheer exhaustion in her words.

It's the sound of someone who's hanging on to life by a thread, and I fucking hate it, but I know offering to pay for the repairs will only piss her off.

"I have a great mechanic," I start to say, "and he—"

"It doesn't matter," she whispers. "It's a *Mercedes*. An oil change is five hundred bucks."

I want to point out that she shouldn't be driving such a costly car but that won't be productive.

"I was going to say, I'm sure he'll give you a payment plan once I tell him you're a friend. He's a good guy."

"I don't really have a choice."

"It's going to be okay, Aspen."

"You don't understand." She still hasn't lifted her head and for the first time in a long time I realize how lucky I am. The only thing I have to worry about in my life is whether or not I'm going to get traded. Not how I'm going to get to work or put food on the table. Not whether or not I have to work a second job to make ends meet.

Dammit.

I need to be better.

And maybe I can start here.

"Look, let me call Briggs. He'll tow the car at no cost and—"

"No cost?" Her head snaps up and the fire is back in her eyes.

Good.

I don't like the defeated version of my little spitfire.

"If you're planning to pay for it behind my back because he's your friend," she grits out, "and then thinking I'm going to pay *you* back another way, you've got another thing coming, you—you—"

I shake my head slowly, trying to tamp down the edges of my temper. "We've already had this conversation, little spitfire. That's not the man I am, and I'd like you to please stop insinuating it. He's my friend, and this is how friendship works. Period. If I call him and say I need a favor, he will get in his tow truck and come get the damn car. No charge. He won't fix it for free, and I wouldn't expect him to, but he'll do us a solid on the tow because I ask him to. Is that so hard to understand?"

It must be.

Because she stares at me for a lot longer than the conversation warrants, her eyes searching my face. I'm not sure what she's looking for, but I decide to let her work through it. Whatever is going on in her head isn't really about me. This is about her demons, her past, whatever it is that makes her so distrusting. I don't know if it's men in particular or all people in general, but there's only so much I can do to prove to her I'm the real deal.

"I…fuck." Her forehead drops to the steering wheel again. "Why are you so nice? You can't be that desperate to get in my pants."

I am, but it probably isn't prudent to say so.

It also isn't the only thing I'm interested in.

Sex isn't some kind of bedpost notch to me.

It was in the past.

It potentially might be again, depending on the circumstances, but I'm thirty years old and have slept with dozens of women. I don't need to chase a dark-haired spitfire who insults me every time we're together just for sex.

"Because I find you interesting. Beautiful—"

She interrupts me with a snort.

"You might need your glasses," she mutters. "So you can take a closer look."

"I know exactly what I see," I say patiently, "and I think you're beautiful. Not to mention hard-working, independent, and a bit of a spitfire. Personally, that's a trifecta of interesting in my book."

She slowly raises her head and gazes at me again, something inscrutable lurking behind her eyes that I can't begin to decipher.

"You say really nice things," she says at last. "But I can't figure out what your end game is."

"Is everything a game?"

"With people like you?" One slender shoulder lifts then drops, her pretty hazel eyes locked on mine. "Absolutely."

"People like me?"

"Wealthy, successful, and handsome. That's the trifecta of *entitlement* from where I sit."

Ouch.

That's as thought-provoking as it's insulting.

But I'm starving and it's getting late.

I still need to help her and eat something before practice, so I don't have time for a conversation like this.

"Do you want me to call my friend or not?" I ask, unable to hide the hint of frustration in my voice.

She sighs, long and deep, and then nods. "Yes, please."

I pull out my phone and dial.

———

MY BUDDY, Briggs, shows up thirty minutes later, hooks up her Mercedes to his tow truck, exchanges information with her, and is gone before she can protest too much. The good-looking bastard has that effect on women. Hell, sometimes he has that effect on me, and I'm as straight as they come. He's a force of nature, in a good way, zipping through life like hell on wheels. Literally and figuratively, as cars are his job, his obsession, his life.

"I feel like a tornado just swept through the parking lot," Aspen confesses as she gets into my SUV.

"He's a good guy," I say, pulling out of the arena parking lot and onto the street, thankful she accepted my offer to take her home. "You hungry? I need to eat before practice."

"I…" Her constant hesitation is starting to irk me.

One more refusal from her and I'm going to have to rethink all my life choices when it comes to women.

"Yes. Thank you. That sounds nice."

I stop clenching the steering wheel so hard because—

She's letting me drive her home *and* she didn't immediately shoot me down for breakfast.

I'm finally getting somewhere.

We wind up at a diner near her apartment—she said she can walk home from here—and though I figure she just doesn't want me to know where she lives, that's okay. I can understand her wanting to be cautious.

Once inside and seated across from her in a booth, I order a full breakfast.

Eggs, fried potatoes, bacon, fruit, and a stack of pancakes.

I'm starving so there's no way am I following my diet this morning.

She orders the watered-down version of my meal, omitting the fruit and pancakes. "A little hungry, big guy?" she says once the waitress has gathered the menus and disappeared.

I fucking love that there's the barest twinkle of humor in her hazel eyes. "I've just had my ass kicked on the ice and I'm about to do it all over again." I shrug, take a large sip of the water the server dropped off before taking our orders. "I need fuel." My trainer will probably kill me for all the carbs, but I'm fucking starving.

Her lips twitch, but she doesn't comment further, just sips her water and stares out the wide plate glass window.

"Are you a native?" I ask, unable to *not* break the silence.

She's a puzzle I need to know every piece of.

"No." A brisk response, no sign of a smile now. "I'm from back east."

"What brought you to SoCal?"

She hesitates and I don't think I'm misreading the caginess in her frame. "I needed a change of pace. My family is…" Another sip of water. "Old school, I guess, and they were trying to nudge me into marriage to a business associate of my dad's. I didn't want to. So I left."

"I'm sorry. That sounds—" Our food arrives, and I sit back, making room for the plates that nearly fill the surface of the entire space. "Rough," I finish softly once we're alone again.

She doesn't sugarcoat the truth. "It was. It still is. But I'm happier away from it all." Sighing, she nibbles the end of a piece of bacon, clearly done discussing herself. "What about you? Are you from here?"

Stomach rumbling, I pick up my fork, dive into my pancakes. "No. I'm from South Dakota originally. I went to college in Boston because I got a scholarship, and then I played in Boston and Pittsburgh for a few years before I got myself traded to the Vipers."

Hazel eyes on mine, deep pools of brown and green in the morning sunshine. "You wanted to come here?"

"This is where my friends—well, really, they're my family —are." I scoop up a bite, chew and swallow, aware of those eyes on me, seemingly focused on every word. As though it's unfathomable that someone might want to be close to family. "Atlas settled here after college, and Royal made this his home base because of his band. Then Atlas hired Dash's sister, Briar, and Dash didn't want to miss out on Frankie's life, so he came out here too."

She blinks, her brow slightly furrowed…

I realize that was a lot of info and a lot of names.

"Sorry." I rumble out a laugh. "My friends from the other night? You probably know Atlas because he's more hands-on at the club, even though we own it jointly."

"Yes." She makes a face at the bacon in her hand.

"What's wrong?" I ask.

"Too chewy." She waggles the floppy piece in my direction before setting it down and going after her potatoes.

"Here." I take my two pieces—far superior in their crispiness—and put them on her plate. "I like it chewy." Not exactly true, but I'll suck it up for her.

"Oh," she whispers. "Um…thanks." Her face is soft and she closes her eyes as she takes a bite. "Perfect. Yum."

It makes me happy to see her happy, so I keep talking, hoping not to ruin the moment. "Anyway, Royal is Royal Ewing from High on Midnight."

"The one who lost the use of his hand in the car crash," she says softly. "God, that must be so hard for him."

I wince. "Yeah. We've had a rough couple of years. Between losing Colt and then Royal's accident, we've had to dig deep to be there for him."

"You all went to college together?"

I smile. "Yes. Me, Atlas, Royal, Dash and Colt. We played hockey together too, but I was the only one who was drafted to play in the pros. Atlas has a dual computer science and business degree, Royal majored in music, and Dash and Colt were in ROTC and went into active duty military after we graduated. I think they both majored in political science. Anyway, we all kind of went our separate ways for a while, but after Colt was killed in action, we found our way here to SoCal."

"Who's Frankie?" she asks.

I smile. "Frankie is Dash's sister's three-year-old. I'm her godfather." I immediately pull out my phone and find a picture.

"Oh, she's beautiful," Aspen breathes, the first genuine smile I think I've ever gotten from her. "How sweet that you're so close."

It hits me in the solar plexus so hard that I forget to breathe for a second.

"Is that Frankie's mom?" she asks, pointing at the screen.

I nod. "Yup. Briar's a few years younger than us, but we're family, you know?"

She jabs at a fried potato. "No, I guess I don't know," she murmurs. "I mean, I *have* a family, but we were never there for each other like you guys seem to be. Everything is transactional. You want money? Show me your report card. If you have enough As, you can have it. You want a new pair of designer jeans? Make sure you make us proud at church on Sunday." She shakes her head, sighs. "It doesn't matter now, anyway."

I think it does.

But I don't push her, not when we're sitting across a table and sharing more than a meal.

I'll take what she's willing to give.

For now, anyway.

"It was just me and my dad growing up," I say, "but we were close. My mom died right after I was born so we just had each other. But he was my biggest fan and was never afraid to show it."

She pauses. "Was?"

I nod. "He died of cancer when I was in college."

"Damn," she whispers. "I'm so sorry." She reaches across the table to rest her hand on mine and the jolt of electricity that shoots through me is hard to ignore.

When I look up at her, the spark in her eyes tells me she feels it too.

"Thanks," I say quietly.

I need to move my hand but it's like I'm rooted in place, fixated by this first true contact between us.

Would it be bad to close my fingers around hers?

Will she throw her coffee at me?

Call me names again?

Well, we're about to find out because...

Fuck it.

I turn my hand over and lace our fingers together.

CHAPTER NINE

Aspen

He's touching me.

He shouldn't be.

But some part of me can't pull away.

So much tragedy in his life…

And I judged him to be a pretty playboy without a care for anyone else. Banks is shaping up to be far more than that, and the kernel of guilt—the one that's been brewing in my belly since I was harsh with him at The Sapphire Room, since I snapped at him at the arena (more than once)—grows.

He's more than what he seems.

I feel like a jerk to have assumed otherwise—though, in fairness, that's been the role of all the men in my life.

Sit down. Shut up. Look pretty. And let the big, tough men take care of everything.

And when I didn't want to live that life anymore?

No support. No love. No…nothing.

No longer a Rockwell.

Just Aspen who works two jobs and scrapes by the best she can.

I haven't touched anyone like this—with comfort and gentleness and without any ulterior motive—since Nanny.

My grandmother.

She was sweet and lovely and the one person whom I knew loved me.

And, one day, she was gone.

Then I was alone in a pit of vipers, never good enough. I wonder what they would think of me now if they bothered to find out what I'm doing with my life.

No, I suppose I already know how far down their noses they would look at me if they learned I was bartending, let alone spending the early hours of the morning scraping gum off the bottoms of chairs.

It was one thing to work in a restaurant my family owned —one of a chain of hundreds across the world—but that was to learn the ropes, to understand the business.

To be working for someone else?

Yeah, that wouldn't fly any more than my gum-scraping.

Banks's fingers flex in mine and I jerk myself out of the past.

A big, warm hand engulfing mine, deep emerald eyes searching for something in my expression—probably wondering if I'm going to bust out my keys and go rabid raccoon on him.

But I only have the fob for my apartment. My only effective stabby key is with Briggs, the mechanic.

Who towed my car. For *free*.

Because of Banks.

My heart does a little somersault in my chest.

Definitely misjudged him, and definitely feeling…*feelings*.

Panic coils in my stomach and I jerk my hand back, clutching it against my chest like I've been burned.

"Easy, little spitfire," he murmurs, leaving his hand where it is for a moment before drawing it back into his lap. "I'm—"

But he doesn't get the chance to finish whatever he's about

to say because there's a cry and we both whip around to watch a lady who's seventy if she's a day, falling toward the black and white tiled floor.

"Oh, shit—"

Before I can so much as move, Banks is out of the booth, hustling toward the woman who's fallen to the floor, the contents of her purse spread out on the floor around her. He crouches at her side and my icy cold heart stutters in my chest as I watch him carefully help her to her feet and settle her in a chair.

It's also what finally gets me moving.

I slide out of the booth, step between the other customers who are all just standing around and staring, and start picking up her belongings.

A tube of lipstick, a baggie of cough drops, a compact, various coins, her wallet, and an older style flip phone—I snag them all and tuck them safely in the black leather handbag then bring it over to her.

"...just take a breath," Banks is saying. "There's no hurry."

"I'm so embarrassed," the lady says. "I didn't see that lip there and—"

"People trip all the time."

She just shakes her head.

"What's your name?" Banks asks gently.

"Gladys."

"Hey, Gladys. I'm Banks." He lifts his arm, shoves up the sleeve of his sweatshirt. "See this bruise?"

A tiny nod.

"I tripped on a dumbbell at the gym and totally ate it. And I did it in front of all my teammates." He shakes his head. "The teasing they've unleashed on me since is no joke."

"*You* tripped?"

One of those big shoulders lifts then drops. "Yup. I wasn't paying attention and—" Another shrug. "Next thing I know, I was on the floor."

Gladys exhales quietly. "Really?"

"Unfortunately, yes," he murmurs. "So, suffice to say, it happens to the best of us. Now"—he stands up, extends his hand—"are you sitting in a booth or at the counter?"

———

GLADYS CHOSE a large booth in the back of the restaurant where she and the friends who came in just a few minutes later to meet her held their weekly coffee and pie book club meeting.

This just in—I want to be Gladys when I grow up.

Cackling over refined sugar and copious amounts of coffee while discussing spicy books and hot heroes. One of which was a real-life hero in Banks. Him swooping in to help her was something Gladys relayed loudly and in great detail to her friends.

I didn't miss the way Banks's cheeks went bright red during the dissertation—and I had to admit it was cute.

Cute.

The big, sexy hockey player is *cute*.

Who would have thought?

Both that he's cute—and that I would dare to think such a thing.

A dangerous, slippery slope I can't bring myself to avoid. I'm staring down at the decline, and instead of turning and marching away, I'm inching closer to the edge.

One wrong move and—

I'll go tumbling down.

"Here you go," Banks says, popping the trunk to his SUV and pulling out one of the totes I'd crammed with the stuff from my car. He passes it over to me, but before I can snag the rest, he grabs the handles and hangs them over his shoulders. "Don't ask me to make you carry all this however many blocks it is to your place," he says quietly when I open my mouth to protest. "Either you get back in"—a nod toward the SUV—"and I drop you right in front of your building, or I help you share the load on the walk back."

There my heart goes again, turning over in my chest as I study the hard set of his expression, the tension in his leanly muscled frame.

If I really fight him, he'll give in.

I know it.

But…some part of me is tired of fighting.

Stupid, but I still step away from the back of the SUV, jerk my chin in the direction of the apartment building that's across the street and just down the block. It's seen far better days, but the rent is cheap, I don't have a roommate, and I have my own bathroom.

It's a fucking unicorn when it comes to southern California real estate.

"You weren't kidding when you said it was close."

"No," I murmur. "I wasn't."

He snags the bag he'd passed over, bleeps the locks on his SUV, and then heads for the crosswalk.

"I—"

But he's already crossing the street, and I have no choice but to hurry toward him, matching my strides to his much longer ones, making quick work of the short distance to my building.

Once there, I dig my keys out of my purse and wrestle the old lock open.

Then I pause on the threshold.

"Up to your door, little spitfire," he murmurs.

And…I don't argue.

I should.

But I don't.

I just hold the door wide enough for him to slip inside, and then hurry to the stairs on the opposite side of the lobby, taking them up to the third floor.

He's close behind me as I struggle with this lock as well, and I'm so flustered, so *aware* of him and the heat of his body, the spicy scent of him filling my nose that I don't do the smart thing and snag my bags back. Don't slam the door in his face. Instead, I step inside and hold the wooden panel wide, hold it for him to step inside.

Allowing the dragon into the treasure hold.

Leaving it open and vulnerable to pillaging.

And clearly I've been reading too many fantasy books of late…

Something he's walking right toward I realize, snapping back into myself in a rush, watching as he sets the bags on the tiny table I found thrifting that takes up most of my kitchen and turns to study the battered bookcase I snagged at a flea market that I use to separate my dining and cooking space from the sleeping portion of my studio apartment.

"I—"

He picks up a thick hardback that I got from the used bookstore down the street. "I love this book."

My eyes go wide. "You read?" I blurt and then immediately wince.

He's been nice and that…well, that sounds rude as shit.

But he doesn't get mad, just shrugs, one half of his mouth curving upward. "Yup," he says dryly. "I can even manage the big words and everything."

"I—" Damn. That kernel of guilt has popped, joining others in my belly to fill it uncomfortably full.

"I'm teasing, little spitfire. No offense taken." He moves toward me, flipping through the pages, showing me the map in the front. "I'm a sucker for a book with a map, and I have to admit that my high school self wouldn't have minded learning how to ride a dragon—"

"A wyvern," I correct softly.

"What?"

"They call them dragons in the books, but they're really

wyverns. Dragons have four legs and wings and wyverns have two legs and wings."

He's still, emerald green eyes locked on mine, staring so deeply it feels as though he can see right into my soul. "Why do I think you imagined being a dragon rider too?"

I inhale sharply.

God, how many times had I sat in my window seat, books all around, desperate for any form of escape.

What I wouldn't have given to be the lead in my own epic fantasy adventure?

Certainly, my life wouldn't have been this—barely eking out an existence, alone and sad and—

Fingers brush my cheek.

I gasp slightly, realize that my eyes had closed without me meaning to.

Now I peel open my lids, see that Banks is standing there— *right* there. Close enough to touch, to smell his spicy scent, to see the embers of gray in his eyes, the scar mostly hidden beneath a tumble of dark blond hair.

"You're so fucking beautiful," he whispers, stroking the backs of his knuckles over my cheek. "A gorgeous, perplexing puzzle that I want to piece together."

That should be a threat.

And maybe I would have taken it that way if not for him stepping even closer, the toes of his shoes brushing mine, those deep green eyes darkening with desire. Maybe I would have still retreated if he hadn't kept talking. "I don't like that your boss talked down to you, and I hate that you're pulling as many hours as you do, but I respect you so damned much for holding your ground with me, for keeping your head down and working your ass off, for putting in the effort to get what you want—"

Is this what I want?

To live in a crappy apartment? To have no life outside of working and sleeping?

Or is it a prison I've locked myself in?

"I think you're incredible, little spitfire." He cups my cheek. "And I hope that when you look in the mirror in the morning, you think that too."

He's charming and sweet and…too damned wonderful.

I need to show him out, throw the lock, slam that cell door. It's safe in my prison, and what he's saying, what he's making me feel…

Dangerous.

So damned dangerous.

But before I can shove him into the hallway, his mouth curves into a smile that's so beautiful it takes my breath away. "Just like I hope you'll go to dinner with me some time and tell me"—he holds up the hardback—"all about the different kinds of fae."

How is a woman supposed to resist the temptation of this man?

I just know I can't.

So, I give into the feel of his hand on my cheek and his scent in my nose and his knowledge of a book that means so, *so* much to me…

And I rise on my tiptoes, close the distance between our mouths, and I kiss him.

He goes so still that I know I've surprised him.

But then he bursts into a flurry of movement—his fingers clamping onto my hip, drawing my body flush against his. He groans quietly, his tongue finding the seam of my lips and slipping into my mouth to tangle with mine, stroking in a rhythm I know we'll find when we're naked, our bodies pressed together, his cock sliding home, thrusting deep over and over again. One hand slides into my hair, tilting my head back, deepening the kiss, making me forget about my need for oxygen, making me forget about everything.

Until his tongue slows, his fingers tense, and he slowly draws away from me.

I protest when his lips leave mine, realize that I'm plastered against him, my nails digging hard into his shoulders, my leg wrapped tightly around his hip.

"Fuck, little spitfire," he groans quietly, dropping his forehead against mine. "But you can *kiss*."

My pussy spasms.

"Banks," I whisper, and yeah, my tone is pleading.

His eyes burn into me, but when he takes my hand, he doesn't draw me over to my bed. Instead, he guides me to the door, pausing and staring at the handle for long enough that I step close, murmur his name again.

He shakes himself, turns back to face me, brushing his lips over my forehead, emerald eyes unfathomable.

"I'll see you soon, little spitfire," he murmurs.

And then he's gone.

CHAPTER TEN

Banks

Sometimes, a kiss is just a kiss.

Other times, it hits hard and becomes representative of something else.

Something more.

And with Aspen, the word *more* doesn't quite articulate what I'm feeling.

It's been a long time since I've met a woman who brings out the protector in me.

I want to sweep her off her feet, fix every single one of her problems, show her that life can be beautiful. And that's before I even take her to bed.

Because that's where we're going.

The only question is whether or not I'm the guy she needs me to be.

Christ.

What the hell am I doing?

Aspen is pretty much all I've thought about since our first encounter that morning at the arena. She's fiery and spirited, but also a fascinating mix of vulnerable and independent. It's a combination I'm not used to, so maybe that's what has me twisted up inside.

The truth is, I'm not a relationship kind of guy.

Probably because I'm a little broken.

Between growing up without a mother, and then watching what my friends have gone through over the years, I'm not sure I ever want to be that emotionally invested in someone. Losing Colt was gut-wrenching, so the thought of falling in love with a woman, having kids, and building a life together is daunting.

My gut tells me that's what Aspen wants.

I should walk away and leave her alone, but I already know I'm not going to.

I want her.

It's that simple.

And that's why I'm heading up to The Sapphire Room late on a Thursday night just before a road trip.

I have to see her before I go, make sure she has a way to get back and forth to work, even if I have to surreptitiously pay for it myself. That will piss her off, so I'll have to find a way to make it work. There's no way in hell I'll be able to think about hockey while I'm gone if I'm worrying about her, and since she's almost all I think about lately, I might as well do something to mitigate the issue before I go.

It's still fairly early when I get to the club, visions of the kiss Aspen and I shared vivid in my mind. I don't see her anywhere on the floor or behind the bar, and I look around curiously.

"Aspen here tonight?" I ask Johnny, our other regular bartender.

He nods tightly. "She's in the back with Leo."

The way he says it makes the hair on my neck stand up and I frown, but instead of asking him what's going on, I turn and head in that direction.

I can hear Leo's loud voice the moment I get into the hallway that leads to the offices and I slow down, listening.

"...it'll be deducted from your next paycheck."

"You can't do that," Aspen protests. "It's more than I make all week!"

"Then I guess next time you'll be more careful when you're handling three-hundred-dollar bottles of whisky."

"The step stool isn't sturdy on the mats behind the bar. Johnny has fallen a couple of times too and—"

"Listen, there are rules, and you don't get special treatment just because you have a great rack. You'll pay for the bottle you dropped or you can find another—"

I don't need to hear any more.

"Leo." I step around the corner and fix him with a glare. "What the hell are you talking about?"

He shrugs, seemingly not intimidated by my sudden appearance. "Atlas said we have a lot of waste and that if the servers spill more than two drinks per shift, they have to pay for them. And the bottle—"

"I'm talking about your comment about her rack." I emphasize the word. "We promote a safe work environment here and talking about an employee's *breasts* is not acceptable."

"I just meant—" He begins to sputter, but I hold up a hand to stop him..

"Apologize."

His mouth falls open as he gapes at me.

The look on my face must be pretty intense because he swallows hard, his Adam's apple bobbing nervously—*now* he's intimidated—and then he finally looks at Aspen. "I'm sorry about the comment about your chest. I was just trying to say we don't show favoritism here and we have rules."

"I'll talk to Atlas," I say before Aspen can respond. "We'll find a compromise about the drinks but the employees are *not* going to have accidents deducted from their paychecks unless it becomes excessive. And we're going to get a different step stool or ladder that will make it easier for them to get what they need. Do you know what kind of lawsuit we open ourselves up to if someone gets hurt?"

Leo is quiet, and Aspen is nervously shifting from one foot to the other.

"Go on back out to the bar," I tell her. "Everything is fine. Leo and I are going to have a chat."

I can see the worry on her face, but she nods and hurries in the other direction.

As soon as she's gone Leo scowls at me. "You fucking her?"

Before I can stop myself, I have my hand around his throat, and I slam him against the wall.

"Watch your fucking mouth," I hiss. "Who I fuck is none of your business, but even if it was, you work for *me*, not the other way around. If you don't like the way I want my club run, *you* can find another job. You don't get to lord the tiny bit of power you have over the employees. Do you understand?"

He gasps, quickly nodding, and I release him with a shove.

Then I stalk back out toward the bar before I do something I regret.

―――――

ASPEN IS behind the bar cleaning furiously, her brow furrowed in concentration.

Cleaning seems to be what she does when she's upset and for some reason I hate seeing it. I'm also starting to hate the fact that she works so hard. She needs the money, I get that, and I respect her hustle, but there's a part of me that just wants to make it so she doesn't have to worry about that shit.

My balls twinge at the thought of how she'd react if I said those words out loud.

Definitely knee-in-the-junk territory.

So…thoughts to keep to myself, and a good reminder that I need to tread carefully.

She's special, and I have no plans to hurt her.

I plunk down on a barstool and watch her for a few minutes, but she doesn't make eye contact.

"You okay?" I ask after a few minutes.

"I'm fine," she mumbles.

"Liar." I reach out and gently catch her wrist. "Hey," I say when she tries to jerk back. "Just stop for a second and look at me, Aspen."

She sighs and slowly lifts her eyes to mine. Her lips are pressed flat, her shoulders tense.

But I press forward anyway. "Has he spoken to you like that before?"

She exhales. "Not really. I mean, he's made a few off-color remarks, but this is a bar." She shrugs. "I'm used to it."

I shake my head vehemently. "No. He's your boss. It comes with the territory when it's the customers making inappropriate comments. They're always going to hit on an attractive bartender or waitress." I squeeze her wrist lightly. "But from your boss? The person who manages the club? No. *Fuck no*. I'm going to talk to Atlas about this right away. It's not acceptable."

Her eyes suddenly fill with tears. "Please don't fire him on my account. I don't want to be responsible for someone not being able to pay their bills, especially since you and I…" Her voice trails off, as if she doesn't want to label what's happening between us.

For a moment, I'm speechless. Leo has been a jerk to her and she's worried about *his* finances?

"Where's my little spitfire?" I lightly stroke the inside of her wrist with my thumb. "Even if there wasn't this thing between us, his behavior tonight was totally unacceptable. I'm not doing anything for you I wouldn't do for any other employee."

"I know." She sighs, her gaze dropping to where I'm caressing her skin. "But I know what it's like to worry about how I'm going to afford groceries, and I never want to be the cause of someone else going through that."

She's fire and spine and…

Nice.

"You're too damned sweet for your own good," I say gruffly. "I'm sorry you've struggled so much. Is this all because you wouldn't marry the guy your family wanted you to?"

She nods, gently pulling her wrist free and going back to wiping down the already squeaky clean bar.

"They didn't believe I could make it on my own," she says as she works. "They laughed when I started packing. My oldest brother bet my next older brother a thousand dollars I'd be back in a month. At least I have the satisfaction of knowing he lost that bet."

I grimace. "How long has it been?"

"Almost two years. In the beginning, it was easy, because I'd saved up money in a bank account my family didn't know about, but when you live in a protective cage, it's hard to know just how expensive life can be. First and last month's rent and a security deposit to get an apartment. Car repairs. Health insurance. Freakin' groceries…how is it five bucks for a dozen eggs?"

I don't respond because she's on a roll.

Also, because I have groceries automatically delivered to my house, with a housekeeper to put them away and place the orders when we start running low. I have no idea how much eggs cost. Or anything else, for that matter.

"And then buying things like mattresses and pillows," she exclaims. "I blew through my savings just getting settled in my apartment. Then it took a lot longer than I anticipated to find a job. Apparently, a degree in English Lit doesn't do much for you on the job market, which is why I'm bartending even though I have a Bachelor's degree from Notre Dame. On top of that, one job wasn't enough. This position fell into my lap—Johnny and I worked together before, and he let me know there was an opening—and I was hoping with it I would finally be able to breathe financially."

"But it's not enough?" I ask softly.

"It's *never* enough. I heard from Briggs. It's going to cost a thousand dollars to fix my car. But he was nice enough to say I can pay for it a hundred dollars at a time. So it'll take me almost a year." She stops moving and dips her head. "I'm so fucking tired of being broke, Banks."

"How many shifts a week are you getting here?" I ask.

"Three."

"Would you like a fourth?"

She lifts her head and makes eye contact. "Leo said we don't need two bartenders on Sunday, Monday, Tuesday or Wednesday. And again, I don't want to take work away from anyone, least of all Johnny. He's been here longer."

She's right about that, but there has to be something we can do.

"Let me think about it," I tell her. "We'll work something out." I can talk it over with Atlas, come up with some way to—

"Don't worry about me. I'll be fine. I always am. And anyway"—she tilts her head to the right as a group of men sidle up to the bar—"I can't do this now. I have customers."

I nod.

She turns away, stops, and then rotates back to face me. "But…thanks for listening."

"You're welcome."

Turning the situation over in my head, I stay on my stool and watch her making drinks for a few minutes but movement at the club's entrance catches my eye. When I look, I'm surprised to see Atlas, Dash, and Briar coming in.

"Hey!" I go over to greet them, hugging Briar tightly. "Missed you, kid."

"Hey, Banks." She smiles up at me.

I tug a strand of her hair. "Where's Frankie?"

"Uncle Royal is babysitting," she responds with a grin.

I laugh. "I wonder who'll get worn out first?"

"No question," Dash says. "My money's on Royal."

"I'm going to agree," I say, casually putting an arm around Briar's shoulders and drawing her to my side. She's like my little sister, and it feels good to have her here, to know that she's okay and see her out on the town living it up a little. Her life has been so focused on work and Frankie that she hasn't had much of a chance to let her hair down. "But it's good for him to do something that isn't moping."

"And it's good for me to have an evening that doesn't revolve around bath time and reading 'Good Night Moon' forty-two times before bed," Briar adds with a smile.

"Let's order drinks," I say to Atlas, starting forward and dragging Briar along with me, forcing her little legs to keep up. "And then I need to get your thoughts on something."

"Uh-oh," Briar says. "I sense shop talk is about to commence."

"It'll be quick," I promise, kissing the top of her head.

"I don't want to talk shop," Dash protests, following us.

"Stop whining," Briar teases him. "I work all day and then go home and parent. You work part-time and then spend the rest of the time womanizing."

"I don't work part-time!" He protests.

"You sure?" she asks. "Because any time I call, you're home."

"I work from home sometimes!" he says, rolling his eyes.

"Eh. I don't know if I believe that." Briar giggles then dances out of reach when he tries to give her a wet willy. "Ew!" she snaps, batting his hand away. "Don't make me break out the blackmail material."

Dash affects innocence. "What blackmail material?"

"I don't know?" she says, mischief in her eyes as she taps a finger to her chin. "I mean there *is* that time with Becky Sullivan—"

Dash clamps a hand over her mouth. "Don't you fucking dare."

"And now we all need every detail," Atlas says.

"Dead," Dash tells her. "And you two"—he jabs a finger in our direction—"are dead too."

"Well," I say to Briar, "if death is imminent, you might as well tell us."

Dash scowls, but not for long.

Because Briar begins regaling us with tales of Becky Sullivan and her obsession with 80s teen romcoms…and how it ended with her blaring a Bluetooth speaker outside Dash's window at two in the morning.

"Mom and Dad were so mad."

Dash shakes his head, but he's smiling. "That they were."

"And then you made everything worse because you let her crawl in your bedroom window," she says, punching him in the arm.

"Ow," he mutters, rubbing the spot. "I was a teenage boy. My decision-making skills weren't top tier."

"They still aren't," Atlas says.

"Asshole."

"Bigger asshole," Atlas counters.

"Bigg*est* asshole," I add for good measure.

"Children," Briar warns.

This is such a familiar rapport that no one can keep a straight face.

And then the four of us are cracking up as we move toward our regular table.

CHAPTER ELEVEN

Aspen

"ANYTHING ELSE?" I ask, sliding the Gamebreaker over to the middle aged man who fills out the suit he's wearing in the best possible way.

And who does absolutely nothing for my libido.

Nope.

Every cell in my body is fixated on the man across the room.

Banks is wearing a white button down shirt with slacks that hug his powerful thighs, caress an ass that's made for holding on to when he fucks me deep and hard and fast, and…

He has his arm around a woman who's beautiful and curvy and has spent more time laughing and smiling than scowling.

So, the opposite of me.

Completely.

"That'll do it, sweetheart."

I shake myself, focus on Suit Guy and force a smile. "Should I put it on your tab?"

"Yeah, gorgeous. Thanks." He passes over a twenty.

I freeze, momentarily confused before figuring that it's

loud in here and he probably didn't hear me clearly about putting it on his tab. "I'll get your change."

A warm hand on mine. "That's for you."

"Oh." I blink. "I—"

He folds my fingers over the bill, lifts the cocktail in a silent salute. "I'll see you later for another one." A wicked smile. "And maybe I'll be able to convince you to join me for a drink later."

Banks with his arm around a beautiful woman.

A handsome man in front of me, flirting and offering to buy me a drink.

It's tempting to tiptoe toward self-destruction.

But every cell in my body is…fixated across the room.

"Thank you," I say, letting him down gently, "but we're not allowed to date patrons."

"Disappointing," the man says, taking a sip. He salutes me again. "At least you make an excellent Gamebreaker."

"Sometimes it's the little things," I quip.

A grin. Another tip of his glass.

And then he's disappearing into the back of the bar, joining a table filled with equally handsome men in suits.

He won't be alone for long.

Of that I'm sure.

Smiling and shaking my head, I turn to the next person waiting for a drink. But before I can make it that far, I spot something that sends a chill down my spine.

Leo's standing in the opening of the hallway, shadows clinging to his body.

But not his face.

And his expression…makes me shiver.

I don't think Banks confronting him about the bottle of whisky did me any favors.

I reach for my towel, nerves dancing out my fingertips, giving me the urge to clean everything within arm's reach—

"Hey, Aspen!"

Jerking, I clench the towel hanging on my apron, glance down the bar at Johnny. "Yeah?"

"Can you make an empties run?" he asks. "Marissa's on break and we're running low on glasses."

"On it," I tell him, making quick work of the group in front of me—four men who just need bottles of crappy beer put on their tabs—and then I grab a tray. I zip through the tables, not wanting to leave Johnny on his own for too long, but knowing we need clean glasses more. I load up the circular platter, my arms protesting the weight even as I try to squeeze on a few more empties.

We need them.

And maybe part of me wants to get close to Banks's table.

He's the boss, after all. I should make a good impression, make sure he gets great service.

Is that what the kiss was?

My feet screech to a stop, and I nearly topple the tray…*and* down the slippery slope I'm traversing.

This is stupid.

This is—

"Aspen!"

I freeze, gaze whipping toward Banks, seeing that he's waving me over.

My stomach tenses and I brace. He has a beautiful woman clamped to his side and likely wants to impress her. Probably, he'll order me around and show off his power and—

"This is Briar," he says, when I reach him, taking the tray and setting it on the table.

I let him because…

Well, because *this* is Briar? The woman who's like a little sister to them?

Shit.

I lift my hand and shake Briar's. "Nice to meet you."

"You too," Briar says, her eyes drifting between Banks and

me. "Are you the new bartender?" she asks. "Or are you working the floor?"

I force a smile, feeling like far too many eyes are on me, studying me like I'm a bug under the microscope. "I'm working behind the bar." I nod to the tray. "Just getting a jump on empties so we don't run out of clean glasses during the rush."

The man wearing a suit—and doing it beautifully—flicks his brows up, exchanging a look with Banks.

"Well, I should get back to work," I begin quietly, tossing my thumb over my shoulder and reaching for the tray. "Can I bring you all anything to drink?"

"Four Gamebreakers."

I nod as I turn back to the man who's spoken.

"Atlas," he says, confirming my assumptions. Suit equals businessman. Great deduction, huh? "Nice to meet you." He lifts his hand and I shake it before reaching for the tray again. "Sorry I haven't been around much to meet you before now. I've been traveling for work."

"Because he's a big-time important businessman," Briar stage whispers.

"Doing important businessy things and all," the other male in the group—wearing a black tee and jeans— chimes in.

"*So* important," Briar says with a grin.

Atlas sighs and rolls his eyes, but I don't miss the barest bit of a smile edging into the corners of his mouth.

"And this dumbass is Dash," Banks says, nodding to the man with arresting hazel eyes and curly brown hair with a hint of red.

"Hi," I say softly as my free hand is engulfed and gently shaken by the big man.

"Did you give Banksy boy your number yet?" he asks, waggling his brows and reminding me of the bets the men made my first night here.

Banks scowls, but Briar reacts before anyone else, swatting him on the back of the head. "Cool it, dipshit."

"Ow!" Dash mutters, releasing my hand to rub the spot. "What the hell, Thorny?"

Briar shifts close, puts her face right in Dash's, and jabs her brother in the chest. "Two words," she grits out. "Becky. Sullivan."

I don't know what that means, but apparently Briar knows how to handle these men because Dash stops giving Banks a hard time and mutters, "Rude" before slumping into the booth and crossing his arms.

He's cute.

But definitely a handful.

And now I find that I'm fighting a smile of my own.

"There's more to the Becky Sullivan story?" Atlas asks.

Briar smiles evilly as she stares down her brother. "There's *always* more."

"I'll just"—I tilt my head toward the bar—"make those drinks for you all."

"Aspen," Banks begins, taking a step as though to follow me.

I heft the empties on my shoulder, inching away from him. I can still feel his fingers on my wrist, his thumb brushing lightly over my skin. Still see the way he burst into the office, hear his sharp words for Leo. "Johnny's going to be drowning if I don't get back."

He looks as though he wants to protest, but he doesn't, just says, "You'll let me drive you home tonight?"

"Johnny and Marissa already offered," I say, nodding toward the bar again.

More protest in those green eyes, but he doesn't give voice to them, only nods quietly. "Glad you'll be safe. Just…" He glances at the table then back at me. "Don't be a stranger, okay? If you get a free moment, I'd love to catch up before I head out of town with the team."

"Out of town?" I ask.

"Road trip," he explains.

Because he's a professional hockey player and does things like go on road trips and play in front of tens of thousands of people.

"Right," I say. "I'll, um, try to make time. If not, good luck with the games."

His face gentles, but I don't stick around to watch it like I want to. Instead, I hightail it for the bar, running the dirties to the kitchen so they can be put through the industrial dish-washer. I bring out a fresh case on my way back to the bar, sliding it into place between Johnny and me.

Noise rises—laughter from Banks and company, chatter from the kitchen behind us, from the patrons pouring in through the entrance, filling up the available space. In fact, I barely have time to make those four Gamebreakers and have Marissa bring them to the table…

Before we're utterly slammed.

It means I don't have to find a way to work up the courage to make small talk with his crew, to deepen my dangerous connection with Banks.

I'm barely keeping up, making drinks as quickly as possible, trying to keep orders straight, and forcing my gaze away from that table.

The latter is a losing battle.

My focus is drawn like a beacon to Banks, Atlas, Dash, and Briar, heart squeezing at their obvious camaraderie, at their smiles and laughter.

I never had that.

I wish I could sit close to them, just be a fly on the wall.

Just have *that* for a few minutes—

"Aspen, do you have any lemon juice?"

Shoving the thought down, I snag the container and bring it to Johnny, smiling when he thanks me before getting back to orders.

I don't have that.

I never will.

I just need to accept it.

And move on, keep making my way, continue grinding out a life that may be small and more than a bit lonely…

But at least it's mine.

———

KNOCK. *Knock. Knock.*

Groaning, I shove my head under the pillow and clamp my hands to my ears.

It's my day off.

I didn't get home until almost four—mainly because I had to walk home.

Johnny's a good guy, but when he's dating a new woman, he doesn't have a lot of space in his head for anything, least of all a promised ride home.

He and Marissa rode the high of the rush, hurried through their parts of closing down, and then…

They disappeared.

Which meant a long, cold walk in the dark hours of morning.

Knock. Knock. Knock.

"Go away," I moan, clamping the pillow tightly against my head. "I just want to sleep in."

Knock. Knock. KNOCK!

Groaning, I toss the pillow aside, curse when I'm momentarily blinded by fucking Southern California sunlight blasting me through the windows.

"Stupid sunny state," I grumble as I yank on a pair of pajama pants and stomp to the door.

Fuck my downstairs neighbors.

They're all probably at their nine-to-fives anyway, I tell myself to assuage the guilt that hits me halfway to the door.

I soften my steps anyway, reach for the handle—

Knock. *Knock.*

"For fuck's sake," I growl, whipping the door open…

And revealing Mrs. X—or really, Mrs. Xavier, but because she has a not-so-secret crush on Patrick Stewart and is obsessed with the X-Men movies, she has demanded all of her friends (not me) and broken little creatures she collects (this *is* me) call her Mrs. X.

"Hi, Mrs. X," I say, rubbing the remainder of sleep out of my eyes. "Did you need something?"

"Why else would I be pounding on your door?" she says, briskly moving by me and marching across my apartment.

It's not far.

Which is why it only takes her a moment to reach my makeshift closet—a rolling rack and a banged-up dresser and…

A laundry basket.

Which Mrs. X scoops up.

"What—"

She lifts her chin, marches back toward the door, basket in hand. "It's laundry day," she says, brushing by me and stepping into the hall. "Get dressed and meet me downstairs."

Then she's gone.

And I'm left holding the door open as the whirlwind that's Mrs. X disappears.

I shake myself, grab a sweatshirt and yank it on, and then get my bag of quarters and follow her downstairs.

"Who was the man hanging around your place the other day?" she asks the moment I stumble through the door to the laundry room to find my clothes in the washing machine and a cup of coffee waiting for me.

I see that the washer's going already and try to pass her the correct number of quarters.

She waves them off, shoves the coffee into my hand instead.

"What do you mean?" I ask, trying to play it cool.

Either my family has found me—unlikely considering where I'm living and the lengths I've gone to not draw attention to myself, or Mrs. X has been spying through her peephole again and she caught Banks leaving my place.

"I'm talking about the hot hunk of manflesh that was leaving your apartment bright and early the other morning." She wiggles her brows. "Did you have a fun night?"

A fun night scraping gum off concrete.

Yup, I sure did.

"He's a…" I snag my laundry basket, avoiding her razor-sharp gaze as I try to formulate what exactly Banks is to me. "...a co-worker," I finish.

She snorts. "Liar, liar pants on fire."

"Mrs. X," I sigh. "I work all the time and sleep the rest of it. I don't have time for a man."

"Even one who carries your bags up to your door?" she asks pointedly.

"Didn't you just insinuate he spent the night?"

She takes a sip from her mug, white curls bouncing as she shrugs. "I have many tools in order to access the necessary gossip."

"You're terrible."

"Nope," she says, popping the p. "I'm persistent and I'm glad there's a man in your life who looks at you like he does."

Looks at me how? I want to ask.

I don't because…I can't know the answer to that.

"He's just being nice," I tell her. "My car is in the shop, and he gave me a ride home."

"Hmm," she murmurs, but it's clear that's not the extent of what she's thinking. Not at all.

"What?" I can't help but ask.

"I wouldn't be opposed to *any* ride that man offered up to me."

Groaning, I drop my chin to my chest, not lifting it until she squeezes my forearm.

"You deserve happiness," she says. "And deserve it with a person who'll look after you."

I scowl because those words are far too similar to those I heard in my life before I moved here. "I don't need looking after. I'm strong and independent and not reliant on anyone, let alone a man, to take care of me."

"No," she agrees. "You're right. You *can* take care of yourself. It's just"—she squeezes my arm again—"you don't always have to do it alone."

"I'm happy alone," I tell her and before she can press me further, I divert her by saying, "Did you see that there's an X-Men marathon on TV tonight?"

Her eyes widen. "When? What channel is it on?"

I tell her and then we do the usual, shooting the shit (thankfully not about Banks and hot hunks of *manflesh,* barf), dishing gossip, talking about her grandkids. She forces another cup of coffee on me, along with a half dozen muffins—though I don't fight very hard because she's an excellent baker.

Then she's off for her morning walk and I'm back in my apartment with my clean clothes.

I putter around for a few hours, doing some long overdue cleaning, making a grocery list and adding a couple of treats for myself since the rush last night means that I have a pocket full of cash tips. Checking emails and paying bills and…

Stumbling onto the SoCal Vipers' website.

Banks is there, handsome and smiling and…

My eyes slide down and I see they're playing tonight against the L.A. Phantoms.

Playing—my gaze slides to the upper right corner of my laptop screen—right *now.*

I tell myself it's not Mrs. X's words that has me turning on my TV and putting on the game.

It's *not*.

But I still have them bouncing around my brain anyway.

You don't always have to do it alone.

CHAPTER TWELVE

Banks

FOUR MINUTES LEFT in the game and we're down by two.

The first line—my old line—has been out there for about ninety seconds and they're gassed. I can see it. Our opponents, the Phantoms, can see it too, and if we can't make a line change soon, we're going to be down by three.

I look over my shoulder at Coach, hoping for a sign that I'm up, but he's watching the ice with zero emotion on his face.

Figures.

"Come on," I mutter under my breath.

We can't seem to get the puck out of our zone long enough to make the line change, and I'm on the edge of my seat. I should be out there with them. It's *my* line, *my* teammates and—

The crowd roars and I jump to my feet as one of the Phantoms' defensemen high sticks my buddy, West. He goes down holding his face and Coach snarls a string of profanity when the refs don't call a penalty.

At least the boys can come off the ice now.

West is still holding his face and one of the trainers runs up with a towel.

Coach taps my shoulder and I immediately throw my legs over the boards, soothed by the familiar crunch of my skates hitting the ice.

I'm itching to play.

To score.

To fight.

Anything to get out of this slump.

I take my place near the faceoff circle, watching my center, Ace, lean in.

He wins the draw and the puck all but lands on my stick. I one-time it to my linemate and he takes it behind the net before sending it back to me. This is something we've done a thousand times in practice, but somehow I miss the puck and it slides past me to one of the Phantoms.

Motherfucker.

Frustration surges through me with such ferocity I can't breathe for a minute.

I can't catch a simple pass?

What in the ever-loving fuck is wrong with me?

I tamp down the urge to yell a plethora of obscenities and chase down the puck at full speed, getting it back with ease, adrenaline pumping through me. My reward for all those extra practices is a burst of power, and it feels good to move like this, to dominate the ice as we head back into the zone. I should be passing, looking to make a play with my teammates. Instead, I'm driving forward, focused on the spot just over the goalie's right shoulder. That's one of his only weaknesses, so if I can just—

A Phantoms D-man comes out of nowhere, drives his shoulder in my chest and I lose my footing, crashing into the boards hard enough to knock my helmet loose.

"Keep your head up!" the Phantoms defenseman chirps as he skates past me.

This time the feeling surging through me is fury, and I'm back on my feet despite a burning pain in my shoulder. I chase him down, hip checking him a fraction of a second after he releases the puck, and he whirls, pissed that the hit was late. I give him a shove—I've been working up to this all night—and he shoves me back. Then the gloves come off and it's a free for all. He's a good four inches taller than me, but I'm powered by desperation, frustration, and a few other emotions I can't articulate at the moment...

His fist connects with my jaw and the jolt of pain infuriates me even more. I hit back, two quick jabs that catch him by surprise. He comes at me, getting a grip on my jersey, but I've been around the block way too many times for that bullshit, so I twist my body away, continuing to swing, despite the refs trying to pull us apart.

"Whassamatter, Christianson?" the guy taunts. "Forget how to score?"

"Fuck you, D'Marco." I swing once more, but the ref catches my arm and he and the linesmen have managed to pull us apart.

"Bye-bye now!" D'Marco calls after me as I turn for the tunnel. With only a minute left in the game, there's no point in my going to the penalty box since the infraction would probably be four minutes—two for instigating and two for fighting.

I don't give him the satisfaction of a response, opting to catch my breath and figure out if I need someone to check my shoulder. It's throbbing, which isn't good, and the last thing I need is an injury.

"Fuckin' D'Marco can suck my dick," West says as I skate past him.

"Better you than me," I quip, chuckling.

Fuck.

I grab my water bottle on the way out of the arena, and my shoulder isn't happy about the quick movement.

Coach is going to kill me if fucked up my shoulder from fighting.

More than likely, it's from smashing into the boards, but it's hard to tell at this point.

I'll have to let our head trainer, Norris Lawton, take a look.

He appears as if he's read my mind.

"How bad?" is all he says as I follow him into the locker room.

"I don't know," I admit, sinking down and pulling off my jersey.

He checks me out but doesn't seem overly concerned.

"Doc'll probably want you to do an X-ray, just to be sure, but it's probably just bruises. I don't think it's serious."

Thank fuck.

———

BETWEEN TALKING TO THE PRESS, getting an X-ray done, chatting with the team doctor, and finally getting into the shower, it feels like hours until I'm on my way back to the hotel. I pull out my phone and I'm not surprised to see a bunch of texts.

BRIAR: ARE YOU OKAY? TEXT ME!

I chuckle as I send her a quick note letting her know I'm good. She may be younger than all of us by five years but she's still the mother hen of the group.

ROYAL: You should have knocked that
asshole into the middle of next week.
Shoulder okay? You hit the boards hard.

Those are a lot of words from my reclusive buddy, and I take a minute to assure him there's no permanent damage.

There are also messages from Dash and Atlas, as well as from Briggs and my housekeeper, Zelda, who watches every game without fail and then gives me a critique of my performance the next time I see her. She's a Polish immigrant who's in her sixties, but she knows almost as much as I do about hockey. Our conversations tend to be pretty epic, so I take a minute to reassure her, and the others, that I'm fine.

But it's the last text that catches me off guard.

> ASPEN: That hit into the boards was terrifying…are you okay? Please just let me know.

For reasons I don't want to overthink after the night I've had, it means a lot that she reached out. Yeah, I know we only exchanged numbers because Briggs has her car, but the fact that she reached out first is monumental. It's possible I might have even put a tiny chink in her seemingly impenetrable emotional armor.

And since I can't text while driving, I call her instead.

"Are you okay?!" she demands by way of greeting.

"I'm good, little spitfire," I respond. "Driving home now. Doc said it's just a bruise. I'll ice it tonight and tomorrow and should be good for the next game."

"Jesus. It scared the crap out of me when you went into the wall like that—shouldn't that be a foul or something?!"

I chuckle. "They're called penalties in hockey—and yeah, they usually are, but if the ref misses the hit, or doesn't think it's an illegal one, there's nothing we can do."

She pauses and I can picture her scowling. "Is that why you punched him?"

"Yeah." I sigh, my energy dissipating like a deflating balloon. "Well, one of the reasons."

"I—are you okay?" she asks, her voice suddenly softer. "I

mean, you just said your shoulder is fine, but…you sound…I don't know, exhausted in a way that has nothing to do with being tired."

As if she's familiar with the feeling.

I hate that.

"Yeah." It's hard to put what I'm feeling into words. "I'm fine."

I don't talk about this stuff.

I *can*. My friends would listen. They would try to understand. They know the pressure I'm under. They have lots of their own pressures in their lives. But they never played sports at this level. The scrutiny we get is unlike anything I've ever experienced.

"It's okay if you don't want to talk about it."

I don't…but I do.

"I've been struggling," I admit after a moment. "It's still early in the season, but I haven't scored yet. That's not like me. They paid me a lot of money to come here and get results. Last season was okay, but not great, and so far, I'm not starting off strong."

"What do you consider strong?" she asks.

"I don't know, but it's definitely not zero," I mutter.

"It's a team sport, though," she says. "It's not on you to do all the scoring, is it?"

"Yes and no. Yes, it's a team sport, and no, it's not all on me." I shove a hand through my hair in frustration. "But in a way, it is. That's why I'm here. I bring a very specific skill set to the table, and without it, why are they paying me? They have a couple of tough guys. Magnus Forsberg and Aaron Shaunessy are the guys that fight and get gritty out there. Colby is the first line center who wins all the faceoffs. West is a playmaker. He's the one with this incredibly high hockey IQ who can visualize what's happening almost before it happens. He's so intuitive, he gets us into position to score. And *scoring* is what I do. My shot placement and accuracy are some of the best in the league, and I study so much tape it makes my eyes cross, just so I know all of the goalies' weaknesses. I can pick a corner, choose where I'm shooting, and bury the puck in the net more often than not. *That's* why I'm here." I sigh. "Or why I'm supposed to be here, anyway."

"And without that you're…useless?" Her voice holds no censure, and I know she's trying to make me think about my place on the team as a whole, but it's not that easy.

"I'm not useless, but there are a dozen guys the team can pay half of what I'm making to perform at this level. They're taking a huge cap hit to have me here. And the truth is, if I don't step it up a notch, I'm afraid they're going to trade me."

There.

I've finally vocalized my biggest professional fear.

"And you don't want to leave your…family."

The way she says *family* should have given me pause, but I'm too wrapped up in my own shit to take the time to analyze it.

"Exactly. I can't be in Florida or Ottawa or some shit while Frankie's growing up in SoCal. And Royal, he needs all of us to check on him, because while we're not particularly worried he'll hurt himself, we *are* worried about his mental health. He hasn't been the same since he lost the use of his hand. Atlas and Dash both have lucrative businesses that require a lot of travel, so having all of us based here to be there for Briar, Frankie, and Royal is important."

"You think they'd trade you because you're having a slow start?" she asks.

"No, but my numbers last season were pretty mediocre too. The sports writers are all saying that I may not be a good fit here, shit like that. And it doesn't help that Coach dropped me from the first line to the third." I say *third* like it's a dirty word and she doesn't miss it.

"That's some kind of punishment?"

"He said it wasn't, specifically, in those words, and all four lines are important or we wouldn't have them, but yeah—that's how he incentivizes me to be better. Play better. If I want to be back on the number one line, I need to earn it."

"Is there anything I can do?"

A handful of crude, inappropriate responses come to mind, but I immediately turn off that train of thought. This is too important for me to screw up with sexual innuendo.

She texted me because was worried. She's asking me questions and trying to understand my job. Not to mention, we're actually having a civil conversation for once. So yeah, I'm sharing some heavy shit, but this rapport between us feels good.

It's something I haven't had with a woman in a long time, and…I don't want to lose it.

"Just keep listening," I say solemnly. "It feels good to be able to vent without feeling judged or, worse, pitied."

"No judgment or pity here," she says. "I'm happy to listen to you talk about dribbling the puck around the ice. Whenever or wherever."

"Dribbling, little spitfire?" I tease. "Really?"

She laughs. "Look," she says. "I'm a newbie to the whole hockey thing. I just watched my first game tonight."

"Dribbling's for basketball."

"I'll mark it down in my notebook under useless things I've learned today," she says dryly.

I grin. "So what else did you do today?"

"Why do you ask?" Some of the lightness leaves her tone.

"Well, obviously, you know what *I* was up to," I say. "It's your day off, right? Did you have any time to relax?"

A long pause.

"Come on," I coax. "I gave you mine."

This pause is a little shorter, and then I'm rewarded with a small piece of Aspen.

"I did laundry with my Patrick Stewart obsessed neighbor, Mrs. X."

I blink.

"Tell me more," I order.

And when, after a brief blip of quiet, she does, I forget about the game, about my sore shoulder, and the lack of goals.

I'm just here with her.

Why does that make me so happy?

CHAPTER THIRTEEN

Aspen

A SHORT PEOPLE problem is not being able to reach the top shelf, even with the biggest step stool the bar has.

I strain, rising higher on my tiptoes, fingertips just brushing the polished edge of the glass ledge.

It was a slow night, which is sad for the stash of tips in my pocket, and the carton of ice cream I was hoping to splurge on (since I have no self-control and the one I bought the other day is already gone).

Instead, it'll be water and electricity and ramen noodles for the next few days.

Sighing, I stretch a little higher, trying to reach the bottle of expensive alcohol and to do it without breaking anything.

I know that Leo's asked me to clean all of the shelves because he's pissed at me.

Banks standing up for me was sweet, but it definitely didn't endear me to the man who oversees The Sapphire Room day-to-day. In fact, if I had a dollar for every time I caught Leo glaring at me tonight, I'd be able to afford a dozen cartons of chocolate chip cookie dough.

He's hoping I'll fuck up and break something else, that I'll be a liability and so he'll have an excuse to fire me.

Well, I have no intention of allowing that to happen.

Carefully, I stretch a little further, snag the last bottle of expensive ass swill.

Exhaling, I climb down, set it on the bar top.

And then I set to work, grabbing the towel and glass cleaner and starting with the top shelf.

Stretch. Spray. Wipe until the glass gleams and there isn't a fingerprint or speck of dust in sight. Stretch. Spray. Wipe.

Rinse. Repeat.

Until the top shelf is clean and I'm readying myself to make a careful descent.

"You missed a spot."

I like cleaning. Some might even say that it's my safe space, my *happy* place. When all the thoughts in my head are twisted and disordered, it's sometimes my only distraction, the only way for me to find balance again.

But I *really* hate it when my bosses tell me that.

I grit my teeth together, look over my shoulder at Leo. "I'm happy to go over it again," I grind out.

Eyes cold, Leo stares at me for long enough that my nape begins to prickle.

Then he nods sharply, turns away, and stomps down the hall.

Distantly, I hear the door to his office slam.

Sighing, I go over the top shelf again then repeat the process with the others. It doesn't take much time, and so before long, I'm wiping bottles and setting them back into their proper positions.

"There," I say, placing the last one and surveying my work.

The shelves and mirror behind them are pristine, glittering like jewels in the soft overhead light.

"Not bad," I murmur, mentally patting myself on my back as I toss my towel to the side and begin to climb down.

I've managed this without incident dozens of times in the last hour, but this time when I go to descend the step ladder, it wobbles. I reach for the bar, trying to steady myself.

Too late.

The leg of the stool slips on the black rubber mat, skidding off the edge and slamming into the cabinet on the back wall.

And…

Fuck.

I go down, the ladder toppling beneath me, tangling up my legs, and I land hard, ankle rolling.

Pain is a scalding burst of agony that shoots up through my foot and into my leg.

"Fuck," I hiss, grabbing at my ankle, kicking away the useless stool with my other foot.

The frame is bent now, one of the steps missing.

"Bastard," I mutter as I lay there, clutching my foot, trying to even out my breathing, hoping the pain will subside.

It does after a long moment.

But it's renewed when I manage to push up to my feet, when I test the joint with the slightest bit of weight.

"Christ." I slam my eyes closed, gripping the counter as black clings to the edges of my vision. It hurts, but it's subsiding, like a stubbed toe making it so you can barely breathe until the worst of the pain has passed. I keep still, inhaling and exhaling slowly and steadily, waiting until it calms, and then try again.

It's bad and I grit my teeth.

But it's not as bad as before, which has the lovely side effect of meaning other pains come to light.

My wrist hurts, a bruise is blooming on my elbow, and a throb has begun in my knee.

Great.

Love it.

Just like I love that no one heard the commotion and checked on me.

Which means it's likely that Johnny and Marissa have skipped out on giving me a ride again. Those newly-in-love hormones strike again. Too busy getting out of here so they can fuck like jack rabbits to remember pesky promises like making sure their carless friend doesn't have to walk home during the darkest part of night.

Sighing, I right the ladder, using it to help me hobble down the hall to the break room, forcing my ankle to take a bit more weight with each step.

It hurts like hell and sweat has broken out on my back, beneath my breasts, but I just keep moving.

I stow the stool in the storeroom and then go next door to clock out, retrieve my coat, and purse.

Leo's in his office when I tell him I'm leaving, and he doesn't deign to look up.

Asshole.

I pocket my cell, toss my purse over my shoulder, cross-body style, and pull on my jacket.

And then I'm hobbling out into the cold night.

———

I'M BARELY three blocks from the bar and sweating like a pig, pain filling each and every part of my body when I see the headlights flash over the road.

I keep moving, trying to hide my limp as much as possible, to not be an easy target, trying not to draw any attention from the driver.

Unfortunately, my efforts are for naught.

The car slows to a stop, and I reach into my purse for my pepper spray, fingers tightening on the canister.

The driver's side door opens, and I lift the metal container. "Back off!" I shout, assuming rabid raccoon position.

"We've got to stop meeting like this," comes the dry, male voice.

I blink against the shadows, see that the man is leaning one broad shoulder against the roof of his car.

"Banks?"

His smile is a flash of white in the dim light.

"Yup, little spitfire." That smile fades, a note of anger entering his words. "Care to clue me in on why you're walking down the street in the middle of the fucking night?"

"Don't snap at me," I snarl, shoving the canister away and starting to walk down the road again.

Silence, then even angrier words.

"Want to clue me in why *the fuck* you're limping?"

I close my eyes. "Dammit," I whisper, moving faster.

Or trying to anyway.

Because my ankle is getting worse, not better.

The thought has tears prickling in my eyes. I can't afford a trip to the doctor's or the medical bills that will follow. I can't afford a fucking brace. I can't afford to take time off work.

I can't—

Suddenly, I'm in the air.

I screech.

"Quiet," Banks growls, striding toward his car with me in his arms, my body cradled against his chest. "You have got to be the most fucking stubborn woman on the planet." He shifts me as he opens the door then bends, settling me carefully on the seat.

"I'm—"

"You're limping down the sidewalk in the middle of the night in a not-great part of town," he says, sounding like he's chewing on broken glass. "I don't want any sass. Just sit there and let me drive you home."

He doesn't want any *sass*?

My temper spikes, retorts crawling up the back of my throat.

But they don't make it out because then he slams the door shut.

I watch as he rounds the hood, his body barely a shadow in the headlights. Then he's climbing into the driver's seat.

"Fuck. You," I grit out.

"You can be mad at me," he snaps, putting the car in drive and speeding down the street. "Because I'm pissed at you too."

For a minute, I sit there, anger roiling through me.

Then I ask, "Why are *you* pissed?"

"I went to Sapphire to check on you," he clips out. "Leo told me you knocked off early because it was quiet."

My eyes go wide as I turn to stare at him. "You're mad I didn't finish my shift?"

"No," he says, words frost-filled. "I'm pissed you don't seem to give a fuck about your personal safety."

"I was supposed to get a ride from Johnny, but he left without me again."

A pause that's long enough for me to feel the tension ramp back up. "Again?" he asks dangerously.

"I'm fine," I say instead of answering that.

"He left you." A beat. "Again."

"I'm not Johnny's responsibility," I remind him, "and I'm not yours either."

We pull to a stop at a signal, and he pinches the bridge of his nose, exhales sharply. "I don't want to fight with you," he says quietly.

"Then don't order me around and act like a goddamned caveman."

He exhales sharply before he nods once, releasing his nose and lifting his head, glancing over at me. "Noted." A breath, his voice even and calm. "Now, is it okay if I drive you home?"

I narrow my eyes, waiting for him to pull some other caveman bullshit.

When he doesn't, and just waits for me to answer, I nod. "Yes," I say, projecting some calm and even of my own. "Thank you."

The light turns green, and he accelerates forward.

"What happened to your foot?"

My ankle throbs in response to the question. "Nothing."

"Aspen," he warns.

"No caveman," I counter.

A breath that lifts and drops those big shoulders. "Please tell me?"

It's the *please* that does it, and I find myself saying, "I fell off the step ladder when I was cleaning the shelves behind the bar."

"Please tell me it was a new step ladder that Leo purchased."

Since I can't tell him that, I just look out the window.

He curses, but we've reached my apartment building and he's pulling into my empty spot. "Did Briggs say how much longer your car would be?"

"Not too much longer." I reach for the handle, pop open the door.

By the time I unbuckle and start maneuvering out, Banks is there. "I'm going to carry you up—"

I shoot him a glare.

"*May* I carry you up?"

"I should refuse on principle." But my ankle hurts and I'm exhausted and he might say that *I'm* stubborn, but I can see the resolution in his face. He'll fight me on this.

And…I'm too fucking tired.

"But…" he prompts.

"Yes, you can carry me up."

A second later, I'm in his arms again. But almost immediately, guilt courses through me. "Your shoulder—"

"—is fine," he finishes. "Like I told you, it's just bruised, and I don't know if you know this, little spitfire"—his voice lightens—"but you're tiny."

I lift my chin. "I'm five-six, I'll have you know."

"And I have half a foot on you."

I sniff. "Maybe on a good day."

He smirks, snagging my keyfob from my hand and yanking open the bottom door. Then he's moving to the stairs, not remotely out of breath by the time we reach my floor.

Bastard.

But I can't complain—not about the strong arms wrapped around me, or the hard chest behind my back, or the gentle way he settles me on my good foot so he can unlock and push open my door.

I *can* complain, however, about how he doesn't give me a chance to protest…

When he barges inside.

God, Mrs. X is going to have a field day with this.

CHAPTER FOURTEEN

Banks

I'M NOT sure whether I want to seduce her or spank her.

And I'm not talking about the fun, sexy kind of spanking.

She's the most infuriating woman I've ever met and despite how attracted to her I am, it's starting to wear on me. I like a little sass, I enjoy a fiery personality, and butting heads sometimes is fun. But this is a lot. Too much. She has walls up that feel impenetrable, and if that's the case, what the hell am I doing?

It might be time to cut my losses.

I have enough going on in my life with my hockey career, I just don't have it in me to chase someone who genuinely doesn't want to be caught. Playing hard to get is one thing— what Aspen is doing is something else altogether.

"I can take you to an urgent care center if you need it," I say once she's settled on the couch with a towel, a bag of ice, and a pillow beneath her foot. It's swollen and turning purple, which isn't good, and it concerns me.

"I can't—" she begins, but I cut her off.

"I know. You can't afford it. But if you were hurt at work, the company will pay for everything."

She looks up with a wariness that's impossible to miss. "Banks...I can't afford to *miss* work."

"You also can't afford to have an injury not heal right. Even a hairline fracture could heal wrong and then you'll wind up with a limp—or worse."

She closes her eyes and leans back, as if all the fight has drained out of her.

"I'm so tired," is all she says. "Of everything."

"I know, baby. But I'm here. If you'll just let me in." I settle on the couch next to her, moving her legs over my lap. I gently run my hand up her calf, noting the tension in her muscles. She's coiled tighter than a drum, and I feel another wave of guilt.

Money is something I take for granted.

I'm generous, sometimes to a fault, but I still never give a second thought to going to the doctor. Or whether or not I'll be paid because I need a sick day. Even with the worst of injuries, I get my paychecks on time. Without question. Not to mention, the money in the bank, in my savings account, and my extensive investment portfolio.

Not having any of that is obviously weighing heavily on Aspen.

And now on me.

I want to tell her I'll pay her salary anyway, but not only is that not a Sapphire Room policy, it's also not enough. She relies on tips, not the twenty dollars an hour we pay our service staff. It's more than most places pay, but she doesn't have enough hours to make her rent that way.

It's complicated—and something I can't easily fix—which pisses me off.

Her eyes are closed and her breathing has slowed, so if nothing else, I'm helping her relax. That's the best I can hope for at this point.

I continue to stroke her calf, the bony sections of her knees, and the top of her thigh. Her skin is soft, like the finest silk, and my eyes drift closed as well.

If this is going to be the last time we're together, I want to remember her like this.

Relaxed and quiet and enjoying my touch.

I've done everything in my power to show her who I am, and it's beginning to feel like it's not enough. So I'll sit here until she falls asleep and then it's time for me to go. If she wants to see me, or talk to me, or anything else, it'll have to be her move.

───────

I WAKE up with a stiff neck and Aspen's back pressed tightly to my front.

My very *awake* front.

Shit.

I don't remember falling asleep or getting into this position, but I wouldn't move now if someone paid me.

It feels so damn good, any thought of leaving her long gone.

I run my hand along the curve of her hip, wondering if my touch will rouse her.

It's still dark out, so it can't be morning yet, and my watch is on the wrist of the arm I'm lying on. I nuzzle her hair and it smells like coconut, reminding me of the islands. Would she ever let me take her on a trip like that? Buy her a different bikini for every day of the trip? Peer across the table at her while she sips a fruity drink with an umbrella straw?

I'm harder than stone now, my cock aching against my slacks, and I start to shift away from her.

To my surprise, she presses back against me, a soft moan of protest escaping her. "Don't stop," she whispers.

I freeze, positive I can't have heard her right. "You want me to keep touching you, baby?"

"Yes." There's no mistaking the sureness in her voice.

It doesn't make sense, but I don't care.

I want this.

Want her.

In any way she's willing.

"You want me to keep touching you, baby?"

"Mm. Yes. I want you so much."

"Show me," I say quietly.

I want her, but I need her to feel what I feel.

Before I have time to overthink it, she's shifted so she's facing me.

Kissing me.

Fingers drifting beneath my shirt and skimming the skin beneath.

Fuck.

That feels so good.

My lips drift to the side of her neck, kissing the soft skin there and watching the gooseflesh break out.

"You're so soft," I whisper. "So beautiful."

Then we're kissing again and her lips are just as sweet as I remember, but this time I don't keep it chaste or casual. I cup the side of her face with my hand and plunge my tongue into her mouth. She meets me stroke for stroke, giving as good as she gets, and we slowly shift positions until she's fully on top of me, our mouths practically fused together.

Her body is warm and soft, firm breasts pressed into my chest.

I want to touch her everywhere, all at once, and for a second I feel like a teenager about to get his first blow job.

Nope.

Aspen isn't the type of woman you fuck without finesse.

And frankly, I don't want to fuck her.

I want her to know me, feel me, understand the man I am in ways other words and actions haven't managed to convey.

I slide my hands beneath her blouse and loosen the bra strap there. Then I gently explore. Her back. Her shoulders. The dip in her waist. The curve of her ass.

All while making love to her mouth in the same way I hope to make love to her body.

"Banks." The way she says my name—a soft, breathy whisper filled with longing—brings out the beast in me. I need to win her over, take her—*own* her. This cat and mouse game she's been playing ends now. I'll make her mine or walk away. That's my only course of action at this point.

I use both hands to pull her top off and am gratified when she drops her mouth right back to mine as if pulled in by a magnet.

Good.

I want her to be needy.

Raw.

Open.

Mine.

"Off," she orders, pushing at my shirt.

Buttons go flying as we fumble on the small couch that's nowhere near big enough for me, much less both of us.

Then she lowers her head and kisses a trail along the underside of my jaw, lightly nibbling my Adam's apple. Her lips feel like heaven on my body, and I relax into the cushions as she kisses and sucks and teases my torso. When she closes her mouth around one of my nipples, I groan, digging my fingers into her hair.

"Fuck, baby, that feels good."

Her eyes darken as she gazes up at me. "*You* feel good."

"You're wearing too many clothes."

Mischief in those hazel eyes. "So are you."

I chuckle and reach down to unzip my slacks, lifting my

hips as we push them off, along with my boxers. Then I tug at her skirt, and she wiggles out of it.

Jesus, Mary, and Joseph.

She's beautiful with clothes on, but she's fucking breath-taking naked.

"Grab the condom out of my wallet and climb over here," I instruct in a gruff voice.

She doesn't hesitate, picking up my slacks and fumbling around until she gets to my wallet and the condom within.

"Put it on me," I say, my eyes locked with hers.

We stare at each other for an extra beat. I can see the conflict in her eyes, as she wars with herself. She's torn between wanting to give in to this magical feeling between us and being irritated because I'm telling her what to do. Again.

But she likes it—in the bedroom, or couch, anyway.

Because a moment later she's sliding the condom down my cock, her fingers cool against the overheated flesh. I let out a soft hiss when she cups my balls with her hand, squeezing lightly. My breath catches when she straddles me, and I reach up to stroke my thumbs across her pretty pink nipples. They harden against my touch, so I keep going, squeezing and pinching and stroking until she sighs happily. Her eyes are closed again, and she's settled against my crotch, though I'm not inside of her yet.

So many things I want to do to her.

So many ways to make her feel good.

Yet I'm not in a rush.

In fact, I plan to let her take the reins. Initially, at least.

"What do you want, baby?" I ask, resting my hands on her hips.

She braces herself on my chest, bringing her knees in closer to my sides. "You."

"You have me. Take whatever you want."

Her eyes soften with a look I can't quite decipher, but then she's kissing me again, her sweet mouth opening over mine.

Our tongues collide hungrily, greedily, everything amping up no matter how hard I'm trying to slow them down and savor these first moments of intimacy.

My cock is gliding between her warm, wet folds and I can feel how aroused she is.

For me.

It's killing me not to flip us over and drive into her. Hard and fast and deep. To make her scream my name and dig her nails into my back. To give her the pleasure I know is coming.

But I wait.

It *has* to be her move.

I don't know why, because I've already asked her what she wants, but it feels important.

"Banks…" Her forehead is pressed to mine, her body molded against my torso.

"Take what you want," I repeat quietly. "It's all for you."

She reaches between us, and I feel her hand on my cock, lining me up at her slick entrance.

She sits up and her eyes seek out mine as she slowly slides down, taking me inch by methodical inch.

"That's it, baby. Take it all."

"Banks. Oh fuck…Banks!" She lets out a soft cry when I'm fully seated, her pussy clenching and pulsing around me.

I reach up and rest my hands on her hips, as if that will somehow help me stay in control.

"That's it, rock yourself home," I grit out as she starts to ride me, pleasure thrumming through my veins.

It feels so fucking good, I don't know how long I'm going to last.

"Please, Banks…" Her voice is a whispered cry.

"What do you want, baby girl?"

For once, she doesn't hesitate. "Everything."

The word I've been dying to hear.

And she has no idea the beast she's about to release.

CHAPTER FIFTEEN

Aspen

FOR A SECOND, he doesn't move.

Then he's a flurry of motion, pushing off the couch with him still inside me and walking the five feet to the bed. He dumps me on the mattress, and I lose him for a second, my protest welling up in my throat, but before it can escape, he's notching himself at my entrance and sliding in to the hilt.

I gasp at the intrusion, so hard, so full, so—

"Banks!" I cry as he pulls back until he's barely inside and then slams home without warning.

Fast and furious, hard and deep.

This isn't me riding him slowly, seeking an orgasm that's just out of reach.

This is Banks fucking me with purpose, sending us both toward a glorious peak. It's just on the right side of rough and when he palms my breast, squeezing it like he owns it, I feel desire pool between my legs.

I don't like orders in real life.

But in bed? When I can submit without worry to a man who…

I still for a second as the truth rolls over me.

I can submit here because I *know* he's the man he says he is.

Because he's *shown* me that.

He hitches one of my legs up and tucks it around his waist then leans in and nips my bottom lip.

"Pay attention."

To the man who's fucking me like he owns my body. The man who smiled at me from across the bar while giving a woman who might as well have been his sister a noogie. The man gave me a ride home, even though I was being a bitch. The man who kissed my bruise and got ice for my ankle— which is feeling surprisingly good right now.

In fact, I can't feel it at all.

"I said"—a stinging smack to the side of my ass that has my arousal flaring, my need drowning out any coherent thoughts—"*pay attention.*"

"Shut up and fuck me," I snap, leaning up and biting his pec hard enough to leave a mark.

If I'm doing this, if I'm diving down a slippery slope that may end up with me crumpled and broken and alone at the end of it, I might as well own it.

"Ow," he growls.

"Mine," I say.

For now. For as long as we both want.

Until he gets tired of my bullshit and moves on.

"Yours," he says, hips still pistoning, hand pressing my thigh wide, strokes growing faster, deeper—

And then he hits it.

The magical spot inside my pussy that has my orgasm closing in.

I drop my head back, arch up to meet his stroke, seeking that same bolt of pleasure.

But I don't have to *seek* it.

Banks, who as I know, pays attention.

He gives it to me.

Once. Twice. Again. Paired with his thumb on my clit, pressing on the bundle of nerves.

No mercy as he works my body. No quarter as he drives me higher.

No—

"Banks!" I scream as I fall.

Down that slope, sliding so rapidly that I can't breathe, can't see, can't think.

But I can hear, can feel.

So, I don't miss his strokes losing rhythm, don't miss my name on his tongue, don't miss how he comes apart inside me.

And it's the most glorious thing I've ever experienced.

For about two seconds.

Because just as I manage to catch my breath, to begin peeling my lids open, I hear—

Knock. Knock. Knock.

Banks tenses where he's braced above me, not crushing me beneath his weight—because of course, he'd pay attention to that too. His eyes come to mine, a silent question in their green depths.

"I don't know," I murmur.

Knock. Knock. KNOCK!

He scowls then shifts off me with a grunt and snags the blanket from the bottom of the bed, wrapping it around me before he snags his slacks and disappears into the bathroom to presumably take care of the condom.

A few moments later, he's out of the bathroom, pants on but not buttoned and hanging low on his hips in what may be one of the sexiest looks I've ever had the pleasure to witness.

Of course, my yummy sight is interrupted by another knock.

"I'll get rid of them," he says, coming over to me and pressing a kiss to my forehead. "And then we'll figure out the rest of it."

Like why my stomach is suddenly churning with nerves.

Or why part of me wants to show *him* the door.

I close my eyes, nod. "Okay."

A thumb brushing over my cheek and then he's heading to the door in the midst of yet another knock. "All right," he bellows. "I'm coming."

The knock cuts off mid-sound, but I barely have time to process that because he's whipping open the door to reveal—

Mrs. X.

We stare at each other like we're in the middle of a romcom—mouths gaping, eyes wide, no words forthcoming—but Mrs. X recovers first.

"Well, aren't you a live one?" she says, eyes tracing the same sight I'd just appreciated as she barges right past Banks who, presumably, is too shocked by the sight of a tiny, gray-haired lady with a bag in one hand and a T-shirt with Patrick Stewart's face dominating her torso to stop her.

She marches into the kitchen and begins unpacking the bag, setting containers on the counter with aplomb.

"Good morning, children," she says.

Banks chokes.

"I'm sorry," she says, not sounding sorry in the least. "Good morning delectable hot *man* who my Aspen is definitely not interested in."

With that, her gaze flicks to mine, mouth hitching up when she takes in the sight of me on the bed, naked but for the blanket Banks wrapped around me. "And it looks like *you* had a great morning."

My cheeks heat, but I lift my chin and narrow my eyes. "I don't recall it being laundry day."

Mrs. X shrugs. "I had the grandkids over. They eat a lot"—a nod to the containers—"and then they don't."

Banks lifts a brow and closes the door. But he hovers there and I have the feeling that he's assessing me, seeing what I'll do with the pushy busybody.

Considering how unwilling I've been to accept his help.

But here's the thing.

Mrs. X has proved herself many times over.

I know I can trust her.

"Will you at least turn around so I can get dressed?" I ask.

"If you get dressed does that mean the hot hunk of man meat"—a nod toward Banks—"will get dressed too?"

I gag. "Please don't ever say that again." I lift my chin at her. "And *turn around*."

A huff. "Fine," she says. "But only because your fridge needs organizing—ho, mama!"

Banks, who's bent to pick up his shirt, freezes like a poor frightened gazelle.

"*That's* a sight."

I know what she means.

That ass of his should be in a museum. Listed under Prime Specimen of Biteable Bums.

"Around," I order, spinning my finger at her.

Another huff but finally Mrs. X obliges, giving us her back as I scurry to the dresser, yank open a drawer, and snag some undies, dropping the blanket as I shimmy them up my legs.

"Now *that's* a sight," he murmurs, coming close, nipping at the hinge of my jaw.

I look down, see that my shimmying means that my boobs are bouncing.

"Cute," I grumble, but I don't push him away when cups my bottom, draws me close to him and tugs his tee over my end.

"For my eyes only."

I flick my brows up. "Really?" I ask dryly. "Caveman first thing in the morning?"

"You like it."

I do.

Something he clearly knows because he winks at me. "Don't be scared, little spitfire, not now that we've finally had some fun."

"I should threaten to stab you with my keys again."

He winds an arm around my middle. "I might like it if it means you'll let me feel that tight pussy of yours again."

My mouth falls open and before I can find a retort—and I have to face it, one would be a long time coming, especially with that smirk he's sporting and those twinkling eyes and the way his pants are just barely staying up...

One tug and—

Now *that's* Mrs. X talking.

Speaking of whom, I whirl around, see her watching us unabashedly. "Seriously?" I ask her.

"I waited until you had the shirt on," she chirps.

Which begs the question of exactly *how* she knew when I had the shirt on.

But I don't go down that road, just shake my head, grab some pajama pants and pull them on, wincing slightly when they snag on my foot.

"Your ankle," he murmurs a flash of guilt crossing his face.

"I promise you I wasn't feeling my ankle," I say.

He bends, pulls the PJs up and examines my foot. "It looks much better."

"It feels better," I tell him. "Minus me yanking on my pajamas."

"Good." Rising, he touches my cheek then buttons his slacks, prompting Mrs. X to sigh disappointedly.

I just shake my head as he grins and moves to the kitchen, surveying the haul she brought in curiously.

"Homemade mac and cheese," Mrs. X says pointing to the first one. "Almost a whole batch because they only eat the blue box. Brownies." Another much smaller container. "Because they liked those. Chicken noodle soup because they love it, but I can't stand to have another bowl. And Caesar salad because getting them to eat anything green is nearly impossible. Oh—" She lifts one last container. "And apple strudel because we all need something sweet. Good with ice cream or heated up with a cup of coffee. So, what do you say, green eyes? Want a bite of my strudel?"

I choke, laughter bubbling up in my chest.

"I bet your strudel is delicious," Banks says lightly, meeting my eyes, the emerald depths dancing with mirth.

"It sure is," Mrs. X says, bustling to my cabinets like she owns the place and pulling out two plates and two mugs. She looks in the coffee maker, frowns, then goes to the freezer where I normally keep my coffee grounds.

I'm out.

And because I'm saving for my car, I hadn't bought any this week.

Banks' gaze is on mine again, but it's not amused now, and I hate that I feel small and ashamed and…like a failure who can't even afford coffee.

"I'll go to the diner—" he begins.

But Mrs. X is her usual flurry. She shoves a plate into Banks's stomach, making him grunt, and then hurries to the door with the mugs in hand. "You serve up the strudel, hockey hunk," she trills, "and I'll be right back with the coffee."

I open my mouth to refuse then slam it closed again.

There's no arguing with the force that is Mrs. X.

And, indeed, she *is* right back with the coffee, setting two steaming mugs on the counter and supervising Banks as he cuts her strudel.

"Bigger," she orders. "Nope. *Bigger*." A wink in my direction as I wander carefully toward my beat-up counters. My ankle is ginger but holding. "Aspen likes it big."

I choke again.

But this time my laughter escapes.

"That's better," she says softly, cupping my jaw for a brief second before marching to the door.

I open my mouth to tell her to stay but she's already shaking her head and mouthing, "Enjoy *his* strudel."

And then she's gone, the door clicking closed behind her.

Silence descends and I feel awkward all of a sudden, not knowing what to do with Banks in my kitchen. My apartment is clean, but it's not luxurious by any means. He's probably got a million-dollar mansion with a fancy coffee machine and—

"Come and eat," he murmurs, nodding toward the table.

Two plates with strudel, the two mugs next to them.

"Courage, little spitfire," he cajoles when I hesitate.

I should refuse on principle.

"That's it." He grins, like he knows exactly what's going on in my head.

Frowning, I lift my chin and move to the chair, dropping down into it.

"There now," he teases. "That wasn't hard."

I lift my fork. "Don't push it," I warn.

He just grins and sits down next to me.

Slippery slope—I've jumped on and I'm careening to the bottom.

At least the strudel is delicious.

I shove a giant bite into my mouth—

"So, where are we going to dinner tonight?"

—and promptly exhale a cloud of powdered sugar as I choke for a third time.

But, by the end of my near-death experience, I've still somehow agreed to go on a date with Banks Christianson.

CHAPTER SIXTEEN

Banks

DATE NIGHT.

When's the last time I went on an official date?

I go out with friends and teammates, hook up with an attractive woman every so often, and keep busy with hockey. But dating? The romantic kind with candlelit dinners and flowers and all the bells and whistles? That's something else.

My gut tells me a little romance will go far with Aspen, but I'm not a hundred percent sure what direction to go. Flowers and candy feel a little old-fashioned, like I'm trying too hard, but at the same time, I think she *needs* me to try harder than any other man in her life. She isn't like other women, and since we've already slept together, I don't want to be lazy with the effort I put into dating her.

I hesitate for a minute when I pull up to her building, absently drumming my fingers on the steering wheel. I have a dozen sterling roses and a book I think will fit in perfectly with the other fantasies on her bookshelf on the seat next to me, and one of my Vipers jerseys wrapped in some tissue paper on the back seat. I plan to give it to her along with a ticket to the next home game, but a small part of me isn't sure whether it's the right move.

Will she feel obligated to go?

Will she understand how serious I am if I invite her to a game where she'll meet my friends and teammates? Not to mention the other wives and girlfriends.

Fuck me loud.

I'm totally overthinking everything.

I need to get my ass out of the car and go get my woman.

Yeah, it's a done deal in my head.

I just have to be cautious about how I present the concept to her.

Instead of sitting there driving myself nuts, I take the steps up to her apartment two at a time. I've just lifted my hand to knock when she opens the door.

"Hi." She smiles, her eyes falling to the roses in my hand. "*Oh*...sterling roses. How did you know?"

"How did I know?" I'm a little confused. I'd picked them because the silver-purple color seemed exotic and beautiful. Like her.

"That they're my favorite." She frowns suddenly. "Did I mention it?"

"Pure luck," I say, leaning in to lightly brush my lips across hers. "I stopped at a florist, and these were the only roses they had other than red...and you're too beautiful for something as common as red roses."

One side of her mouth quirks up a little as she accepts the bouquet. "There's a part of me that wants to be snarky and remind you that I've *already* put out, but that seems a little impolite. Even for me. Come on in and let me put these in a vase."

I follow her inside and watch as she pulls a beautifully ornate vase out of a cabinet.

"Is that Murano?" I ask in surprise.

She glances up. "Yes, it is. Are you a connoisseur of art glass?"

"A little. Atlas makes us invest in all kinds of shit, and I have a few rare pieces."

"This was a gift from my grandmother on my eighteenth birthday," she says quietly, her eyes hooded before she turns to fill the vase with water. "One of the few things I took with me when I left."

"It's beautiful," I say.

"So are the flowers." When she turns around again the haunted look is gone and she's smiling. "Thank you."

"That's not all."

Her eyebrows draw together. "Um…what?"

I hand her the book. "I thought"—I tilt my head to her bookshelf—"you'd like to read this. It's one of my favorite series."

Her face…

It's fucking beautiful—soft and sweet, like I've just pulled a Kool-Aid man through a bunch of her carefully constructed walls.

She slowly takes the book from me, smooths her fingers over the cover, flips it and reads the back. "You pay attention."

"What?"

Her smile is gentle, her hazel eyes a mix of that soft and sweet and something else I can't discern as she carefully sets it on her bookcase. "I can't wait to start it," she whispers, moving back over to me. She lifts her hand, lightly cups my jaw, and presses her lips to mine. "Thank you, honey."

My heart rolls over in my chest, offering itself up to this woman.

"You're welcome. Ready to go?"

"Yes." She picks up her purse and I settle my hand on the small of her back as we leave the apartment.

She looks gorgeous tonight in tight black leggings and a form-fitted gold sweater that shows off her figure. She has on flat black ballet slippers, probably because of her ankle, and she looks so sexy I almost wish we weren't going out.

Almost.

As much as I'm hoping to get naked again tonight, I'm also looking forward to sitting across a table from her, sharing a bottle of wine, and just talking to her. With minimal arguing. Maybe actually getting to know her better. I thought about Dash doing a background check on her because I have so many questions about her past, her family, and more, but I changed my mind.

I have a feeling she'd lose her shit if she ever found out—and let's be honest—she would find out eventually. So instead, I'm going to try to do things the old-fashioned way—by getting to know her. Hopefully, she'll open up more than she has to date.

"I've never been here before," she muses as we're seated at a table by the window, overlooking the city. This rooftop restaurant is casual but expensive, and I come here often.

"It's one of the places I come for dinners with the team," I respond. "They have great steaks and an extensive wine list."

"Sounds heavenly." She picks up the menu. "I haven't had a good steak in…a while."

"I try not to have them more than a few times a month. Too much fat compared to chicken and fish, but luckily, I work out a lot."

She chuckles. "I don't do a lot of working out, per se, but I spend a lot of time on my feet so I think that counts."

"It definitely does. How do you feel about merlot? The 2019 Duckhorn Three Palms is fantastic."

"Oh, I love that one. Yes."

She knows something about expensive wine, which solidifies my feeling that she comes from money. It doesn't seem prudent to ask outright, though.

Once we've ordered and the waiter has poured us a couple of glasses of merlot, I take a moment to drink her in.

Sitting across the table from me, candlelight glinting off her hair, she's stunning. She also appears to be more relaxed than I've ever seen her, and I'm surprised when she starts telling me a story about when she was in college.

"...and of course, none of us were twenty-one, but we had five cases of wine in the kitchen that no one knew what to do with. So we just start opening them and trying them all." Her eyes crinkle in amusement. "Thousands of dollars of wine, and we're tossing half of it in the sink because we have unrefined pallets and don't like it."

"Did you ever find out who sent it?" I ask, chuckling.

She grimaces. "My father's secretary made a mistake. He'd recently had her send me a package from my mother, and she just clicked the previous address instead of the client they were supposed to go to. By the time they figured out what happened, it was all gone."

"Did you get in trouble?"

"I was eighteen and it wasn't my fault. What could they do? I got a stern lecture about underage drinking, but again—what was he going to do? Turn me in to the police?"

"I'm guessing you weren't close to your parents growing up?"

She snorts. "Not hardly. My mother is a closet alcoholic who does whatever my father tells her to as long as he keeps paying the bills."

"And your dad?"

She wrinkles her nose. "He's...successful and singularly focused on work. All of us kids were nothing but a nuisance until we were old enough to be useful to him."

"What about the grandmother you mentioned?"

A genuine smile lights her face. "Grandma was amazing. Unfortunately, she died not long after my eighteenth birthday.

That's partly why that vase is so important to me. It's the last thing she gave me."

"I'm sorry."

She sighs. "She was in her eighties. I guess it was inevitable."

"The women in my family don't seem to live very long," I admit softly. "My mother died right after I was born, and her mother died of breast cancer when she was in her forties. My dad's mom died when she was in her forties or early fifties, so I never knew any of them."

"Really?" She looks surprised. "Your mom or either of your grandmothers?"

"Nope." I shake my head. "My dad did his best to make my mom real, if you know what I mean. Pictures and stories and stuff. It's not the same, though."

"No, I imagine it's not. I'm sorry you missed out on that. Were you the baby? Do you have siblings?"

"I was the first and only child. My dad never remarried, so basically it's just me now that he's gone."

"And your chosen family. The guys from the club." She meets my gaze across the table, and it seems as though she suddenly understands my bond with Dash, Atlas, and Royal.

"Yes. And Briar and Frankie."

"Is Frankie's dad in the picture?"

I make a face, always unable to hide my irritation about that particular subject. "No. We don't even know who it is. Briar said it was a one-night stand and she never knew his last name."

She cocks her head. "Why do you look like you don't believe that?"

"Because that's not who she is. Don't get me wrong. I'm in no way being misogynistic in this case, and I'm not judging women for one-night stands or anything like that. I've just known Briar since she was a teenager. She was shy and awkward in high school. Like, *really* awkward. She had frizzy red hair and buck teeth that she wore headgear for. And these thick glasses that made her look almost cross-eyed. Not to mention, she barely had any friends and never went out. That didn't change in college. Yes, eventually the headgear went away and she got contacts, but she kept to herself. She wasn't even dating, much less sleeping around, so there's no way she randomly hooked up with a stranger."

To my surprise, Aspen throws back her head and laughs. "Spoken like an overprotective big brother."

"What does that mean?" I ask.

"A one-night stand is *exactly* what someone like that would do. She's been the ugly duckling all through school, probably still a virgin, so she goes out one night and finds a stranger to do the deed. It's what I would have done in that position."

"Well, hell." That sounds plausible. "I figured she was protecting some guy who didn't want to man up to his responsibilities."

"Because she knows her big brothers would pummel him into submission."

I shrug. That goes without saying. If we ever find the guy, he'll do the right thing, no matter what. "Well, yeah. Even if she wasn't like a sister to me, what kind of man walks away from his kid? Not a man at all, in my opinion."

"I agree, but she may be telling you the truth about not knowing who he is. Or how to reach him."

"Dash owns a security and bodyguard company. He can find almost anyone. If she would give us anything—a first name, where they met, the date they hooked up…he'd find him."

Aspen lifts one slender shoulder, allows it to drop in a careless shrug. "Maybe that's not what she wants? She might have a good reason. And honestly, I don't know what role this guy could play at this point. Frankie seems to have all the love, money, and attention she'll ever need. Whoever that guy is, it's his loss. Him showing up now would probably just mess up her life."

"For sure." I'm grateful for the break in conversation as the waiter drops off our food because Frankie's father is such a sore subject for me.

"On a totally different subject, I have a question for you," I say once the waiter's gone.

"Oh?" Her gorgeous hazel eyes meet mine.

"Will you be my guest at an upcoming game?"

I'm not sure what I expected her reaction to be, but it's not the disappointment on her face.

"I-I can't," she whispers, suddenly dropping her gaze.

"Hey." I reach across the table for her hand. "*Hey.*"

Her gaze drifts back up to mine.

"What's wrong?"

"I can't," she repeats. "I'd have to give up shifts at the bar, and I honestly can't afford it."

Okay, I can work with that.

It's not personal.

It's not that she doesn't want to be my date or guest at a game.

This is about money.

"There has to be a game coming up that falls on one of your nights off," I say gently. "Or you can switch a shift with Johnny."

Her nose wrinkles. "He won't give up his weekend nights."

"He will if Atlas tells him to."

She vehemently shakes her head. "*No.* Please, don't do that. I don't want any special treatment because we're sleeping together."

I want to roll my eyes, but I manage to refrain, digging deep for patience and reminding myself that she's worth it.

"Little spitfire, you need to listen to me. *Really* listen. You can be as independent as you want. I'm never going to take that from you. I promise you that." I pause, holding her gaze, needing her to *feel* those words. "As long as you try to understand that it's okay to let people who care about you—you know, like maybe the man in your life—spoil you once in a while. Is that so hard for you to accept?"

She doesn't answer right away, and I steel myself.

Because the worst-case scenario?

I'm afraid she's going to say yes.

CHAPTER SEVENTEEN

Aspen

I TOUCH the jersey that's hanging up in my closet, the jersey I've somehow agreed to wear to an upcoming Vipers game and feel my heart skip a beat.

Banks is…

Well, he was wonderful last night.

I've never been on a date like that before—well, I suppose I've never really been on a date with someone who was interested in *me* before. In the past, it was a business venture, a coming together for my family's corporate interests. It certainly wasn't with someone who wanted to know all of the little details that make me tick. Usually, they were looking for the best way to punch their ticket to the family coffers.

But…I have nothing and Banks—

Is different.

He likes me—prickly, rabid raccoon me with a crappy apartment and no manicure and hair that isn't perfectly styled, with minimal makeup, and an outfit cobbled together from clothes that aren't at the cutting edge of fashion.

Back home, I would have been laughed out of town.

Instead, he brought me flowers and the book. We drank wine, ate a heavenly steak, and he talked to me, *listened* to my answers, and…

Looked at me like I was the most beautiful woman he'd ever been lucky enough to lay eyes on.

So, even though I know it's dangerous to keep getting closer to him, I can't stop myself.

It's okay to let people who care about you spoil you once in a while.

I *want* to believe.

And now I've got a hockey jersey with Christianson on the back hanging in my closet.

I sigh, but I'm unable to keep the smile from my face at the memory of those sure words and the conversation that had flowed so effortlessly afterward, not to mention the confident way he'd kissed me before leaving me at my door. "Get a goodnight's sleep for a change, little spitfire," he said before striding away.

Of course, then he turned on the top of the stairs and caught me staring at his ass, which was embarrassing, but—

The message he sent me minutes later was hot enough to burn that memory from my mind.

And the dreams I had of him…

Smile widening, I pull out my uniform for The Sapphire Room, trying to shift my mind into work mode, but unable to stop thinking about the book, the roses, his willingness to work around my schedule, or putting those dreams of mine to good use.

Or, most of all, the protective way he talked about Briar.

What would it be like to have someone like that in my life?

Looking after me, taking care of me, making sure I'm safe and protected and—

Ignoring the fact that he's already doing those things, I get dressed.

It's temporary. He's interested in me, I've let him in. The

sex is off the charts. But eventually, he'll move on and I'll do what I always do.

Survive.

I keep thinking that, *willing* myself to remember it…

But I still can't stop from brushing my fingers over the velvety petals of the roses before I leave for my shift.

"Jesus Christ!" I snap, clamping a hand over my chest when I open my door and get a faceful of Banks's strong, hard chest.

"Hey, baby," he murmurs, steadying me with his hands on my shoulders.

"Wh-what are you doing here?"

"Briggs says your car still isn't ready." He winks and gestures down at himself. "So, Banks's taxi service is at your disposal."

I narrow my eyes, but, secretly, I'm more than pleased. "Don't expect a tip," I say tartly.

He tugs at my ponytail. "Likewise," he says. "I can't wait to keep you busy making Gamebreakers all night."

"You're staying then?"

He waits for me to close and lock my apartment door. "No hockey tonight. And there's a certain woman I'm desperate to spend more time with."

"Desperate?" I ask archly.

He leans close, nips at my bottom lip. "I was a good boy last night because I could see the dark circles under your eyes, could practically feel your exhaustion across the table—"

"I was fine," I protest.

His fingers lace with mine and he draws me down the stairs, outside to his car. "Fine or not," he says. "You were tired."

My pulse picks up.

Because…he pays attention.

"You could have stayed."

Orgasms would have made me sleep deeply.

A thought he seems to pick from my mind.

"I could have," he agrees. "But I couldn't. For me."

There my heart goes again, fluttering in my chest like an overgrown butterfly. "You're sweet."

He tugs my ponytail again as he helps me into the passenger's seat. "Don't tell anyone," he stage whispers.

But I have the feeling the universe already knows what a good guy Banks is.

He closes the door, rounds the hood, and a few moments later, we're heading to The Sapphire Room, zipping through the city streets, the sun setting in the distance.

We talk about everything and nothing—the practice Banks went to that day, the fact that I did, indeed, get a good night's rest (and was able to sleep in without an interruption from Mrs. X). I tell him that Briggs says my car will be ready by the end of the week and that I'm not looking forward to my cleaning shifts at the arena.

"I wish you didn't have to work so hard," he murmurs as we turn into the parking lot.

"I don't," I tell him. "I like working. I like being useful."

One less job would be nice, and I'll be happy to never clean a cupholder ever again or scrape gum off concrete, but working, surviving has shown me what I'm capable of.

I'm not a doll on the shelf.

I'm a grownup who can take care of herself.

He touches my cheek. "I know. Wait there," he adds before I can reply, popping open his door and coming around to my side and opening mine.

"Banks," I whisper as he puts out his hand for me to grab, drawing me from the car.

A tug has me plastered against his chest and he closes the door behind me. "Pretty little spitfire." He runs his hand down my back, cups my ass, and crowds me, pressing me back against the car.

Cool metal.

Hot male.

I shudder. "What are—"

Before I can finish my question, his mouth is on mine and he's kissing me senseless, tongue slipping between my lips to tangle with mine, stroking in a rhythm I know he can match with his dick. He kisses me until I feel like my lungs will explode, until my knees shake, and my legs are jelly.

He draws back, laces our fingers together. "That should make you remember me when all the fuckers flirt with you tonight."

———

MY LIPS HAVE BEEN TINGLING for hours and I've stopped myself more than once from reaching up to touch them.

It doesn't help that Banks has been sitting at my end of the bar watching me intently all night. It's busy and many a drink has been served—not to mention several Gamebreakers (with tips, despite his threats) have been placed in front of him—but his focus never wavers.

I sigh as I begin my next order, staring hard at the ticket.

He's pretty and distracting and has been smirking at me like he knows what's going through my head.

Sex.

Sex is going through my head.

I want the bar to be empty so he can strip me down and fuck me on it.

I want to be pinned against the wall in the dark hallway as he strokes into me fast and hard, the threat of getting caught driving us together frenetically.

I want—

Liquid hits my wrist and I curse, shaking myself when I realize the beer I'm pulling is overflowing.

"Fuck," I mutter as I wipe the outside of the glass, start drawing the next beer.

Only to be greeted with foam—and only foam.

Dammit.

The fucking keg's out.

"The Fat Tire's dry," I call down the bar. "I'll grab another."

The beer's been flowing like fucking water all night. It won't last long.

"Want me to get it?" Johnny calls back.

He's been a good partner tonight, and I know it's because Marissa isn't working so he's not mooning over her, too fixated on her smiles to be of use to me.

"I've got it," I tell him, flexing my biceps at him.

"Okay, Schwarzenegger," he calls.

Grinning, I wink at Banks as I blow by him, hustling down the hall and into the storeroom, flicking on the lights and snagging the handcart. The kegs are heavy, but I'm strong, and it's not like I'll be hefting it on my shoulder, carrying it to swap out behind the bar like I'm part of the World's Strongest Woman contest. I just have to get it onto the cart, wheel it down the hall, and slide it into place.

Then I'll swap it out for the empty.

Easy peasy.

I shove the metal plate of the cart beneath the keg, start to lean back, putting my weight into my good foot because my twisted ankle is still a little tetchy. With a grunt, I start to lift it—

Then freeze, releasing the handle, the handcart and metal cylinder atop it dropping back down to the floor with a *thunk.*

Nape prickling, I glance over my shoulder…

And see Leo's standing in the doorway.

Something about his expression has me skittering back a step.

Not helpful, I realize when I bump into the wall.

"Did you need something?" I ask quietly.

"You fucking Christianson?"

My mouth drops open. "Excuse me?" I say in a tone that's

far too sharp for my boss. But I don't like the question and I sure as shit don't like the way he prowls toward me, smirking as he closes the distance between us.

"I saw him all but fucking your mouth in the parking lot," he says, drawing a finger down my cheek, my throat. "A man doesn't kiss a woman like that unless he's been inside her."

Nausea burns the back of my throat. "Don't touch me," I snap, brushing by him.

Or trying to, anyway.

Because I barely make a step before his fingers wrap around my wrist and he drags me to a stop.

He yanks me toward him, tweaking my ankle, and I cry out. "Shut up," he snaps.

"Leave me alone, Leo."

"No," he says, shoving me hard, sending me roughly back into the wall, forcing all the air from my lungs in a painful rush.

I gasp in a breath. "I *said*, leave me alone—"

He ignores me, coming closer, pressing his disgusting body to mine, dragging his nose along my jaw and inhaling.

"If you give it up to him"—he roughly squeezes my breast —"you can give it up to me."

CHAPTER EIGHTEEN

Banks

ASPEN'S BEEN GONE a long time.

I hate being *that* guy, the one who can't stand it when his woman leaves the room.

She could be powdering her nose.

Taking a piss.

She's allowed to take ten minutes to decompress on a night like this.

Except it's crazy busy and we're out of our most popular beer on tap.

She wouldn't do it *now*.

That's not who she is.

Because I know that about her, there's an uneasy feeling in my chest—I can't explain it—and it propels me off the barstool, my legs taking me toward the back.

As I round the corner, I hear a squeak? Shriek? Some kind of distressed sound I can't quite identify. It's muffled between the loud music and the sound of people partying, but I know what I heard and I pick up speed.

The scene in front of me is momentarily frozen in time.

Leo pressing Aspen against the wall, trying to kiss her as she frantically turns her head and pushes at his chest.

"Stop it!" Her voice penetrates my haze and everything in my field of vision blurs as I lurch forward.

I yank him away from her by the back of his shirt and slam him against the wall.

"What the fuck do you think you're doing?!" My fist connects with his jaw.

"She wanted it, man. I'm telling you—" he sputters, trying to defend himself, but I have zero fucks to give at this point. I know what I saw.

"You're a liar." This time, I hit the side of his face and blood spurts from his nose.

"Get off—" He tries to fight back, but he's no match for me. I've been brawling since I was a kid, both on and off the ice.

"I'll listen to you about as well as you listened to her," I growl, hitting him a third time and feeling a wave of satisfaction at the blood streaming from multiple cuts.

"Banks." Aspen's hand on my arm brings me out of my haze of bloodlust and I glance down at her, though I don't release Leo from the death grip I have on his neck. "Don't do anything you'll regret. He's not worth it."

If she only knew how much harder I could have hit him.

Right now, the only thing I might regret is *not* doing exactly what I want to do.

I release Leo with a shove, and he immediately reaches up to wipe the blood from his face.

"Get your shit and get out. Atlas will send you your last check. I don't want to see your face here ever again. And if you show up to hassle Aspen or anyone else, I'll end you. You understand me?"

"She worth the lawsuit I'm going to file?" he snarls.

I throw back my head and laugh. "Oh, please, *please* bring a lawsuit against us. That kind of thing gets Atlas's dick hard."

"Fuck you."

"No thanks." I motion with my chin. "Get your shit and get out of my club." I turn to Aspen as he leaves in a huff. "You okay, little spitfire?"

She nods, though she won't meet my eyes.

I need to make sure Leo doesn't try anything else, especially in front of her, and she definitely doesn't need to see it if I hit him again. I don't want her to think I'm an animal or something.

"Go on back to the bar," I say gently, guiding her out into the hall. "I'm going to make sure he leaves and then I'll come out and find you."

"O-okay." She hesitates for a second but then turns and hurries down the hall, uncharacteristically quiet, and it makes me want to beat the shit out of Leo all over again. It's not like her to do what I say without a protest, and I know it's because of the fuckwad bleeding all over my floor.

The urge to knock him flat is hard to resist, but I don't particularly want to go to jail tonight. Just to be on the safe side, I send a quick text to Dash and Atlas, letting them know what's going on. Then I follow Leo to his office, lounging in the doorway as he packs up some of his things.

"You never said she was your girlfriend," he mutters.

"Doesn't matter if she's my girlfriend or just another employee—I very specifically heard her ask you to stop. No is always no. What the fuck is wrong with you?"

"Women who work at clubs like this are all about the hookup. You should know that."

Jesus, this guy was a tool.

I can't get rid of him fast enough.

"There's no room for someone like you at The Sapphire Room."

He's still muttering as he yanks on his backpack and pauses to grab some tissues from his desk, pressing them against his face. "This isn't over. You broke my fucking nose."

"It better be over." I meet his gaze unwaveringly, hoping he realizes that I'm not fucking around. If he comes back, or approaches Aspen in any way, Dash will eat him for breakfast and use his bones as toothpicks. I can hold my own, but Dash is a scary motherfucker when provoked. And this will absolutely provoke him.

"Keys?" I hold out my hand and he slaps the keychain into it.

"Good luck finding someone to do as much as I do for what you pay." Leo stomps down the hallway and out the back door without looking back.

Good riddance.

I lock the door behind him and stuff the keys in my pocket.

It's going to be a long night if I have to close, but I'm already considering a plan. If it were up to me, I'd offer Aspen the manager's position and be done with it. The problem is that I'm not sure she'll take it and she's also still pretty new. The next logical choice is Johnny, but we'll make that call when Atlas gets here.

It won't be long. He's already texted that he's on his way.

Grabbing the handle of the handcart, I wheel the forgotten keg out of the storeroom and go in search of Aspen.

She's behind the bar talking to a group of customers, no evidence that she's any worse for wear after the incident with Leo.

I'm still pissed about it as I motion for Johnny to take over on the keg.

He makes short work of hooking it up and when he's done, I ask him to pull me a beer. I sip it slowly, hoping it'll ease the burn of my anger.

Aspen's keeping busy but as I watch her making drinks, I realize her hands are shaking.

Not a lot.

Just enough for me to notice.

Dammit.

"Aspen." I know it's busy and she needs to be out here, but…I need her to be okay.

She glances over at me.

"I need to see you in the back for a minute."

She frowns but nods, finishing the drinks she's making before drying her hands.

I wait for her at the end of the bar, and she meets my eyes worriedly. "Everything okay?"

"Yeah." We walk into the back, and I unlock the door to Atlas's office.

"What are we—" I cut her off before she can finish her sentence, closing the door behind us and then pulling her into my arms.

She resists for a second but then melts against me, burrowing her cheek in the hollow of my shoulder.

"How are you, little spitfire?" I whisper as I cradle her against my chest. "Did he hurt you?"

"No. I was just scared. And mad."

"I was pretty mad, myself." I stroke a hand down her back. "I should have checked on you sooner. I'm sorry."

"I'm okay."

"Your hands were shaking."

"I guess I *am* a little off kilter." She shivers against me. "He's always been kind of a dick, but I didn't expect this."

"You don't have to worry about him anymore. He's gone. And we'll make sure he doesn't come back."

She doesn't reply, merely rests against me as if she were made just for me.

The thought of that creep putting his hands on her gets my blood boiling all over again, but I don't want to say anything that might upset her.

"I'll never let anyone hurt you," I whisper.

She doesn't respond but I feel her sigh against me, and I wish I knew whether it was a sigh of relief or one of frustration. Or…if it's because she doesn't quite believe me.

"Hey. Everything okay?" Atlas comes into the room and pauses, belatedly sensing that Aspen and I are having a moment, but it's too late now.

"I'm good." She quickly pulls away and straightens her skirt. "I need to get back out there anyway. See you later, Banks."

She slips out of the room, and I watch her for a second before turning to Atlas.

"Where did we find Leo?" I demand. "Were there signs he was a fucking pig?"

Atlas shrugs. "He came highly recommended. No criminal record. And yeah, he's always been kind of a douche, but you have to be to work in this kind of environment. Alcohol, bar fights, staffing issues, scheduling…it's a lot."

"Aspen could do it," I say.

"Probably." He perches on the edge of his desk, obviously taking a minute to formulate his response. "But is she ready? She hasn't been here long. There's a learning curve."

Aspen can do it, but the real question is whether or not she'll accept the job from *me*. I don't need to tell Atlas that, though; I've already told him how proud and stubborn she is.

"There is, but she's smart and learns quickly," I remind him. "And we'd be around to help."

"I'm leaving on a business trip next week, and you have a road trip coming up. We don't have time to train her, Banks." His gaze is apologetic but steady.

"So…you're thinking of giving it to Johnny."

"On a trial basis," he agrees. "We'll see how he does. If he fucks up, we can switch gears."

"Right," I mutter. "You think if that happens Aspen would take the job if *you* offered it to her?"

"Maybe in a couple of months." He grins. "After you've had time to wear her down."

I chuckle. Then run a hand down my face and realize it's

sore. "Fuck. Coach is gonna have my ass if I'm not a hundred percent tomorrow."

"How many times did you hit him?" he asks with a knowing grin.

"Enough to make him bleed."

"Ice the hand, take some ibuprofen tonight."

"I'm hanging at the bar until close," I say. "I'm her ride, but I also don't know if Leo will be waiting when we leave."

Atlas's eyes narrow. "He better fucking not. Look, if you need to get some rest, I can stay until closing and take her home."

I shake my head. "Nah. My girl, my responsibility."

"Your girl, huh?" The smirk on his face makes me want to punch him too.

"Fuck off," I grumble.

His laughter follows me down the hallway.

CHAPTER NINETEEN

Aspen

I'VE BEEN in this arena hundreds of times before.

But I've never seen it like this.

Let's just say I get why there's so much to clean up after game nights.

And I'm thankful that I won't be facing off with Cheryl over a speck on the cupholders tomorrow morning.

The place is packed, and people are spilling drinks, dropping popcorn, smooshing candy into the space beneath their feet.

My hands hurt just thinking about the cleanup crew.

And I'm extra careful as I settle my drink in the cupholder and start in on my oversized tub of popcorn.

I didn't buy snacks.

They were delivered to me.

Likely because Banks knows that I can't afford to pay arena prices—or won't pay them, anyway.

My heart actually does a little *pitter-patter* in my chest.

I never realized that's a real thing.

But Banks…well, he's sweet.

We didn't meet up at the arena because he had to be here early to get ready for the game, but he arranged for Briggs to drop off my car today so I have wheels again.

And I still paid for the repairs, even though the sneaky man tried to maneuver around me.

I might like him—might *really* like him—but I've spent too long looking after myself just to let some man sweep me off my feet and forget why I struck out on my own in the first place.

I need to be independent. I need to be able to provide for myself.

I can't lie, though.

Having Banks on my side feels nice.

Walking me to my car after my shifts at The Sapphire Room, making sure I got home safe. Sleeping next to me and helping me polish off Mrs. X's strudel.

And all the while…he isn't mean.

There aren't slicing comments I have to weed through, searching for an insult.

It's just Banks and me.

Ah, there's that slippery slope again.

But I can't seem to stop myself from taking the joyride, especially when the ticket he sent to my phone also came with a VIP parking pass.

And the snacks.

And the seat.

I grew up back east where hockey's more common, but I've never been to a game, so this is…culture shock to me.

The space that's normally cold and quiet, sounds echoing through the concrete stairs, is a cacophony of noise—kids yelling, ushers giving directions, various random conversations surrounding me on all sides. There's the rumble of the ice resurfacer, the vibrations of music being played over the huge speakers mounted on the Jumbotron hanging above the ice.

The lights are bright, but not long ago they dimmed for the

players' entrance, smoke and the team's song blasting, the crowd cheering as the Vipers skated onto the ice.

Now the anthem has been sung, and everyone's taking their proper positions—or at least, I think so.

Five guys on each side of the ice, a goalie in each net. The referees—four of them in their black and white striped shirts—spread out.

There's a hush that has me holding my popcorn closer.

And then the puck drops.

For a second, I don't know what's happening, or I can't keep up. It's so much faster than on TV and I don't have the announcers telling me what's going on.

But between the screen on the Jumbotron and the fans around me shouting, it doesn't take me long to start figuring out where to look.

I gasp as two big bodies collide, the echo of the collision audible even where I'm sitting, but as I'm attempting to track that flash of movement, the puck is still flying and the other players on the ice are still skating.

Even those involved in the hit.

They jump to their feet and rejoin the play.

And…

I'm mesmerized.

Yeah, this is *so* much better than watching the game on TV.

The play speeds back and forth across the ice, the crowd cheering as both goalies see shots that have me leaning forward in my seat, my heart in my throat. Time ticks down and neither team scores, despite the chances making me and the rest of the crowd gasp. The players seem unaffected, though, changing positions in a carefully choreographed and fluid dance, hopping over the boards, skating hard, passing and hitting and shooting and—

Banks is out there.

My pulse picks up.

I'm wearing his jersey and I've kissed almost every inch of his naked body, but that's not why I recognize him.

It's the smooth way he moves.

Liquid lightning, same as during the practice when I spied on him.

He skates hard, face determined, focus absolute, and I find myself holding my breath as he crosses over the blue line and heads straight into battle on the boards.

The collision makes the glass shake and my breath hiss out, but a second later, he's moving again, and this time with the puck.

The other team closes in quickly, almost faster than I can track, but he doesn't seem to have that problem as he does something fancy with his stick and feet and he's suddenly in open space.

"Shoot!" someone screams from behind me.

Banks keeps moving, his head up, gaze searching for something—

I don't see what until the pass is already on his teammate's stick and then I'm in awe as everything happens in a flash.

One second, Banks has the puck.

The next, it's across the ice.

One more, and he's flying toward the net, the puck sliding back toward him.

Electricity in my veins, wrapping fingers around my spine. I grip my tub of popcorn so tightly that kernels topple out and spill on the floor.

But I barely notice.

Because he's snagging the puck—

"Come on," I whisper. "Come on."

Lifting his stick.

I clench my popcorn tighter, hiss, *"Come on."*

A shot flies off the end—

"Come. *On!"*

And the puck sails into the goal.

For a second, everyone is still. Then there's a burst of noise, the crowd roaring their excitement.

For Banks.

Who hasn't scored all season…

Until tonight.

I grin so wide that my cheeks hurt as I watch him celebrate with his teammates.

He did it.

He scored!

After all his hard work, all the stress and worries, he's done it.

I stand up with everyone else, stomping and cheering—and hissing at the right times—along with the Vipers' goal song.

And even though Banks scored, I'm still on the edge of my seat as the game goes on.

The score is tied up by the other team ten minutes later and we go into the first intermission even. Neither side breaks that tie in the second period and so it's not long before the final intermission is over and the teams are heading into the last twenty minutes of play. It's tight—even hockey newbie me can tell that much—with good chances from each side, but no one manages to score.

Not until the final minute of the game.

My popcorn is long gone so I don't have the tub to clench as Banks corrals the puck and skates hard up the middle of the ice, two guys from the other team chasing hard.

They're closing in, but not soon enough.

I can see it from here.

He'll have one chance to score before they catch him.

Over the blue line.

In between the two large red circles that take up most of that third of the ice.

Moving in on the goalie.

Closer. Closer. Close—

"Shoot!" someone yells from behind me.

I clench at my armrests, grind my teeth together.

Banks has time yet.

Time to be calm, to put all that extra work to good use.

Time to do something better than just let the puck go at the net all willy-nilly.

I hold my breath, dig my nails in, and wait for my man to do something fabulous.

It's coming.

I can feel it.

I—

"Oh shit!" the yeller from behind me says.

And…I can't disagree with him, not this time.

Because what I'm watching should be illegal.

Banks shifts his body hard to the left, drawing everyone's focus, making everyone—including the other team's goalie—think that he's going that way, and he's doing it so fast, so smoothly that the change of direction that comes barely a heartbeat later makes my breath rush out.

He was going left.

And now, suddenly, he's going right.

And the puck…I lose sight of it as the goalie scrambles to make that same shift of motion, to keep up with Banks—

But he's too slow as he comes across…

And just misses the puck slipping beneath his spread legs.

Not a hard shot.

Just a tiny little tap that slides home.

I blink, thoroughly impressed, and then I'm on my feet, cheering like a loon, pride filling me so full that I swear I can float right up to the ceiling like a balloon with its string cut.

My man did that. He *did* it.

Two freaking goals.

Hell yeah!

Banks is surrounded by his teammates, and I watch as the group hugs and collides with the boards. They're a flurry of movement—slapping him on the back, patting him on the head, all of them smiling huge.

And the best part?

Just as they break apart and start skating for the bench—

Banks looks up and our eyes meet…

And his smile sets my soul aflame.

CHAPTER TWENTY

Banks

FUCK. Yeah.

My heart is still hammering against my ribs as we push back into the locker room. The rest of the team is almost as excited as I am, the air charged with electricity as we high-five each other.

"You were on fire," West says, with a smirk. "All this because of the new girlfriend, eh?"

"Wait—what?" Aaron Shaunessy, one of team D-men, puts his hands on his hips, squinting. "There's a new lady in the picture? Why weren't we informed?"

"Because you're not my fucking mother," I quip, scowling at West. Leave it to him to spill the beans.

Not that it's a secret or anything, but we're pro athletes, not monks. We tend to walk a thin line between traditional locker room talk and finding a mostly respectful way to talk about women. Wives and live-in girlfriends are off-limits, but us single guys? There's basically no line my teammates won't cross when it comes to ribbing us about dating.

To be fair, this is a great group of men.

There are only a few guys I'm not particularly close to, but we're generally tight as a team. We hang out on road trips, spend time off the ice together, and know each other's families. No one is going to call a woman derogatory names or anything like that, but on the other hand, if I'm seeing someone with big tits? They're not at all shy about letting me know how much they appreciate it.

Now that the cat is out of the bag about Aspen, so to speak, I have to make sure they understand that she is *not* some random hook-up. She doesn't fall under the unwritten no-holds-barred-comments agreement.

She's my girlfriend.

I'm not sure she knows it yet, but these guys are about to.

This means they have to behave, but they'll probably give me a little shit in private because I'm going from single to taken with no warning. Someone is bound to ask if she's pregnant.

"So, are you going to fill us in or what?" Aaron asks.

"I didn't realize this was the hockey version of The Bachelor," I say. "But just so you fuckers remember your manners, she's my girlfriend, so keep the fuckery to a minimum when you meet her after the game."

"She's coming back to the lounge?" West glances at me in surprise. He's my closest friend on the team, and I haven't even told him much about Aspen.

Shit.

My balls are about to be seriously busted.

"So it's serious? Already?" Vinnie gives me a grin. "Good for you. She's not pregnant, right?"

I roll my eyes, annoyed.

I knew something like this was coming.

"That's not fucking happening," I mutter. "Not all women are puck bunnies trying to land themselves a baby daddy with a pro hockey contract."

"They're not? Got me fooled!" Asher Holloway is only

twenty and I've never known anyone who's had more girl-friends than him. Not even me, in my college days.

"You'll meet someone special someday," I respond. "Then everything changes."

Asher shudders. "Fuck that. There's way too much fun to be had to settle down with just one. I might try one of those poly relationships…or sister wives!" His eyes dance with amusement. "How many can I have? Is there a limit?"

"Fourteen," Vinnie deadpans. "Would that be enough? Though, I think you can ask the Elder for permission, and he'll let you go up to twenty."

I cover my mouth to hide my laugh as Asher's eyes widen further.

"Yeah? I could have twenty wives? How fucking awesome would that be?"

"I mean…until they start popping out babies." Aaron is working hard to keep a straight face, but I can see the tic in his cheek belying how close he is to losing it. "You know how expensive it is to raise kids?"

"Oh, no kids. They'd have to be on board for no kids." He's so serious, it's like he's actually contemplating all of this.

"I think at least one has to have kids," Magnus Forsberg, a newer Swedish player on the team, says in his faintly accented English. "Or the Elder will not give permission."

"Oh." Asher looks disappointed. "Well, I guess I could do a couple of kids. Like two. But not until I'm at least thirty-five."

That might have been the first rational thing I've heard him say all season.

"Women get jealous," Vinnie points out. "You'll probably have to make a sex schedule."

"I could probably do three a day if we don't have a game," he says. "One first thing in the morning, one after practice, one before bed."

"Right, right," Aaron nods, playing along. "And you can probably have a few side chicks on the road too."

"Exactly! That's what I'm thinking."

"So…twenty wives and say, half a dozen girlfriends on the road?" Vinnie asks.

"I fucking love my life!" He throws his hands up in the air and struts back toward the showers.

The rest of us can no longer hold back the laughter, and we crack up.

"Please save me from the rookies," Magnus pleads, looking up at the ceiling.

When we've finally calmed down, I look at West. "Do me a favor and keep the comments to a minimum around Aspen? I've just gotten her to trust me—she's had a hard life and doesn't trust easily. The last thing I need is for her to think I talk shit about her in the locker room."

He nods. "No worries, man. You know we're not about that. Wives and girlfriends are off-limits. Ish." He winks as he walks toward the showers.

———

I MANAGE to escape the media tonight. I probably should have talked to someone, but what am I supposed to say? Sorry, I have a new girlfriend and tonight was her first time coming to see me play so I don't have time to answer stupid questions about the game?

Not happening.

So I sneak into the showers, change, and head for the family lounge.

Aspen isn't there when I arrive, so I pull out my phone and text her.

BANKS: You coming down to say hello?

ASPEN: I don't know where the lounge is.

BANKS: Where are you? I'll come get you.

ASPEN: Concourse A elevator.

BANKS: Be right there.

I head in that direction and find her standing there when the doors open.

"Hi." I reach out a hand and pull her into the elevator.

"Hi." She smiles up at me.

"You brought me luck tonight," I say, palming her ass and pulling her up against me once the doors close. "I owe you a big thank you."

Before she can respond, I dip my head and capture her lips. Her mouth parts without hesitation, tongues instantly tangling, as if our bodies know what to do before we do. Her breath is warm and sweet, mingling with mine, and I can't keep my cock from taking notice.

Fuck.

This is neither the time nor the place, but she feels damn good in my arms.

"Banks…" Her voice is breathy as the elevator doors open and we pull apart.

"I know, baby. I want you too." I press her hand to my erection. "I don't know how the hell I'm going to make *that* go down."

Her eyes shine with arousal. "I know a place. One floor up."

Without breaking eye contact, I press the button on the panel and the doors close again.

"Where?" I ask when we get off.

"Trust me." She slides her hand into mine and tugs me down the hall.

I never come to this floor. It's one above ice level, but below the concourses. As far as I know, there are some random offices and storage areas here, and not much else.

Aspen seems to know where she's going and we're practically running down one hall, up another, and then she takes a quick look around before throwing open a door.

"This," she says with a smirk, "is Cheryl's unofficial office. She's not supposed to have one, but since nobody uses it, she does." A wicked glint in her eye. "The thought of you fucking me on her desk turns me on."

"Is that so?" I kick the door shut behind us, hit the button on the handle to lock it. "How do you feel about me licking your pussy on her desk?"

"Excellent." Her smile is mischievous as she begins to unzip her jeans.

"Leave the jersey on," I say, shrugging out of my jacket as I lean forward. "I like seeing you in it."

"Yes, sir." She slides down her jeans as our mouths come together again, and I realize she's not wearing panties.

Fuck.

I love that.

"Up you go," I growl, lifting her onto the desk. I push her onto her back and then drop down to my haunches. "You're wet."

"Is that a question or a statement?" she asks.

I move her thighs apart without answering, trying to decide if I should start slow or just dive in. Oral is one of my favorite things and I can't wait to get my tongue inside of her, but I don't want to rush. So I compromise and kiss a trail along the inside of one thigh before tossing both of her legs over my shoulders.

"Banks!" Her cry is soft, but her hips lift off the desk when I press the first kiss on her clit.

"Quiet, little spitfire—we don't want security to come see what the noise is about."

She moans in response, and I slide my tongue along her slit.

She tastes like honey and bourbon and musky woman.

Like a sexy Gamebreaker.

The tanginess tingles on my tongue as I nibble the soft skin there.

She's making the hottest little sounds, wiggling against my face.

I lightly slap her ass. "Keep still."

Then I dive in, taking a swipe right down the middle and slip my tongue inside of her.

"Banks!" That was definitely not quiet but I'm too busy enjoying myself to pull away.

Fucking her with my tongue isn't nearly as much fun as it's going to be when I use my cock, but it's a good start.

And she tastes so damn good.

I don't go down on a lot of women.

It's intimate in a different way, without the barrier of a condom, and though I've never really articulated it before, I guess it's saved for special women.

And this woman is rapidly becoming the most special woman I've ever met.

Which is why I want to make her come.

Hard.

I lighten my touch for a moment, gently nibbling the delicate lips, letting her settle into a rhythm. My fingers are squeezing and kneading her ass cheeks, keeping her right where I want her. Then I shift her up a bit more, putting her clit right at my mouth, and I bite down.

She squeals, trying to move, but I'm holding her tight.

I suck her clit into my mouth, alternately biting and sucking, until she's writhing like a wild woman, desperate to get away and simultaneously anxious for more.

So I give it to her.

Two fingers inside of her, her clit firmly between my lips, and I find the spot that I already know makes her go wild.

"Baaaaanks!" her shriek is loudly and raspy, and I fucking love hearing it.

"That's my girl," I whisper when she finally collapses against the desk.

I straighten and pull out the condom from my wallet, rolling it down my aching cock.

"Do. Not. Move," I order.

And she doesn't.

CHAPTER TWENTY-ONE

Aspen

AFTERSHOCKS OF SENSATION are still ricocheting through my body as he notches the head of his cock between my legs and begins to push inside me.

I groan at the stretch, at the slight burn as he threatens to overfill me.

It's that perfect mix of pleasure and pain.

Almost too much and not nearly enough and—

"Look at me when I fuck you, little spitfire."

My eyes fly open, locking with his, and my pussy convulses at the heat in his eyes, the desire. This is a man who sees me, who wants me.

Not a woman with a trust fund.

Not a connection to a family name.

Just…me.

"Banks," I whisper.

His hand clamps onto my hip and he holds me in place, the edge of the desk biting into my ass as he pulls back and thrusts in.

It's hard. It's a little rough.

It's not gentle and slow and sweet—

And I fucking *love* it.

"Your pussy is like a vise around my dick," he rasps, leaning down to nip at my bottom lip. When I gasp, he slips his tongue inside and I can taste myself on his kiss.

"Banks," I whisper again when he lets me breathe.

"What do you need?"

"You."

My heart pulses with fear, but only for a moment.

Because I don't think I've ever said anything *more* true.

He cups my jaw. "I'm already yours."

My exhale is shaky, but I'm not weak. I'm done with the fear, with hiding, with living a half life.

I'm *his*.

"Then show me," I whisper. "Show me hard and fast and deep."

He grins…

And then he does exactly that.

"Oh god!" I moan, my head falling back onto the desk as he grips my hips and fucks me without quarter, each stroke sending the desk shifting back a little.

I hear a crash, something falling from the wooden surface to hit the floor, but I can't bring myself to care.

Fuck Cheryl.

"Goddamn, little spitfire," Banks groans, picking up the pace, sending any thoughts of my boss skittering right out of my head. "I. Can't. Get. Enough. Of. This. Tight. Wet. Cunt." Each word is punctuated by a hard thrust, one after another that send me shooting toward completion, toward another orgasm, headlong for blissful oblivion.

He's right there with me, that heat in his eyes blazing bright, his jaw clenched tightly enough that it looks like it's made of marble, every muscle I can see taut with unraveling control.

"Harder," I order softly. "Fuck me harder."

That control snaps.

And, lucky me, I'm on the receiving end of his rough thrusts and even rougher words when it does.

"*Fuck*," he growls. "You're going to come around my cock, baby. You going to come so hard that you're going to squeeze my dick until it feels like it might break, and to punish you, I'm going to fuck you even harder, so damned hard that you'll feel me every time you sit down tomorrow."

I tremble.

He feels it—the effect those words have on me, the deep thrusts—and the wolfish grin he gives me in response is almost enough to topple me over into orgasm.

Almost.

But not quite.

Thankfully, he doesn't stop fucking me..

Another powerful stroke has me calling out his name, my nails biting into his arms.

One more has my entire body shuddering.

"Now," he orders, yanking my hips down as he thrusts up hard enough that I see stars.

My orgasm blasts through me, incinerating me with pleasure. My elbows slip out from beneath me and I drop back on the desk as he continues to fuck me, as he chases his own orgasm, as his strokes lose their rhythm and become frenzied.

"Aspen," he growls.

And I feel it then.

I feel him come apart.

———

"SHIT!" he exclaims, sharply enough that I'm roused from my blissful oblivion.

"What's the matter?" I ask, shoving my arms beneath me and pushing up to my feet.

"*Shit!*" He whips around before I can reach him, hands

balling into fists, one of which he punches against the wall. "Fuck," he hisses. "Fuck, I can't believe this shit."

I search the room for some sort of threat, for the reason why he changed from my sweet sex god of a man into the furious ball of male energy currently punching walls, but I don't find anything. The door's closed. Cheryl's desk is slightly worse for wear, but it's not obvious that we had a fuck party in her office.

Nope, that's just for me to remember every time she tries to play Hot and Cold with a fucking kernel of popcorn.

But there's nothing I can see that would make him react this way.

"Banks?" My throat has gone tight, but I push out, "What's happened?"

He's silent for a long time, long enough that I reach for my jeans and start pulling them on.

Maybe this was a mistake—

"The condom broke."

I immediately relax because...I'm on birth control.

This is not a big deal.

"I—" I exhale. "It's okay," I say, lifting my arm to show him. "I have the implant. See?"

"Wh-what?" he rasps.

"It's a birth control implant." I snag his hand, turning him to face me before I place his fingers over the bump on the inside of my bicep. "Feel that? They insert the implant under my skin so I can't accidentally get pregnant."

His eyes are worried, panicked even, but that fades as I explain, as he runs his thumb along the edge of the implant.

"You can't get pregnant?"

I try to study his face, but it's a perplexing mix of emotions.

"Not with this guy in here," I assure him. "It lasts for three years."

And with that, the mix is gone, my Banks starts to come back.

I smile and zip up my jeans then attempt to smooth down my hair. "Here," I say when that's done, snagging my purse from the floor and digging out a wad of tissues.

He touches my cheek then reaches down and takes the tissues, making quick work of the cleanup. "Sorry," he says. "I didn't mean to freak out. I'm just…I'm not ready to be a dad."

I laugh softly, the knot in my stomach loosening. "God no," I say. "I barely have my life together as it is. Being a parent isn't even in my Five-Year Plan."

He shoves the condom and wad of tissues in the trash can, picks up the pencil cup we must have knocked over earlier, then turns back to face me. "What is?"

My pulse hiccups in my veins. "Wh-what?"

"What's your Five-Year Plan?" he asks, pulling on his pants and tee.

"I don't know." I guess I haven't really thought about it. Not with how hard it's been since I left home. "I—"

His phone buzzes.

Cursing softly, he pulls it out of his pocket and glances at the screen.

"Who is it?"

He rolls his eyes. "My teammates are anxious to meet you."

———

I DON'T THINK I've done a good job of fixing my sex hair because when I walk through the door to the family lounge a little while later, my legs beyond shaky, my pussy very aware —and happy—of the pounding it just took, it's to see a handful of the men, whom I presume are players because they're tall and built and have the same great ass that Banks possesses, smirk.

Banks's fingers tighten around mine and he draws me a little closer to his side.

"Everyone, this is Aspen," he says, and I don't miss that his voice is filled with warning. With protectiveness.

I slip a little further down that slope.

One of the men saunters forward and extends his hand for me to shake. "Hi."

"Hi," I say. "I'm—"

But before I can finish the introduction, another of the guys swoops in, snagging my hand and lifting it to his lips. He presses a kiss to my knuckles and says in a soft European accent, "Hi, beauty, I'm—"

Someone else moves in, blocking him from view. It's nice to meet you." He looks me up and down then winks at Banks, as though to say nice job. "I'm—"

A younger player steps forward, and God, he can't be more than twenty. "I'm—"

"Shoo, Rookie," the first man mutters, shoving the kid who's barely a man back. "Take your sister-wife searching elsewhere."

I frown up at Banks, but he just shakes his head. "You don't want to know," he mutters before drawing me into the circle of his arms. "Okay, knuckleheads. Stop being weird. This is Aspen." A beat, his hand tightening on my shoulder. "My girlfriend."

Shock hits me hard in the stomach.

Something that Banks must see as he leans down to murmur in my ear, "Mine."

Then he straightens and starts making introductions, starting with the first man and finishing with the rookie. "West. Magnus. Deacon. And Asher."

"Nice to meet you," I say, feeling oddly shy with them all staring at me.

"You didn't mention that she was hot," West says, mouth tipped up into a smile. He waggles his brows.

"That hair alone is enough to give a man ideas," Deacon says.

I resist the urge to smooth down the strands again.

"Definitely," Magnus agrees.

"Yup," Asher, the rookie, says.

Banks stiffens behind me.

"Well, he certainly didn't mention that you were pigs," I retort without really thinking about it.

Certainly, without considering that me insulting his teammates isn't the right way to make friends with them.

But…ew.

"Pigs with"—I give them a taste of their own medicine, sniffing as I drag my gaze down their bodies then back up—"teeny tiny penises."

The guys rock back on their heels, eyes widening in shock.

Then they start laughing.

West claps Banks on the shoulder. "Don't fuck it up with this one, yeah?" Then he lifts his hand for me to fistbump. "You've got fire, baby. I like it."

"I'm not your baby," I tell him.

"No?" He lifts a brow.

Oh, this one's trouble.

"Don't make me bust out my keys," I threaten.

"She *will* stab you with them," Banks adds with a chuckle, tugging lightly at a strand of my hair.

Magnus looks back and forth between Banks and me.

"Explain."

So, I do.

And my tale of meeting Banks outside the arena, not recognizing him, then threatening to go full rabid racoon on the Vipers' captain has the men in stitches.

Deacon snags Banks's arm, lifting it and turning it from side to side.

"What the fuck are you doing?" Bank snaps, yanking away from him.

"Checking for claw marks."

"Teeth marks," I say, rather helpfully, I think. "You're looking for teeth marks."

Asher sputters.

Magnus grins.

And West…well, West fistbumps me again before heading to the fridge and grabbing a drink. "You'll do, Aspen," he says, saluting me with a bottle of beer.

"You'll just do."

CHAPTER TWENTY-TWO

Banks

Sunday dinners at Briar's house don't happen often, but we look forward to them when they do. Atlas, Dash, and I all travel regularly for work, so it's hard for us to all be in town at the same time. Briar's good about staying on top of our schedules, though, and puts together what we call Family Time whenever she manages to wrangle us.

And today she suggested I bring Aspen.

So that's what I'm doing.

I want to bring Aspen into the fold, let her get to know the people I love most in the world, and for them to get to know her.

If she's going to become a permanent part of my life—and we're heading in that direction—this is the next step.

She was startled when I invited her, but said yes, and when I pick her up, she asks me to carry a massive bowl of pasta salad down to my car.

"My grandma used to—" She stops, and I watch her throat work for a second before she says, "well, it was something she taught me to make," she says. "It's a little different than a traditional pasta salad, but most people love it."

"My mouth is already watering," I reply. "Although you didn't have to bring anything. Briar usually cooks enough to feed an army."

"You never show up to a party empty-handed," is all she says.

Old-fashioned but polite and honest.

I like that.

I like everything about her, and I close my fingers around hers on the short drive to Briar's house. She only bought it last year, and we all helped her get settled. Royal spear-headed decorating Frankie's room and it's a gloriously artistic combination of rockstar and little girl. That's the only way to describe it. Musical instruments—guitars, keyboards, drum sets and the like, versus violins or flutes—done in soft pastels. Black and white family photos grace the walls—including some of Royal in his rock and roll heyday, as well as me on the ice, Dash in his military uniform, and the four of us guys standing in front of The Sapphire Room just before its grand opening. Somehow, it all blends together perfectly, and Frankie loves it.

I'm looking forward to showing it to Aspen.

"Are you sure I look okay?" she asks me as we pull up.

She's wearing gray leggings with an emerald-green tunic that hugs her curves, and knee-high boots. I don't know much about fashion, but she looks both beautiful and casual, which is all that matters.

"You look perfect," I say. "We keep things simple during Family Time."

"You really consider them your family, don't you?" she asks.

"I do. And hopefully, you will too."

She doesn't reply and I don't press it.

It'll take time for her to bond with everyone, but I have no doubt they'll love her as much as I do.

I haven't truly articulated my feelings until now, because it's still pretty new, but I can't deny what's going on in my heart. She's everything I never knew I wanted. That sounds like a cliche, but it's true. I've never thought about who the perfect woman would be. The woman I'd settle down with, build a life with. She was always some mystical, faceless entity with no specific set of attributes. I've just always assumed I would know her when I found her.

And I'm pretty sure I have because…

I'm falling hard and fast, and I feel it deep in my bones, my heart, my soul.

I must have a smile on my face as we walk up to the front door because she asks, "What's funny?"

"Just thinking about how excited Frankie's going to be to show you her room," I hedge. No need to send her running for the hills just yet. "Royal decorated it, and new people always get the tour."

Her mouth curves. "I'm looking forward to it."

Briar throws open the door before I can knock and she's smiling huge. "Hi, guys! Come on—" She snags the bowl in my hands. "What on earth did you bring?"

"My grandmother's pasta salad," Aspen says shyly.

Briar peers into the bowl. "Well, you didn't have to, but it looks heavenly. Thank you. Should I refrigerate it? It'll be a while before we eat."

A nod. "Yes, it's better when it's cold."

"Ooo, are those sun-dried tomatoes?" Briar asks.

"Yes, and chunks of fresh mozzarella."

"That sounds delicious! I'm getting hungry already. What else is in it?"

And just like that, the two of them take off like old friends. They've only met briefly that night at the club, and it's nice to see them pick up where they left off.

"Hey, man." Dash comes over and shakes my hand. "Beer?"

"Is that even a question?" I follow him out to the back patio where Royal is sitting on a loveseat with Frankie on his lap, and a child-sized acoustic guitar on hers.

"Whatcha doin', tiny tot?" I ask her, using the nickname we've had for her since she was a baby.

"I'm playing guitar," she replies, giving me a look that indicates I'm an idiot.

She's full of piss and vinegar sometimes, but we love that about her. She's nothing like her mom, who's shy and quiet and introverted outside of our little family. In fact, Frankie's never met someone who isn't her best friend, and she's made more of them in her one year of preschool than I've probably made in my entire life.

"Well, let's hear it," I tell her, giving Atlas a nod and grinning at Royal.

He's always been a moody fucker, the one out of all of us who was most likely to go off the grid for a while, and that increased tenfold after his accident. With Frankie, however, he's almost like he used to be. Lighter. Happier. He even smiles sometimes.

"Remember, you start here," he says, moving her little hand onto the fret of the guitar.

Watching him handle the guitar is gut-wrenching.

He hasn't picked one up—as far as I knew—since the day the physical therapist told him he would never have full use of his right hand again. Obviously, that doesn't apply when it comes to Frankie.

Sometimes I think the little girl is the only reason we still have him in our lives at all.

"What are we playing?" Dash asks, dropping in the chair across from them.

"Just shut up and listen," Royal grunts at him.

"Sorry." Dash mimes zipping his lips.

"The farmer in the dell," Frankie sings, playing a soft chord on the guitar. "The farmer in the dell...hi-ho the derry-o, the farmer in the dell."

She's playing basic chords, barely changing with each line, but it doesn't matter.

The music is right, her singing is surprisingly on key, and her excitement is infectious.

"G," Royal stage whispers when she falters with the chords.

She quickly adjusts her fingers, stops singing, stares intently at the frets, until Royal gently encourages her to keep going.

"The wife takes a child...the wife takes a child..."

Aspen and Briar have just come out and Aspen nestles against my side while Briar sinks down in a chair as we all listen intently.

Frankie ends the song—all ten verses—on a high note and we applaud loudly.

"That was wonderful!" Briar gushes. "You're getting so good."

"Thanks to Uncle Royal." Frankie turns and wraps her little arms around his neck. "I love you," she whispers, and I hear Aspen's breath hitch.

Hell, even I might shed a tear, it's so sweet.

"I love you too, tiny tot." He squeezes her tightly.

"Mommy, I'm hungry!" Frankie announces, moving on from all things music and Royal in that typical kid fashion.

"First, I want you to meet our guest," Briar says. "This is Uncle Banks's friend, Aspen."

"Hi." Frankie eyes her curiously then proves how smart she is by asking, "Are you Uncle Banks's girlfriend?"

Aspen's breath hitches again, and I know it's for a completely different reason.

"She is," I say before Aspen can commence running. "What do you think?" I tease. "Can we keep her?"

Frankie frowns, obviously taking my question far more seriously than it's intended.

"First, she has to see my room," she says. "Then we decide."

I glance at Aspen, thankful to see that she's now struggling to keep a straight face.

She nods, her tone serious. "Absolutely. Shall we go now?" She holds out her hand to Frankie, who immediately takes it.

"Yes. Come with me." Frankie all but drags her into the house.

Briar chuckles. "I hope Aspen is prepared."

"I'm going to join them," I say, getting up and following them inside.

Frankie's chirpy voice greets me as I approach her bedroom.

"...and this is my Uncle Royal. He's happy here, with his band. He can't play guitar anymore after he broke his hand. It makes him sad. That's why I'm learning."

"You're learning to play guitar so he won't be sad anymore?" Aspen asks her.

"He's happy when he shows me how to play. That's when he smiles most."

That breaks my heart a little.

Watching Royal lose the thing he loved most—his career as one of the hottest lead guitarists in rock and roll—has been devastating for all of us. We try to be there for him, but there are no words to adequately convey his loss. So we just do our best to drag him out once in a while, keep his spirits up when we can, and stay as close as he'll allow.

And apparently, little Frankie picks up where we leave off.

There's a reason he's her favorite uncle.

"And who's this?" Aspen asks her just as I reach the door. I lean back against the frame, watching them, though I can't see which picture she's pointing to.

"That's my Uncle Colt. He's in heaven. Mommy says he would have loved me *lots* if he was alive."

"I'm sure he would have."

"Mommy said he was cute." Frankie giggles.

Aspen chuckles too. "Yes. I can see he was very handsome."

"Do *you* play guitar?" Frankie asks, switching gears again.

"No, but when I was little I took piano lessons."

"Uncle Royal says I should play piano too. Mommy said I can start lessons next year."

"That sounds like a good plan."

"Oh, look at my Barbie!" I grin as I watch Frankie zoom around the room, grabbing different things and presenting them, as if it's important to show Aspen every aspect of her life.

Aspen turns and catches my eye, giving me a soft smile.

"She's adorable," she whispers.

"She is."

Frankie runs over, stopping right in front of me. "Uncle Banks, when do I get to learn hockey?"

This question has come up multiple times and Briar always vehemently opposes it, but Frankie doesn't seem to forget anything.

"Whenever Mommy says it's okay," I remind her. "But first, you have to learn to skate. Once you can skate forward and backward, we can start with hockey."

"Okay." She flings herself onto the floor and dramatically puts her arm over her eyes. "I'm starving."

Aspen giggles.

I walk over and tickle her. "Well, you're not going to get anything to eat on the floor of your room," I say. "How about we go downstairs and see if Mommy has a snack?"

"Okay!" She jumps back up and blows past us like we're not even there, practically racing down the hallway.

"She's a force of nature," Aspen says, laughing.

"She is."

"But also very insightful. I'd even dare to say protective of her Uncle Royal."

"Very protective. Those two have a special bond. He was in the room when she was born."

"Really?"

I nod. "Originally, her mom was going to be in the delivery room with her, but Frankie came early, and Dash and Briar's parents couldn't make it back in time." I shake my head. "Dash was traveling with a client, Atlas and I were both too far away, but, luckily, Royal was playing a gig nearby. The minute he heard she was alone in the hospital, he dropped everything and was there for her and Frankie. And he's been there ever since."

"That's beautiful."

"It is." I sigh. "I truly believe he might not be alive if not for Frankie. She's like his kid in some ways."

"And there are no romantic feelings between him and Briar?"

I shake my head. "No. Honestly, we all think of her as a little sister. I wouldn't be mad if something like that happened—Royal needs someone like her to love him—but there is zero evidence of those kinds of feelings between them."

"Well, I'm sure there's someone out there for her. I barely know her, but she seems wonderful."

"She is. She works hard, is a great mom, and is basically the glue that keeps our family together. I don't know what we'd do without her."

"You're very lucky to have them," she said softly. "It's the kind of thing people like me only dream of."

I pull her against my chest and wrap my arms around her waist. "Well, consider it a dream-come-true. You're part of me now, Aspen, which means you're also part of our family."

She gazes up at me, her eyes wide and full of confusion.

Then she bursts into tears.

CHAPTER TWENTY-THREE

Aspen

"I-I'm s-sorry," I force out through my sobs, turning my back on him and frantically wiping my eyes, trying to stave off the flow of tears.

It's just…

Family isn't *this*.

It's not cheering on a little girl playing guitar or sitting around shooting the shit while sharing drinks. It's certainly not stepping up and holding their surrogate sister's hand as she's pushing out a baby.

And Frankie—

God, she's so sweet.

And loved. I can feel how much they all love her, can see how she's blossoming into something wonderful because of that unapologetic affection.

She knows she's safe.

I never had that.

"Ig-ignore m-me," I manage, chest hitching, my tears little assholes who won't stop. "I-I'll be f-fine in a m-minute."

To give the man credit, me turning into a damned watering pot doesn't seem to faze Banks.

He just gently turns me to face him.

"Hey," he whispers, cupping my jaw, tilting my face up.

Meeting his eyes like *this*—when I'm so fucking vulnerable—is terrifying.

But I make myself stare into the gentle emerald depths.

He tenderly wipes his thumb beneath each eye then wraps his arms around me and tugs me against his chest. "Let it out, little spitfire."

It's an order, but I can't fight it.

I don't want to.

Because being held by him, held safe against his chest, those strong arms around me, is quickly becoming one of my favorite places to be, even though I'm likely getting his shirt all gross and snotty.

He doesn't seem to care as he strokes his hand down my back, fingers sliding through my hair, not ordering me to get it together, to stop crying. Instead, he's in no hurry. He just… holds me, comforts me, consoles me with gentle words.

"Cry if you need to, baby. I'm here. I've got you."

For a few minutes, that makes me sob harder.

I've never been allowed this.

I've always had to be strong, to keep it all locked up inside.

Emotion is weakness. Love is a blade slipping between your ribs to pierce your heart. Caring is a vulnerability.

Anger is okay.

Rage and ruthlessness are valuable tools.

It's the only way to survive in a pit of vipers.

But this man, who's shown me he's good, he's safe…he's saying it's okay to let down my walls, it's okay to cry…

Because *he's* here.

Eventually, I'm able to pull myself together and I push away from his chest, dash a hand over my cheeks.

And yup, I sure ruined his shirt—it's damp and streaked with makeup.

"I'm sorry," I whisper, waving a hand at his torso. "I'll replace it."

Now that Johnny's taken over as manager, I've been getting more shifts. More shifts mean more money, more tips, and I'm close to being able to quit the arena job.

Bye, Cheryl.

Can't wait to flip you off on my way out the door.

"No, you won't," he says simply, and then before I can process that—or really, argue with that—he wraps his fingers around my wrist and tugs me from Frankie's adorably decorated room.

A moment later, we're inside a bathroom, the door closed behind us.

The glimpse I get of myself in the mirror is terrifying— streaky mascara, puffy cheeks, foundation that's half rubbed off (the other half being on Banks's shirt).

"Up you go," he says, and before I can freak out about the fact that I'm about to hang out with his family with Puffy, Crying Face after I just met his hockey family with Sex Hair, he lifts me up and settles me on the counter.

"Wh—?"

But he's already grabbing a hand towel, gently wetting it in the sink, rubbing it lightly beneath each eye.

Cleaning off the mascara.

Then my cheeks—wiping away the remains of my makeup.

"So much for my smokey eye," I whisper because this is so much worse than crying. I feel flayed open in the aftermath of those tears, of his care, and even though he isn't pressing me for an explanation, I know I owe him one.

People don't just randomly burst into tears after touring an adorable little girl's room.

"You're beautiful," he says simply.

Which is even worse.

I exhale, shore up my courage, and whisper, "I don't know what to do with this."

He freezes. "With what, baby?"

"With you being so nice. With Frankie being adorable and sweet and *loved*. With Briar and the guys welcoming me, even though I'm intruding on your Family Time—"

"You're not."

"—with you holding me as I cry and not telling me to shut up," I continue, because if I don't, I'm going to start sobbing again. "With you welcoming me into your family like I belong here. I'm not related to you guys, to them. I don't have a place here—I didn't even have a place in my own family, and they were supposed to be the people who—" I run out of steam because this is all so scary and confusing and—

I *want* it so badly.

The Family Time.

The dinners with Briar and the guys and Frankie.

Going to the games and watching Banks kick ass.

Sitting at their table in The Sapphire Room, sharing in the reminiscing and the inside jokes and—

I want it so badly that I can taste it.

"When your own family didn't love you as they should have?"

My chin drops to my chest because…yes, exactly that.

"I know this isn't the time for us to have a heart-to-heart," he says softly.

"You mean after I slobbered all over your chest?"

His expression gentles further, and he taps a finger to the tip of my nose. "Little spitfire." A quiet admonishment before he goes on, "But I need you to know that you're amazing, baby girl. You're smart and hardworking. You've got a steel spine I can't help but admire. And"—he cups my jaw, rests his forehead on mine for a moment—"you deserve to be loved for all of those things, but also because you're a human being who has value, not because of who you marry or how many drinks you pour or if you clean a cupholder well enough. You deserve kindness and love and care because you're *you*."

"Goddammit," I mutter.

"What?" he asks, eyebrows yanking together.

"I'm going to cry again." Even now I can feel the tears burning the backs of my eyes, the sob creeping up into my throat.

"Can't have that," he teases, setting the towel aside and lifting me down from the counter. "Should I start giving you orders? Give you a set of keys so you can threaten me, rabid raccoon style, with them?"

I swat him on the shoulder. "You're impossible, you know that?"

"Impossibly good looking," he quips, lacing his fingers through mine and reaching with his free hand to open the bathroom door.

And that's why I'm laughing when we walk out into the hall and see his friends—no, his *family*—waiting for us.

―――――

THEY DIDN'T GIVE me a moment to be embarrassed, I realize several hours later.

They just swept me downstairs, busted out the board games, and locked us in a battle for Connect Four dominance that was more intense than anything I've ever experienced.

By the time Atlas was declared the ultimate winner in the round robin style tournament, I was feeling almost normal.

Mostly because Banks disappeared out to his car in between rounds and came back in a clean shirt.

No more evidence of my tears.

Now we've demolished my grandma's pasta salad along

with the lemon garlic chicken and cheesy mashed potatoes Briar made. Oh, and the bowl of "green leafy shit," as described by Atlas.

Apparently, the businessman isn't a fan of vegetables—though, to be fair, none of the guys seemed particularly excited about Briar including that addition with the spread.

They all ate it though.

(Of course, I think this is mostly because Briar threatened to not give them dessert unless they had a helping).

In my opinion, the pie was totally better than the "green leafy shit."

And the salad was delicious—mixed greens with dried cranberries and walnuts, a dash of feta, and a raspberry vinaigrette that had me begging Briar to share the recipe.

She did…as long as I gave her the one for the pasta salad.

So, all in all, it's been a lovely night filled with laughter and love and a light bit—okay, a *lot*—of board game competition.

But, I have to say, my favorite part is right now.

Watching these four big, strong men, being manipulated by a tiny, adorable human into a game of Who's the Better Uncle as they all vie to be the one to put Frankie to bed.

"I'll read you *five* bedtime stories," Dash says, upping Atlas's previous offer of four.

"Well, *I'll* read you those five books *and* I'll sing you your favorite song," Royal chimes in.

Frankie, holding court as she sits on the edge of the kitchen table, taps her bottom lip. "Hmm." Then her eyes go to Banks, clearly waiting for him to present his best offer.

"Little troublemaker," Briar says, nudging my shoulder and passing me a glass of wine. "Why don't we go sit out back and let them duke it out?"

I laugh quietly then nod. "Sounds like a plan."

Banks looks up as I follow her, our eyes connecting, and I don't miss the hint of concern in his, but I just nod, letting him know that I'm fine, that I'm not going to randomly burst into tears again.

That's a once in a decade thing.

Mouth quirking, I step onto the patio and pause, feeling the gentle strokes of the cool evening air, hearing the faint chirp of birds in the distance. "It's a beautiful night," I say with a contented sigh. I take a sip from my glass and drop into the seat next to her. "And this is a great wine. Thank you for sharing."

"One of my favorites," Briar murmurs, her gaze on the sky.

It's a gorgeous sight, the sun has dropped below the horizon, turning the heavens into a canvas of pinks and oranges and blues.

"How long have you lived here?"

"Just about a year," she says.

"Well, you've done a great job with the place."

"Thanks. I've really enjoyed decorating it, even though it's taken a while."

"I go to a lot of yard sales and thrift stores," I admit. "Buying little things here and there and saving them for when I can get a bigger place."

"I do a bit of that myself," she murmurs. "I just don't have as much time as I'd like."

"Same. Work keeps me busy."

At the mention of work, she turns, eyes coming to mine. "I heard what happened with Leo."

I wince. "Unfortunately, it's not the first or last time a man's been a dick while I've worked at a bar."

"You've had a lot of experience working at bars then?"

I still because something about her tone has my nape prickling, but I don't lie. I just take another fortifying sip of wine and say, "Yes, my family owns some bars and restaurants. My first job was working in one of them."

"Yeah?" She sets down her wine, holds my gaze. "*Some* bars and restaurants?"

"Umm—"

There's a flinty edge to her gaze now that has my stomach twisting. "Because I think it's more than that."

"Uh—"

"Which leaves me wondering if there's some other reason why you haven't told Banks you're Aspen Rockwell."

CHAPTER TWENTY-FOUR

Banks

WITH THE GIRLS chatting outside and Royal upstairs putting Frankie to bed, Atlas, Dash and I take the time to talk business. Royal is an equal owner in The Sapphire Room, but he doesn't care about the business end. From what I understand, he tells Atlas to just re-invest his quarterly earnings and doesn't even look at the numbers.

That normally works for me too, but I've been paying more attention lately, especially since the Leo situation.

"The nightly receipts have been off since Johnny took over," Atlas says, pouring himself two fingers of bourbon from Briar's well-stocked bar. "I don't know if it's because he's new or too busy screwing Marissa or something else."

"You think he's helping himself?" Dash asks, narrowing his eyes.

"I don't want to accuse him of anything because he hasn't been doing the job very long, but something is bugging me about him."

"I've never liked him as a person," Dash says, "but his background is clean."

"So was Leo's," I mutter.

"He's also setting the alarm right at two on weeknights," Atlas says, leaning against the fireplace. "That means he's closing early. Because if last call is at ten to two, and then they close right at two, count the till, and finish cleaning, he shouldn't be setting the alarm until at least two twenty or two thirty. Leo never set it before two thirty."

"Have you asked Aspen about it?" I suggest.

"Ask me about what?" she says as she and Briar come back inside, empty wine glasses in hand.

"Is Leo closing early?" I ask, meeting her gaze with what I hope is a reassuring look so she doesn't think she's in trouble.

She frowns. "Last time I worked with him, no. We didn't get out of there until after four on Saturday." She pauses. "But on Thursday...he might have. I didn't look at the clock, though. Do you want me to pay more attention?"

"Could you?" Atlas asks her. "His nightly receipts don't match what's in the safe, and the petty cash drawer is a little light too." His voice gentles at the concern rippling across her face. "Like I was telling the guys, he's only been doing it a short time, and it's easy to make mistakes in the beginning since there hasn't been a lot of formal training, but the petty cash shouldn't be off."

"No, it shouldn't be." She shakes her head. "Of course, he and Marissa spend half the night making eyes at each other, so he's probably just anxious to get home with her."

"We're not paying him to flirt with his girlfriend," Atlas says in a stern voice.

Her eyes cut to mine and she nibbles at her bottom lip, another flicker of concern drifting through her expression.

"He's not talking about you." I glare at my friend.

"No," Atlas agrees in his typical brusque fashion. "You and Banks might be together, but you haven't let it affect your performance when he's there." A shrug. "Not that I can see anyway."

Christ. Sometimes my friend needs to learn how to *not* be a CEO.

Charming, he's not.

"What he's trying to say is that you're doing a good job," Briar chimes in.

"Right," she murmurs. "Well, I'll definitely pay more attention."

"To what?"

We all look up as Royal comes back into the room.

"Sapphire Room shit," Atlas explains, sort of helpfully.

"Ugh. Business." Royal cuts his eyes to Briar's. "Frankie's out. Finally. It only took five stories and *three* songs."

"And that's why you're her favorite uncle," Briar says, reaching over to squeeze his arm. "She's got you wrapped around her little finger."

"That hurts," Dash mutters. "I mean, *I'm* her actual uncle."

"But you don't sing to her," Briar points out.

Dash snorts. "That wouldn't end well for any of us."

We all chuckle.

Then talk turns to other things and we spend the next hour or so shooting the shit. Eventually, I see Aspen starting to droop. I keep forgetting that she works two jobs and probably has to be at the arena at three in the morning, so I make our excuses.

"I've got to pack for my road trip," I say, standing up from the table.

"See you when you get back." Briar gives me a big hug. "Thanks for coming today."

"Thanks for hosting. You're the best." I kiss the top of her head.

"Thank you for having me," Aspen tells her as they hug.

They exchange a look I can't quite decipher, but then the guys are coming in to exchange their goodbyes and pretty soon, we're in my car and heading to her place.

"Did you have fun today?" I ask.

"I really did. Thank you for bringing me."

"I'm glad. I was a little worried," I admit, "and wondering if this might be too much for you. Or if…I'm moving too fast." A beat. "With all of it." I don't want to slow things down, but I will if she needs me to. Her emotional meltdown earlier reminded me that she's dealing with a lot. I still have so many questions, but I haven't wanted to push her for answers. Not yet.

Not when it might spook her.

Not when we've come so far already.

"I think moving backward is probably too fast for me," she says with a half-hearted chuckle. "But this—*you*—has been good for me. I wanted to make a clean start in California, but somehow that morphed into becoming a loner. Not trusting anyone. Getting used to the fact that the only people I can rely on are me, myself, and I." She touches my arm. "I know it's not healthy but the only person in my life I could ever trust was my grandmother. And even with her, she loved me, but she would never stand up to my father. She simply did nice things for me behind his back."

"I'm sorry." I reach for her hand. "I didn't have a mom, but my dad was pretty great. He was at every practice, every game, every tournament. No matter how many days he had to take off work or how expensive it was for me to play hockey. He made it happen. We didn't have a lot of money, but there was love and hockey. That's all I thought I needed."

"Love and hockey," she repeats softly. "That actually sounds wonderful."

"I'm probably not as well-rounded as I would have been had I had a mother and a father, and maybe a life outside of sports, but it could have been much worse."

"You have no idea."

She says it with so much sadness I want to reach out and hug her, but since I can't, I wait for her to continue.

At least…I hope she will.

Quiet fills the car, but I let her ruminate for a while. I can easily ask her to tell me, but she needs to open up because *she* wants to. Not because I'm pushing her to.

"There's something I have to tell you," she says after what feels like a million years.

I flick my gaze to hers then back to the road. "You can tell me anything."

"My name is Aspen Rockwell."

Okay?

I'm a little confused.

"I know that," I remind her.

"As in Aspen *Rockwell*. *As in* the daughter of the founder and CEO of The Rockwell Group."

The Rockwell Group?

That sounds familiar but I can't put my finger on why.

"They own all the Pinelli's restaurants. And the Wing Shot sports bars. The Frosty Flavors ice cream chain." Her voice is dull, almost bored, as she lists a handful of other chains and product lines most people have heard of.

Oh shit.

That Rockwell Group.

Aspen *Rockwell*.

It was a fairly common English surname so I haven't given it much thought.

Until now.

Fuck me.

Why didn't Atlas say anything? We do background checks on everyone we hire at the club, so he has to have known who her family is. Right?

"My father started grooming my brothers practically from the day they were born," she says quietly.

"You have two?"

"Four."

I blink. "Four. Wow."

"Yeah," she murmurs. "They're all older. Dad wanted six

male heirs. Imagine his heartbreak when baby number five not only was a girl, but my mother announced that it was her last pregnancy."

"I'm guessing that didn't go over well."

"No. And of course, he blamed me. *I'm* the reason his wife was turned off of pregnancy. Not the fact that she had five pregnancies in six years. Not the fact that he didn't pay any attention to her unless she *was* pregnant. Or the fact that he only slept with her to *get* her pregnant. He never touched her any other time."

I wince. "Jesus."

"Yeah, she'd tell me that story every time she started drinking." Her hand tenses in mine. "Which was every night. Then she'd remind me to marry for money, not for love, because the only thing you can count on is money."

"That's dark."

"My dad isn't a nice man. Most rich men aren't." She won't look at me as she says it.

"We're not all like that," I say. "You know that, don't you?"

"I know that *you're* pretty wonderful," she says. "The jury's still out on the rest of the billionaires in the world."

"Well, I'm not a billionaire. But thanks." I meet her eyes again. "I think."

Her mouth hitches up. "You know what I mean." A sigh. "You have to consider it from my perspective, Banks. You don't know what it was like growing up with a father and four brothers who treated me like a mindless little pet. I literally had no usefulness other than being paraded around at a handful of company events or parties—the pretty little girl in the ruffled dresses who softened up Dad's business partners. Once I got a little older and saw what was happening, I tried to rebel, but there were rewards for towing the line. New clothes. My first Mercedes. Trips. I had to earn them, though, and it didn't take long for me to realize the rewards weren't worth what I had to do."

"Were you…" I don't even know how to ask this question, but thankfully, she cuts me off.

"No. Not what you're thinking." She exhales, shaking her head slowly. "It was about making Dad look good. Winning an award. Being the soloist at a recital. Getting a scholarship. Anything he could use to show the world what a great dad he was, and what wonderful overachievers his kids were. The boys loved doing it, showing off, because he actually loved them. It was different for me. I learned from an early age that there was no genuine affection from anyone in that house. If I wanted them to leave me alone ninety percent of the time, I had to do what was expected the other ten. I just thought once I was an adult, it would change…"

"But it didn't?"

"No," she says. "I wanted to study something in marketing or communication, but Dad would only pay for a Liberal Arts degree. English or Literature or something similar. I love reading, as you know, and always dreamed of writing my own stories, but I wanted to do what my brothers were doing." Her fingers tense in mine. "That wasn't allowed, and when I hadn't met a rich, connected husband by the time I graduated, he put me to work in his restaurants. I thought if I did a good enough job, and learned the ropes, he'd let me work in the company somewhere. Turns out, he just wanted everyone to see how hard-working and devoted his beautiful, educated, marriage-ready daughter was. It was nothing but an audition for the marriage mart. And when the right offer came along, saying no wasn't an option."

"So you left?"

"I told my father I wasn't going to marry a man twice my age, with children almost as old as I was. He told me I would or he would cut me off."

"*Then* you left?"

"Yeah." Her head falls back against the seat, as if even talking about it is emotionally taxing. "Then I left."

"I'm sorry, little spitfire." I squeeze her hand. "I hate hearing how your family treated you, but I'm glad you didn't marry that guy."

Her nose wrinkles. "His name was Edwin Schubert. He's CEO of a liquor distributor."

"Wait…Ed Schubert. Isn't he the guy who runs Carlton Liquors? Atlas deals with them for something."

"Probably tequila," Aspen mutters. "They have the best variety and they're one of the bigger distributors in California."

I scowl. "Well, they won't be distributing to The Sapphire Room anymore."

"Oh, don't be silly." She shakes her head. "Everyone uses them. Really. You'll pay double if you use someone else."

"Then we'll raise our prices." I shrug. "I won't deal with anyone who had any part in hurting you. Not now, not ever. Despite what your mother thinks, it's just money. And they'll all agree. We have something way more important."

"What's that?"

"Family."

CHAPTER TWENTY-FIVE

Aspen

FAMILY.

The word rings through my head more than once over the next few days.

And the fact that family means something completely different to Banks than it does to me—

Or *did* to me.

Because…

I think maybe it can be different.

Especially, when I'm getting ready for the rush and look up to see Briar walking through the back door.

"Hey," I say as she comes over and sits at one of the stools in front of me.

"Hey," she says.

"Where's Frankie?"

"With Royal for Favorite Uncle Time."

My lips twitch as I move behind the bar, checking to make sure we're all ready to go. Johnny is supposed to be here helping me, but he hasn't shown up yet.

In fact, he was late the other night too.

Though, I made sure he didn't close up early.

"I bet she's having a blast."

"Oh yes." She holds up her phone so I can see the screen. "She and Uncle Royal are having mani-pedis and doing facemasks."

I grin. "Please tell me you've saved that for blackmail material."

"Unfortunately, Uncle Royal doesn't care about the potential blackmail implications when he spends time with my daughter." She winks. "He took the selfie."

Oh. Right.

Because he likes approximately five people in the world, and none of those include an assistant or girlfriend to snap adorable pictures of him and his niece.

"She's lucky to have him," I say as I check the container of lemons. "Well, really, you're all lucky to have each other."

"Yes."

I look up because her tone sounds off. "Everything okay?"

She winces. "I feel bad about our conversation the other day."

Frowning, I close the lid and lean against the bar. "What do you mean?"

"I was pushy about you telling Banks—" She waves a hand. "About your family. I'm…protective of the guys and I was worried you were deliberately keeping secrets, but I didn't take into account that the dumb-dumbs who are my older brothers don't follow socialite news like I do. Last I heard you were engaged and next thing I know, you turn up with Banks. He's a good guy, but he's got a soft streak." Guilt lies heavy in the lines of her face. "I just…I didn't want him to get hurt."

I reach across the bar and touch her hand. "Like I said, you're all lucky to have each other." I sigh. "I didn't tell him because I was trying to get away from the Rockwell legacy, trying to pretend that part of my life didn't exist. They're… well, they're nothing like the family you guys have built."

Briar turns her hand over, lacing our fingers together and squeezing lightly. "Yeah," she says. "I've seen enough of socialite TikTok to know that while the Rockwell family seems glamorous, there's a dark underbelly."

I wrinkle my nose. "Especially, if you're a woman and you're only good for putting on a party or popping out a kid."

"Ugh." Briar slips her hand from mine but leans over the bar and grips both of my shoulders tightly. "You are worthy of so much more."

"Great," I grumble as she settles back into her seat.

"What?"

"Now you're just trying to make me cry."

Her mouth ticks up. "I'm sorry."

"You're not." I start mixing her a lemon drop, since that appears to be her drink of choice when she comes in. "But really, I should be thanking you."

"Why?"

"Seeing Frankie so loved and respected and confident even though she was the only kid amongst you adults reminded me that things can be different." I add lemon juice to the shaker and cap it, start mixing her drink. "No one makes her small or unseen and the guys, they value you too. They listen to you, and don't expect you to wait on them hand and foot." I stop shaking and pour her drink into a chilled glass. "And you guys welcomed me into that too. Without hesitation. Without making me feel like an outsider. Banks may have brought me, but you all made me realize that I can have something different." I toss a napkin in front of her and set the glass on top of it. "You made me see that family doesn't have to be what I had growing up, that *I* don't have to be them."

"No, it doesn't." She picks up the drink, salutes me with it. "And no, *you* don't."

I sigh. "So, I'm glad we had the conversation. You just gave me the last push to stop holding back. There was no reason to hide the truth of who I am because Banks isn't going to judge me for it."

"Nope," Briar agrees. "Not with that ooey-gooey center."

I giggle. "Should we share that fact with his teammates?"

"Might earn him a brand-new nickname." She winks. "Thank you for the drink, by the way."

"You're welcome." The host leads a group of men to a table in the back and I know it won't be long until the drink orders start pouring in.

Unfortunately, though, Johnny hasn't shown.

I frown. And neither has Marissa.

Ugh.

It's going to be a long night.

"Any clue why Atlas asked me to find a new tequila distributor?"

My brows shoot up. Then I wince. "That may be my doing. Banks found out the man my dad wanted me to marry was Ed Schubert."

"Ew." Briar wrinkles her nose. "Isn't he like a hundred?"

"Not quite."

"But close enough," she mutters.

Since I don't exactly disagree with her, I just nod and take the first ticket from Beth, one of the servers. "Is Marissa supposed to be working?"

Beth sighs. "Yeah. She's not here yet, though, and she no-showed on Tuesday." She hurries over to another table.

No Marissa. And still no Johnny.

Yeah. It's definitely going to be a long night.

Briar drains her drink and stands. "I still can't believe my dumb brother didn't put the pieces together."

"Spoken like a true little sister."

"Exactly." She winks, puts a twenty in the tip jar. "Well, I'll get out of your hair. I need to go rescue Uncle Royal."

"Make sure to tell him to be careful with his nails."

She grins, waves goodbye.

I barely have the chance to do the same before another ticket comes in.

And then another.

And *another*.

And…

I was right.

It's a fucking long ass night.

————

I LOVE HAVING my car back.

But part of me misses the rides with Banks.

No. I just miss *Banks*.

Ugh. One hockey player with an ooey-gooey center and I'm turning into a sap.

I can't lie, though.

I've never felt this alive, this whole, this much…

Me.

Heart rolling over in my chest, I grab my purse and slowly push out of the driver's seat, slamming the door and bleeping the locks before making my way up to my apartment door.

It's quiet as always and as I climb the stairs I try to pretend that my legs don't feel like they're jelly, like my shoulders aren't aching, like I don't want to kill Johnny.

I don't get what's going on with him—the drawers being short, the no-shows.

We've worked together before, and he was never like this.

Or maybe he *was*, I think with a frown, remembering that other bar and working my ass off. Neither of us dealt with the money at the end of the night but…

There was always a woman he was flirting with.

And I was always this exhausted after a shift.

Right?

"Ugh," I whisper to myself as I unlock my door and push into my apartment. I don't know. Maybe my memory is clouded. Maybe I don't want to believe it because he was the one that told me about the opening at The Sapphire Room in the first place. Maybe——

It's too late to be thinking about this shit.

I toss my purse down, peel off my coat, and grab a glass of water before I head into the bathroom and discard my dirty, sweaty clothes.

I need to take a shower, but my bed is calling me more strongly so I wash off my makeup, slap on some moisturizer and use a towel to wash the pertinent bits so I won't wake up feeling completely gross.

Then I'm crawling beneath the covers, plugging in my phone, and—

My stomach fills with butterflies.

I have a missed voicemail.

Even though Banks is out of town, he's been sweet, checking in with me every night I have a shift, making sure I get home safe.

I must not have heard his call.

Wanting to hear his voice, I hit the button to play the voice-mail on speaker—

"Ms. Rockwell," I hear a familiar nasally voice and those butterflies in my stomach turn into elephants, stomping around. Stomping on my hope and joy and the happiness I've found here.

"Mr. Rockwell would like to speak to you at your soonest convenience," my father's assistant says in the recording, "Please call me back at..."

My soonest convenience.

Meaning right-fucking-*now*.

"Dammit," I whisper, jabbing at the button to cut the voice-mail off. Why now? Why after all this time?

I clench my hands into fists.
It doesn't matter.
I swipe and delete the message then block the number.
I'm not going back.
Not ever.

CHAPTER TWENTY-SIX

Banks

BEING AWAY from Aspen after our newfound intimacy is harder than I anticipate.

I'm like a lovesick teenager half the time, thinking about her, imagining her face as I jerk off in the shower, texting her, calling her. I'm a fucking mess because not only am I falling in love, I'm worried about her. Now that I know who her family is, I realize the reach they have. They can cause problems for her—and for me.

Not that I'm afraid. Atlas probably has more money than her family and all their conglomerates put together, but I don't want to have to ask him for help. Or resources.

On top of that, I'm playing like shit.

I want to say I don't know what's wrong with me, but I do.

I'm distracted.

Horny.

Frustrated.

Scared.

Fuck.

Aspen has turned my life upside down in all the best ways,

but nothing good ever comes without some bad too. The negative is not being able to focus on my job. In some ways, as much as I love hockey, it pales in comparison to what I feel when I'm with her. She needs me more than my team does, and my balls all but shrivel into their sacs just thinking that.

I have to get my game back on track, but I don't know how anymore.

Extra time on the ice and watching videos of my mistakes hasn't helped.

Nothing helps.

Well, having Aspen in the crowd that night made a difference, but it's not like I can bring her on the road.

"You look like a man with a lot on your mind." I turn from where I've been nursing a poorly made Gamebreaker at the hotel bar.

"Hey, man." I lift my chin in West's direction, and he sinks onto the bar stool next to me.

"Anything you want to talk about?"

I stare off at nothing, mindlessly twirling the glass in my hand. "How do you focus on hockey with a woman in your life?"

He snorts. "You're asking the wrong guy. I'm as single as they come. My last girlfriend was so fucking high-maintenance I've kind of sworn off women for a little while." A shudder. "At least until I can erase all those memories. She sucked my soul dry. It's not healthy."

"That's not what's happening with Aspen," I say, continuing to stare off into the distance. "She's...amazing. Not high maintenance at all. Almost the opposite. She works hard, is kind and honest, and we have a lot of chemistry." I run my finger around the rim of the glass. "We enjoy each other, both physically and mentally."

"Then what's the problem? She got a sister?"

I chuckle, taking a sip of my drink. "No sisters. Just a shit-ton of asshole brothers."

And a family that treated her like shit.

Ugh. This Gamebreaker is fucking awful.

Aspen's are so much better.

"The problem is"—I put the glass down and drum my fingers on the bar—"I don't think about anything else. I can't even begin to. I've known her less than two months and I'm ready to marry her. That's not normal." I pause and glance in his direction. "Is it?"

He shrugs. "I dunno. I've never been in love like that. But...if I'm being honest?"

I nod.

"It sounds about right. I don't suggest marrying her just yet, but move her in, make things official. What's the holdup?" He flags down the bartender, orders a beer. "Is it her?"

"Kind of?" I push my glass away. "She's very independent. I don't know how she'll feel about moving in, or even taking things to the next level."

"Have you told her how you feel?"

I shift uncomfortably.

We haven't used the L word.

Duh.

It's too soon for that.

"I take it that's a no," he says, shaking his head. "You can't expect her to give up anything if you're not willing to put your heart on the line, you know? Women need that kind of validation."

"I want to give her anything she needs," I admit.

"Then man the fuck up and do it. I'm not looking for a relationship right now, but if I met someone who made me feel like you're describing, I wouldn't let her go. Not a chance in hell."

"I don't have any intention of letting her go. It's just a matter of convincing her that we're right for each other while not blowing up my hockey career. And if I get traded—" I cut myself off abruptly. I shouldn't have said that.

Dammit.

"You think that's a possibility?" He looks startled.

"It's always a possibility."

He bumps his knee against mine. "You know what I mean."

"They're paying me a lot of money to score." I sigh. "And guess what I'm not doing much of this season? Or last season, for that matter."

He nods, understanding dawning.

He knows this life. Things can change at the drop of a hat.

"You don't have a no-trade clause?" he asks.

"A limited one." I have to give management ten teams I refuse to go to, but anywhere else is on the table. And there's always the possibility that shenanigans will arise, and I'll end up somewhere I don't want to go if the back office decides to put me on waivers.

"Shit, man."

"Yup."

"You don't think she'd go with you?"

That's a tough one.

She worked hard to build a life in Southern California.

What the hell do I have to offer her in Calgary or Nashville or some other city where neither of us know anyone? And will she be willing to go at this early stage of our relationship? She likes me, I know that, but does she love me? Is she ready to take things to the next level and start working toward building a life together?

The sad truth is that I don't know, and until I figure it out, I'm in limbo.

Personally, professionally, and emotionally.

That's not going to help my game at all.

———

I'M HAVING a hard time sleeping and I've taken to going to the hotel gym to work out. It's not ideal but I'm usually alone and the extra workouts are keeping me in good shape.

Of course, it's not manifesting into anything on the ice.

Yeah, I'm fast and have a lot more stamina than I used to. But I still can't score a goal to save my life.

And the lack of sleep is catching up to me. I'm going to have to sort that out sooner than later. I can't keep doing what I'm doing— on the treadmill at midnight, sleeping from one until five, and now wide awake again.

Impulsively, I call Aspen. She's probably on her way home from the arena, so I might be able to tell her good night. Hear her voice.

"Why are you up so early?" she asks by way of greeting when she answers.

"Couldn't sleep."

"Again?" Her voice is soft. "We're going to have to do something about that when you get home. How many more hours is it now?"

"Fifty-one."

She chuckles. "Fifty-one and a half, according to the flight schedule you sent me."

"Fifty-one hours and twenty-nine minutes too many."

"You're sweet."

I recline back against the pillows. "You think so?"

"Always."

"Colt used to say that was my downfall with women."

"Being sweet?" She sounds confused.

"Colt was the kind of guy who charmed women by being a dick. I mean, not physically, and I'm not talking about being verbally abusive. Like, he'd see a pretty girl at the bar and check her out. She'd check him out too, but then he'd turn away and pretend not to be interested. It used to drive them crazy and the more distant he was, the more they chased him.

He said I was too nice, and that's why I always got my heart broken."

"*You* got your heart broken a lot?" She sounds somewhat dubious.

"In college I did."

"Well, I think everyone gets their heart broken in college."

"Except Colt. He went through women like water. He was a force of nature. That broody, distant attitude would nail them hook, line, and sinker. Especially since, you know, once you broke past his asshole surface layer, there was a great guy underneath. He was one of the best people I've ever known."

"I know you really miss him."

"So much." I stare up at the ceiling. Colt would know what to do about this situation with hockey. With Aspen. With a lot of things. He'd always been my sounding board.

"How long has it been?"

"Since he died?"

"Yeah," she murmurs.

"It was four years in September. I remember getting the news like it was yesterday." My throat gets tight at the memory. "It happened at the beginning of my first season here and one of the assistants came into the locker room. She said I had a visitor, that it was an emergency."

"Oh, babe." Her voice is gentle, soothing.

"It was Atlas. He was standing in the office, and I'd never seen him look so pale, on the verge of tears. And you know Atlas—he's not the kind of guy who cries."

"Definitely not."

"And I knew. The minute I saw his face, I knew it had something to do with Colt or Dash or both of them." I exhale slowly, trying to gather my thoughts. Even after all this time, the memories are gut-wrenching.

"Both of them?"

"They were in the Marines, Special Forces. They were stationed in Germany but were always going on missions.

Dash had decided not to re-up, so it was their last one together. We'd had a group video chat a week before, the five of us. The last time we were together, so to speak." I pause and swallow. It's so hard to talk about this part. "Anyway, as soon as I saw Atlas, I knew something had gone wrong. We don't know any details because all the missions are classified, and even though Dash is out now, he still can't talk about it. All we know is that Colt went out on patrol and never came back. They found his burned and charred body a few days later."

"Oh no."

"The worst part is that apparently they'd had a fight—Colt and Dash. Colt was pissed that Dash was getting out and hadn't told him. I guess he said something after the fact and Colt felt betrayed. This mission they were on was supposed to be their last and they weren't talking. Then, to make matters worse, Dash broke a rib doing whatever it was they'd done earlier in the day, so that night Colt took his patrol."

"I hate that for you guys," she says quietly. "Dash must be so guilt-ridden."

"The year after Colt died was hard. We'd just found out Briar was pregnant, we lost Colt, Dash was discharged, and Royal was on a world tour…" I sigh, remembering what a struggle it was to keep us together. "We were a mess."

"You've had more than your share of heartbreak," she says.

"I guess we have."

"So…you opened The Sapphire Club in Colt's honor?"

"We did. It was Atlas's idea, but we all pooled our money because it was such a Colt thing to do—live big and a little wild, you know? Then it became a place where we can honor him every year on his birthday. And any other time the mood strikes us."

"I think that's lovely," she says. "A great way to remember him."

"It is. Of course, now it's also when I met you." I smile

even though she can't see it. "And because of that, his birthday is no longer my least favorite day of the year."

"Banks," she whispers.

"What?" I whisper back.

"There's that sweet again," she says lightly. "You really know how to make a girl feel good."

"Just wait until I get home."

She giggles then yawns.

"Go to bed, little spitfire."

"I can't wait to see you…in forty-nine hours and thirty-five minutes."

CHAPTER TWENTY-SEVEN

Aspen

I STARE DOWN at the screen of my cell phone knowing what I need to do.

And dreading it, wracking my brain to try and avoid having to do this.

But…I'm out of ideas.

"Can I get another, sweetheart?"

I jerk my gaze up from my phone, hurry down the full bar and refill the man's gin and tonic—then do the same for the bourbon on the rocks, the draft IPA, and a few others who flag me down for more drinks.

Raucous laughter from the corner booth prompts me to pick my cell up again. The tables are going to get restless, and I'm barely holding on here.

Gritting my teeth, I allow my thumb to descend.

To select the contact and dial the person I hate to bother.

But…

I'm alone.

As in, I'm *alone.*

It's a Thursday night, which means we normally have

fewer staff scheduled. We're typically less busy, so the lighter crew manages just fine.

Unfortunately, two of those fellow staff members scheduled to work tonight are Marissa and Johnny.

And they're not here. Or not answering my calls.

The other, Beth, is out sick.

I've gone down the roster, called all the other servers, the backup bartenders…and none are available tonight.

All of which to say, I'm in the weeds.

I can run the bar by myself, even if we're slammed. I can even run the bar *and* handle the tables if we're up to say… moderately busy.

However, I can't manage the tables and the bar *and* all the things that come with both of those jobs when a giant bachelor party unexpectedly shows up and all the regulars are here, *and* the post-work cocktail hour folks come in.

Which means I cannot manage right now.

So, I make the call.

It rings—once, twice, three times—and just as panic starts to really set in, Atlas answers with a terse, "Hello?" There's noise in the background, like he's at a party or in the middle of a meeting or something.

Shit. He's busy.

Not a surprise considering that he's got a bazillion businesses he runs—or, you know, a half-dozen multinational companies that gross billions of dollars of revenue every year.

He's certainly not sitting around, twiddling his thumbs, waiting for the bartender of The Sapphire Room to phone.

"Hi, uh, Atlas, it's Aspen."

There's a brief pause, and the noise quiets as though he's stepped into another room. "Aspen, are you all right?"

The concern in his tone…

It unlocks the words from my throat.

"No, I mean, yes. Physically, I'm fine, but I probably won't be by the end of the night if I don't— Never mind, that's not important." I shake my head. This man is busy. He doesn't need to worry about my back and arms and how angry they'll be at the end of my shift if I don't get help. Nor about how exhausted I'll be in the morning. These long hours at the arena and running the bar by myself are taking their toll, leaving me even more tired than usual. "Uh, I'm fine," I say, managing to focus. "I just…Johnny and Marissa no-showed again and Beth is sick. And I called everyone whose number I have but no one is available and there's a bachelor party showed up, all the regulars are here and the office crowd—"

"Yo, baby! Get off the phone," I hear. "I need a drink."

Apparently, Atlas hears it too.

He sighs.

"I'll be there in twenty."

―――――

"GODDAMN," Atlas mutters, dropping the tray on the bartop. "They're relentless."

He's shed his suit jacket, rolled up his shirtsleeves, revealing that he has the same tattoo that Banks has on his forearm. In fact, I've seen it on Royal and Dash's arm too—at Family Time. I'll have to ask if it has any significance.

When we're not so busy that my head is spinning.

I snag the empty tray, nod at the one I've just loaded up with Gamebreakers.

"Table eight needs those drinks."

"Jesus Christ," he grumbles, but he picks up the tray and goes back to schlepping drinks like a pro while I move on to fulfilling the next ticket and keeping the guys occupying the stools in front of me topped up on their libations of choice.

It's a careful and choreographed dance that I'm accomplishing tonight via sheer grit rather than with any semblance of grace.

And it's that grit that has me ignoring the fatigue pulling

on my limbs as I make the tray of cosmos, as I top off that gin and tonic, as I grab refills of lemon drops and Gamebreakers and beers with the perfect amount of foam.

I set the final IPA down, close out the tab like the man asked, and move to the next task.

Or start to.

Because as I turn to reach for a glass, I see Briar standing next to me, her hair tied up in a messy bun, wearing glasses instead of her usual contacts. "What can I do?" she asks.

I blink. Once. Twice.

But, nope, she's still there.

"Um," I ask quietly. "Doesn't Frankie have ballet tonight?"

"That was earlier. Royal was watching her class with me when I saw Atlas's text. He took her home and is going to stay with her until I get back. Now"—she claps her hands together —"how best can I help?"

"Do you know how to make drinks?"

Her mouth hitches up. "Does pouring wine count?"

"A for effort," I tell her. "Okay, so Atlas is taking drink orders and putting them into the system. Can you run the drinks I make to the tables and be in charge of money?"

A salute. "I'm on it."

And she is.

But before I finish the next tray of drinks, I spot Dash walking up to the bar.

"Put me to work," he says simply.

"I—you don't have—"

He reaches over the wooden top. "Family sticks together," he says quietly. "Now"—a squeeze of my hand—"put me to work."

Maybe I should refuse.

But I don't.

And since he has a bit of bartending experience, I set him on helping me pull beers and mix simple drinks.

Before long, we catch up, and I pause for a moment to roll out my shoulders.

Then I open my mouth to tell them I've got this—

"Nope," Briar says, nudging me to the side and beginning to wash some of the shakers that have piled up.

"Nope what?"

"Don't even try to get rid of us," she says. "We're here and we're in it for the long haul."

"But we're caught up and it's quieted down."

"Barely," Dash says, dropping a now filled container of quartered limes into the slot in front of me. "A few tables have left, but we leave and you'll be slammed again."

"I can handle it," I say. "It's late, and you guys have to work tomorrow."

"Well, luckily I know the boss," Briar says lightly, nodding at Atlas, who's delivering drinks efficiently, albeit with a scowl that has the women swooning and the men giving him a wide berth.

Not the best customer service.

But people are still ordering as many drinks as ever, so I suppose it's efficient enough.

"And I *am* the boss," Dash adds.

"So quit arguing," Briar begins.

"And just accept that we're helping you tonight," Dash finishes.

I wrinkle my nose at the siblings. "I don't like it when you gang up on me."

"Get used to it," Briar says, setting the shakers on the drying rack.

"Exactly," Dash agrees.

"Fine. I need six IPAs, two rum and cokes, and a vodka water," I order Dash before turning to Briar. "Tables six and two need refills, five needs their check, and three needs to be bussed."

Twin salutes that have me smirking and shaking my head.

But they don't argue, just go off and do the tasks I ask of them.

Atlas returns with an empty tray and pauses, leaning back against the bar and studying me like I'm a bug under a microscope.

"What?" I ask as I mix up a drink.

"You're good at this."

"At making drinks?" I smile. "Well, Banks *does* say that I make the best Gamebreaker he's ever had."

"He's right," Atlas agrees. "But I wasn't talking about making drinks."

"Oh."

"I mean, you're good at managing people."

"I—"

"Sweetheart, I'm still waiting on that drink," my customer from five stools down calls.

Atlas scowls at him. "Men are assholes."

"Don't worry," I whisper out of the corner of my mouth. "Every *sweetheart* gets him one less ounce of booze."

"Then he must be drinking water by now."

I grin. "Well, *I'm* not going to be the one to tell him."

Atlas stills.

Then something wonderful happens—

He laughs.

Loudly enough that Briar comes over, demanding to know what the hell I've done with her scowly, grumpy boss. Long enough that Dash moves to us and declares that wonders never cease.

And loudly *and* long enough that I hear—

"Yo, sweetheart!"

CHAPTER TWENTY-EIGHT

Banks

I WAS on my way home from the airport when I caught sight of the family's group text thread and changed directions.

Aspen alone at the club.

She needed help.

Royal on babysitting duty.

The whole family jumping in to lend a hand.

I don't know why Johnny and Marissa bailed tonight, but as I drop another load of plates into the soapy water—because the fucking dishwasher is on the blink too—I already know I'm going to make sure Atlas fires both of them.

Emergencies happen.

Beth is sick—and even if she's not, she's been here long enough to get the benefit of the doubt. If it keeps happening, that's different, but this time she gets a pass. Johnny and Marissa can fuck all the way off. They'll be picking up their final paychecks next Friday.

I finish with the dishes, dry my hands, and head back to the dining room.

The scene before me makes me smile.

Briar is bussing the last of the tables.

Atlas and Dash are changing out kegs.

Aspen is wiping down the bar, which seems to be her favorite thing to do.

For the first time since I arrived, I have a chance to really look at my girl and it occurs to me she looks tired.

And there is zero chance I'm letting her work her shift at the arena.

Nope.

Call me misogynistic, overbearing, or whatever other chauvinistic name you want, but she's not doing that shit anymore.

"Hey." I follow Atlas into the back. "We need to talk."

"About Johnny?" He snorts. "We don't need to talk about anything. He's already gone. And yes"—he doesn't even look at me as he tosses the empty keg into the back, where they sit until the beer rep comes to switch them out with full ones—"I'm going to offer Aspen the job." His eyes catch mine. "If that's okay with you."

"Damn right, it is. She ran the whole place tonight, other than the kitchen." I grin. "She was barking orders like she was born to it."

He glances up at me curiously. "Well, I mean, she kind of was."

"What do you—" I abruptly stop talking. "Did you know who her father was when you hired her?" I ask.

"Of course. Dash doesn't do a half-assed job with his background checks. But who her father is, isn't our business."

"You didn't even consider she might be a spy?"

"For what? We're not competition to the Rockwells. We're a single club that isn't open to the public. None of us are interested in a chain, and I think that's pretty common knowledge. But once Dash dug into her finances—because you know I leave nothing to chance—it's pretty obvious she was cut off. At the time she had sixty bucks in her checking account, no savings, no assets other than a car that's seen better days."

"Why didn't you tell me?" I demand, folding my arms across my chest.

"Tell you what?" He looks confused. "Did you want a rundown of Johnny's and Beth's assets too? Do I normally tell you about our employees' parents?"

I grit my teeth in irritation since he's purposely being obtuse. "When we started to get involved."

He arches his brows. "I assumed you two talked. You know, that thing couples do."

I narrow my eyes at him. "You know how hard it's been to get her to open up."

"That's not my job. I'm not the one falling in love with her."

Am I that obvious?

Apparently so.

But…

One thing at a time.

"So, are we going to offer her the job as a group right now or are you going to do it all official-like in a meeting?"

He rolls his eyes. "Dude, you know how many things I had to drop to get here tonight? Which means my day tomorrow will be twice as busy. I don't have time for special meetings. I'm going to talk to her now, unless you have a problem with it?"

"Of course not. I'm just…" I let my sentence trail.

"Afraid she'll say no if it comes from you?"

He knows me too well.

"Yeah."

"She won't. She loves this shit. She's tired but you can see how energized she is to be running things, to be getting things done. She was born for this. Literally and figuratively."

He's right, and I smile to myself as I walk back into the dining room.

Aspen and Briar are behind the bar laughing about something. There's one customer left, a regular, and he's joking with them too. Not the flirtatious bullshit going on earlier, but just a normal, decent guy hanging out with the staff at a place he frequents.

"You okay to drive, Pete?" I ask, clapping a hand on his shoulder as I join them.

He shakes his head. "Fuck no. Uber's on its way. Four minutes out."

"Your last one is on me," Aspen tells him.

"You're a good girl," he says. "Thank you." He gets up, gives me a mock salute, calls out to Dash and Atlas, and ambles out the front door.

I lock it behind him before coming back to the bar, where we've all gathered.

"What a night," Briar says, looking at Atlas. "How the fuck am I supposed to be on a plane at six in the morning?"

"Where are you going?" Aspen asks.

"Meeting in Chicago," Atlas responds, rubbing his hands down his face. "Yeah, let's postpone to Thursday. If you can send out an email before you go to bed, letting everyone know something came up, we can reconvene at the office at noon."

"Perfect." Briar nods.

"So." Atlas turns to Aspen. "I have a question, Ms. Rockwell."

Aspen's eyes widen slightly as she looks at him. I reach across the bar for her hand, letting her know everything is okay, and she laces her fingers with mine.

"What's up?" she asks, more curious than wary now.

"How would you like to manage The Sapphire Club?"

Her mouth falls open.

"Please don't say no," Briar stage whispers. "I can't do this regularly. This is way harder than anything I do for Atlas or at home."

He scowls at her for a split second, but then focuses back on Aspen.

And as I'm watching her face, something shifts.

Sweet, guarded Aspen is replaced by shrewd, calculating Aspen. This is a version of her I've never seen before. She's aloof but sharp, and slowly, she pulls her hand from mine.

"What type of compensation are you offering, Mr. Delarosa?" she counters.

The tiniest movement of Atlas's upper lip tells me he wants to smile but doesn't. He's going to play her game, and watching the two of them negotiate is fascinating.

He gives her a more than respectable number as her salary, and she shrugs, unimpressed.

"Benefits? Paid time off? Vacation? And most of all, health insurance."

"We don't really offer PTO," he says. "It's the service industry, but—"

"That's unacceptable," she interrupts. "Despite him being an asshat, Leo was here seven days a week. Payroll, food orders, dealing with liquor distributors, repairs, creating the server schedule, and a million other things. I can give you a lot of time and as many hours as the job requires, but I need time to recharge. Two weeks' vacation is the bare minimum these days, but like you said, this is the service industry, so I understand that vacation works a little differently. However, I won't be able to accept it if I don't have some guaranteed time off."

Their eyes are locked.

"All right." Atlas nods. "Two weeks."

"Four," I interject.

"I don't think you should get involved," Briar whispers.

"She's my girlfriend," I say, ignoring her. "We're going to be traveling next summer in the off-season. So you're also going to need to train an assistant manager and—"

"I've got this." Aspen cuts me off, putting a hand on mine and effectively silencing me, but her gaze is still locked with Atlas's.

I'm equal parts impressed, turned on, and terrified.

"He's right that you'll need to train an assistant," Aspen

continues in a pragmatic voice. "I can't work twenty-four-seven/three-sixty-five. That's not sustainable, and obviously, you're not going to ride to the rescue every time I get the flu or something."

Atlas nods thoughtfully. "I suppose that's true."

"Also, despite a very fair salary, it really comes down to how many hours I wind up putting in. If I'm here seven days a week, working twelve-hour days, that comes to about fourteen dollars an hour and that's not even minimum wage."

Did she just do that math in her head?

"I understand you don't need me to jump in," I interject dryly, "but I'm going to put this out there right now: *no one* is working seven days a week. We've gotten lucky since we opened, hiring people who didn't have personal lives, but that ends now. Work it out however you like, but I'm putting my foot down on this. Whether it's my girlfriend or someone else. Briar doesn't work those kinds of hours. Nor should Aspen."

Atlas looks a little annoyed, but his eyes are doing this little dance I recognize as him dreaming up a proposal. Contemplating. Ruminating. Doing whatever it is he does that's made him a billionaire by thirty.

"All right, I need a little time to come up with a long-term plan," Atlas says at last, glancing at me. "You're right. We have been lucky so far, but it isn't fair, so I need to pivot with staff and scheduling. However, can we agree on a short-term arrangement where you're here a lot until I can hire more reliable staff and turn things around? Less than three months—you have my word."

"Then I'm going to need another twenty thousand a year." Aspen doesn't seem at all concerned about asking for more money.

And Atlas doesn't hesitate to give it to her.

"And those four weeks of vacation."

Atlas scowls but holds out his hand. "You've got a deal."

Aspen smiles and slowly shakes it. "Pleasure doing business with you."

"Thank god that's over," Dash mutters. "I was scared for a minute there."

"I think it's awesome," Briar says, chuckling. "Very few people stand up to Atlas."

"And live to tell about it," Atlas agrees with a nod.

"It totally turned me on," I whisper in Aspen's ear.

She just smiles and puts her purse over her shoulder as we all get ready to leave. "Are you ready to go? It's late and I have another job to get to."

"You're coming to my place tonight," I say under my breath. "And you're calling in sick. You don't need two jobs anymore, little spitfire."

She hesitates but then breaks into a wide yawn. "You might be right. I'm really tired."

"Tell Cheryl you're done. Seriously, don't go back."

"I don't want to leave them in the lurch and—"

"Fuck that. You're done."

Her eyes narrow like she's going to argue with me.

Then she yawns again, and a little sigh escapes her. "I hate giving into your orders—"

I grin.

"—but I think you're right. My body is telling me it's time to stop burning the candle at both ends."

"Exactly." I slide my arm around her shoulders. "Now let's go home."

I'm half expecting her to protest that it's not her home, or that she should go back to her place, but instead…she just melts into my shoulder and nods.

And I know I've just won a big battle in the war for her heart.

.

CHAPTER TWENTY-NINE

Aspen

I PULL at the hem of the Vipers jersey and stretch my arms.

It feels a little tight across the chest, but that's likely because I've spent the last few weeks getting The Sapphire Room into shape.

It's been a lot of work.

And not purely in the physical sense—getting the stockroom in order, working my normal shifts, doing a complete inventory, and organizing estimates for the uncooperative dishwasher and the dozens of other tasks that seem to have fallen through the cracks.

Long days.

Hard work.

I've fallen into bed, sleep taking me under almost the moment my head hits the pillow every single night.

But I've never been more fulfilled.

Atlas listens to me.

Briar makes sure I have the tools I need to execute the necessary tasks.

And The Sapphire Room has become part of me.

Or I it.

Either way, it's satisfying.

But tonight isn't about work.

It's about supporting Banks—which means it's about hockey.

I'm excited because I haven't seen him play in person since that night a couple of weeks ago, and I know he's still worried about his lack of scoring. But from what I've seen on TV, he looks like he's making a difference.

Still, what do I know?

He's the professional hockey player, not me.

I sling my purse over my shoulder, grab my jacket and keys and I'm just reaching for the doorknob when there's a knock on the other side of the wooden panel.

Frowning, I tug it open—

And freeze.

What the actual fuck?

"Ms. Rockwell," my father's assistant, Thomas, says. "Can I come in?"

No. Fuck no.

"I'm late," I tell him.

"I just need a moment of your time."

"I *said*, I'm late."

He shoves a folder at me and instinctively I take it. "You'll find the terms of the offer very amenable."

Frowning, I flip open the cover and start scanning the first page.

And as the words process, I feel my mouth drop open. I cannot actually be reading what I think I'm reading.

"My father's offering me a job?"

Thomas shifts uncomfortably from foot to foot. "I'm to bring word of your decision back to him."

This man works in the pit of vipers—no pun intended—and I almost feel sorry for him because what I'm going to tell him, the giant fuck off I'm going to have him pass along to my father, isn't going to go over well.

I shove the papers back at him, but he refuses to take them, even though I'm basically jabbing him in the chest with the corner of the folder. "Tell him that there's absolutely no way in hell that I would ever accept anything from him, least of all a job—"

"I suggest you look at the terms," Thomas says. "I think you'll find them most generous and—"

"No." I shove the papers more firmly at him.

He slides a step backward. "I'll just leave that with you, give you some time to read through the offer, and let your father know that you'll be back with an answer in a few days."

"I—"

But he's reached the top of the stairs by the time he finishes saying that, and before I can finish my rebuttal of sharp words for my father, before I can tell him exactly what the fuck I think of the offer…

Thomas is gone.

The door across the hall opens and Mrs. X pops her head out. "Everything okay, honey?"

I'm still holding the papers.

Ugh.

"Yeah," I say. "I'm just running late for the Vipers game."

Her mouth curves up into a smile. "Well, hurry along then. Go get your fill of that hockey hunk."

I shake my head, but I'm smiling. "We on for lunch and thrifting tomorrow?"

One of the benefits of being full-time at The Sapphire Room is that I have time—and money—to do things like go out to lunch and shop for adorable knickknacks I don't actually need with Mrs. X.

She lights up at my question. "Absolutely."

"Everything else okay?" I ask.

She just jerks her head toward the stairs. "Go on. Get to your man. We'll catch up tomorrow."

She gives me a finger wave and slips back into her apartment.

Sighing, knowing that I'm likely going to have to deal with my father—but knowing that at least I have Banks and the others on my side—I toss the papers on the table just inside the door, lock up, and hurry downstairs to my car.

I have more important things to do than think about the vipers that are the Rockwells.

I have my own personal Viper to cheer on.

———

AND I DO a lot of cheering.

Banks gets two gorgeous goals that are likely going to be on the highlight reels on social media.

I didn't even know it was possible to move that quickly, and to do it on skates while corralling a puck, but he manages, and he's truly great doing it.

Now, I'm heading for the elevators and the family lounge a few floors below.

Maybe we'll even have another celebratory session in Cheryl's office.

I'm smiling as the elevator doors ding open and—

I receive the second surprise of the night.

The first was unpleasant.

This…

Well, it fills me with glee.

Because Cheryl's standing in the elevator car in her uniform.

I still for a second and then—fuck it—step onto the elevator. "Good evening, Cheryl," I murmur.

She glances up from her phone and I have the distinct pleasure of watching as her mouth drops open. Then it snaps closed so quickly I can hear her teeth click together before her eyes narrow. "What are *you* doing here?"

"Oh," I say, and I know it's petty as hell, but I can't help it, "didn't you know? My boyfriend is Banks Christianson. He plays on the Vipers." I shift enough to show her the back of my jersey then turn back in time to see the smoke practically pouring out of her ears.

Petty? Yup.

But this feels good.

If only I can come up with a way to play Hot and Cold.

"Can you hit floor one for me?" I ask sweetly. "It's only that I can't reach it around your cart."

She's pushing a cart of cleaning supplies—one I'm very familiar with because of its wonky wheel and the trash can that likes to topple over.

My cart.

Or my former one, anyway.

Ha. Take that, bitch.

Silence greets me, but I just smile and wait.

Some might say like she waited for me to find the odd sticky fingerprint on a piece of plastic, or the stray fleck of salt, or a single crunched-up popcorn kernel. Smiling and waiting as she happily tortured me.

No more.

And eventually, she *does* move, shifting forward and jabbing at the button that will take me down to the family lounge.

The elevator begins descending, and a moment later, the doors open with a ding.

"Here," I say as Cheryl begins moving forward. "Let me hold that for you." I place my palm against the side of the opening, making sure the doors don't close on her as she shoves the wonky cart forward and steps off into the hall.

I don't follow her, since the lounge is still one more floor down, but I can't resist adding just before the metal panels slide closed—

"You missed a spot."

I hear her quiet shriek.

And then I'm moving down again, walking off the elevator, and finding Banks waiting there for me.

"What's so funny?" he asks.

"I'll tell you later." I step into his arms, cup his face in my hands. "You played incredible tonight."

Pink spots appear on his cheeks, which is fucking adorable, but it's the smile he gives me that's a hundred times better.

My heart rolls over in my chest.

Because seeing him like this, feeling the strength of him, the way my words so clearly affect him, being on the receiving end of his care, his teasing, his ooey-gooey center…

And I know resisting the slippery slope was always a moot point.

I've set up the Slip 'n Slide, launched myself on the slick plastic, and I'm barreling right to the bottom.

Luckily, for me, I also know that Banks will be there to catch me.

"Thanks, little spitfire," he murmurs, peeling my hands from his cheeks and kissing my palms in turn. He laces the fingers on one of our hands together, draws me to him, uses the other to brush beneath one eye then the other. "Are you tired? Want to head home?"

I am tired.

I'm always tired these days, it seems.

But I push that aside. "No," I say. "I promised that I'd kick West's ass in Connect 4"—I pretend to stretch—"and I fully intend to follow through."

CHAPTER THIRTY

Banks

I'M NOT AN INDECISIVE GUY.

If I want something I either take it, buy it, or find another way to make it happen. It's been that way since I was a kid and became laser-focused on hockey.

Unfortunately, Aspen doesn't fit into any of those categories. I can't bend her to my will simply because I want to. Not even because I love her.

Anything I want from her, she's going to have to give freely.

Which means having a conversation I'm not sure I'll ever be ready to have.

We're both busy and the fact of the matter is it's exhausting trying to sleep over at her place or figure out what time she's coming over to mine, navigating sleepovers. Even date nights are getting complicated now that she's managing The Sapphire Room.

It seems reasonable for her to move in with me.

That will eliminate ninety percent of our issues and,

246 ELISE FABER & KAT MIZERA

frankly, the idea of waking up next to her every morning when I'm not traveling sounds like heaven.

Now I just have to talk her into it.

She's been exhausted lately, which is weird considering she's only working one job now and I've made a point of letting her sleep in every morning. Despite my frustrated libido. Her health is more important, so I've been sneaking out and letting her sleep, since she's not getting home from the club until three or four most nights.

I understand this is a transitionary period, where she's learning the ropes and trying to get her legs under her, so things will hopefully settle down soon.

And once she moves in with me, things will be that much simpler.

"Hey." I roll over on a Sunday morning in late November. It was chilly last night, so her apartment is cold, and we're nestled under two blankets.

I don't have practice or a morning skate today, and I was at the club with her last night making sure she left at a reasonable hour. It's only been a few weeks since she took over managing the club, but she's putting in more hours than I'm comfortable with and it's cutting into the time we have together. I've barely seen her since the game she came to last week, and I don't like being away from her so much.

"Good morning." She gazes up at me sleepily, a faint smile playing on her sweet lips.

"Good morning." I lean over and lightly kiss her. "I have a question for you, and it's a doozy, so do you want to hear it before sex, before breakfast, or after both of them?"

She giggles, nestling against me, and it occurs to me I've never heard her laugh like that before. I like it—that she can be herself with me, can show me a side the rest of the world doesn't get to see. "Just ask already," she orders. "I won't be able to concentrate on sex or breakfast if I'm wondering what's up."

"I love spending time with you," I say slowly. "And I really love waking up together."

"Me too." Gentle words.

"If this thing with us is going to go forward, and I'm really hoping it does, it would make our lives so much easier if we… live together."

Instead of the usual wide-eyed stare I get when something freaks her out, when I'm pushing her, when she's considering turning into a tiny rabid raccoon, she seems…thoughtful.

"It would certainly be more convenient," she says after a moment. "But there are a lot of logistics to work out."

Suddenly, I'm reminded of her negotiating skills with Atlas. "Such as?"

"My lease isn't up until February."

"You won't pay anything to live with me, so you can keep the apartment until then. That also gives you time to decide if you actually like living with me."

"What about you?" she counters. "What if you don't like it?"

I smile. "I guess anything is possible, but it's doubtful. If I wasn't sure, I wouldn't offer. I've never lived with a woman before." I pause, looking down at her. "But I've never felt about anyone else the way I feel about you. I know it's soon. I also understand how badly you've been treated by pretty much everyone in your life before me. So I guess…I'm asking for a leap of faith."

She stares at me with a look I can only describe as adoration. I don't see this soft, vulnerable side of her often, but I really love it. Especially when she leans forward and presses her mouth to mine.

"I'm willing to try," she whispers, her soft, naked body warm against mine.

My cock is wide awake and alert, but it's not time to play any sex games yet.

There are a couple of things we have to discuss first.

Like the reality of being with a professional athlete.

"There *is* something you need to think about, though," I say, running my hand along the curve of her ass. I really love her ass. One day I want to drive my cock into it and listen to her scream my name while I do it.

Focus, Banks.

"Like?"

"Being with me means…" I take a breath, trying to express myself articulately. "I can get traded at any time. I have some restrictions in my contract that give me a little power, but at the end of the day, if the team is willing to take the financial hit, they can do almost anything they want with me. That means we could wind up in Winnipeg or Tampa or anywhere in between. And if we're a couple, you'd have to go with me."

She reaches up and cups one side of my face with her hand. "Of course, I would go with you. Do you really think I could stay here without you?"

Fuck, I love this woman.

Our mouths crash together in a tangle of passion and urgency and…love.

"I love you, Aspen," I breathe against her mouth.

She doesn't answer with words, but her body tells me so much. Her mouth is fused to mine, her fingers digging into my hair. She's eager, so much so that I'm almost inside of her before I realize I don't have a condom.

"Easy, baby." I reach over and grab one off the nightstand. "I think we should get tested," I say as I roll it on. "Then we can go without as long as you're on birth control."

"I have the implant, so yes, getting tested will make things so much easier." She pushes me onto my back and straddles me, lining up my cock right where I want it, mouth curved into a smirk. "So, what's the plan, Mr. Christiansen?"

"Orgasms?" I ask, arching a brow.

She laughs and then leans down to nip my lower lip. "I mean, for moving in together."

I playfully squeeze her ass. "Whenever you want. I'll be gone a couple days this week, but when I get back, we can make it happen."

She slides down a little, the head of my cock gaining entrance to her slick heat. Even with the latex barrier between us, she feels so damn good. I can't even imagine how incredible it's going to be when I'm bare inside of her. All day, every day.

"You're carrying the heavy boxes," she whispers, taking her sweet time in sinking down on me.

"Absolutely." I try to thrust up, but she wiggles away, a teasing gleam in her eyes.

"Don't rush me," she admonishes, resting her hands on my shoulders and staring into my eyes intently. "I'm a little finicky about where things are in the kitchen, so you're going to have to let me have my way with it."

"You're welcome to rearrange the whole damn house," I growl, hissing as she continues to tease me, only allowing the tip of my cock inside of her.

"And I'll need closet space."

I know she's teasing, and I love this playful side of her, but she's driving me wild.

"How much do you need?" I ask, gritting my teeth from the exertion it's taking not to flip us over and drive into her the way I want to.

"Three-quarters," she deadpans.

"Fine."

There's a flicker of surprise but then she's kissing me again and I don't give a fuck about closet space or where the spoons wind up or anything except touching her. Being with her. Making love to the woman I suddenly understand I'm going to be with forever.

Our tongues are doing a sensual, passionate dance, but still, she won't let me push in any further.

"Why are you trying to kill me?" I groan.

She giggles—a sound I'm starting to love—and slides down another inch. "That better, babe?"

I can't answer. Sweat has popped out on my forehead and I'm about to lose my mind. But I need to let her be in control this time. For some reason, I understand instinctively that she needs some power. I've thrown a lot at her. I asked her to move in followed by dropping the L word. She has to be borderline overwhelmed. That's part of her personality, and if I want her to be okay and happy with such monumental changes, I need to suck it up.

Even if it kills me.

Which it might.

She's wiggling and kissing and touching me, masterfully getting me more worked up than I've been in a long time, and still, she doesn't take any more of my cock. Instead, she pulls up so we're back to it being just the tip, and right when I'm about to scream with frustration, she sinks down.

All the way.

Every damn inch buried deep in her tight, hot cunt.

We groan together, the pleasure more than we can disguise.

"Can I fuck you now?" I grunt through clenched teeth.

"Yes. Oh, yes." She throws back her head and the halo of dark hair fans around her like a chestnut cloud.

"You're so fucking beautiful, Aspen," I rasp, a death grip on her hips, holding her in place firmly. She made me wait way too long, and now I need a minute to adjust or I'm going to blow my load.

Then we're kissing again, her perky little tits smashed against my chest, her tongue pillaging mine, and that glorious hair draped over me.

"I need to fuck you. Hard. You okay with that?"

"You have to ask?"

"So hard it might hurt."

Her eyes glitter with arousal and excitement. "Give it your best shot, handsome."

I pull out to the tip and slam back up, continuing to hold her by the hips. She has no choice but to take thrust after punishing thrust, and I only slow down when her eyes start to roll back. This is too good, I don't want it to end. Not yet. She's moaning, panting, fingernails digging grooves in my skin.

"One day I want to fuck your pretty little ass, just like I'm fucking your pussy," I growl. "You ever done that?"

"No." She takes a shaky breath, but I'm sure it's more because of how hard I've been going at her than fear about anal sex. "But I'll try anything with you."

"We'll go slow," I promise. "Work up to it."

"Mmm, yes."

Hearing her agree to one of my favorite kinks takes me right back to the edge of reason.

"Make me come, Banks." Her erotic words penetrate my lust-filled haze and I flex my hips upward.

"Like that?"

"Please."

I don't know why it turns me on when she begs, but it does.

"Milk my cock, baby girl," I whisper. "Use that pretty little cunt to bring us both home."

She makes a loud, strangled sound, but then she's moving and grinding and squeezing me into oblivion.

I can't remember my name or hers or even where we are as we both crash over the cliff of passion we've been climbing.

I've never loved like this—both physically and emotionally.

"Fuck, I love you." The words slip out against her lips.

And even though she doesn't say it back, I know saying those words are important.

Both to her and to me.

CHAPTER THIRTY-ONE

Aspen

"I BET you're not going to be tired of this when you move," Mrs. X says as we recline back in the cheap plastic chairs of the apartment building's laundry room, waiting for our loads to finish up.

It's taking longer than normal because some lovely person —cough, asshole—decided to not move their clothes on time and so we spent long minutes warring between waiting for them to come back and move them to the dryer and just setting the wet clothes on the washer.

In the end, we waited fifteen minutes.

And now, we're watching the wet clothes slowly dry as our items proceed through their washes.

I yawn and Mrs. X glances over at me. "That hot hockey player of yours keeping you up too late at night?"

"No," I say. "I've actually been getting more rest since I quit my second job at the arena."

"Well, that's the fourth time you've yawned."

I shrug, stand up when the washer dings and start moving my clothes to the dryer. "I just don't feel the greatest today."

A pause as Mrs. X's washer goes and she starts doing the same thing I am, albeit moving her things to her own dryer. "How so?"

"What?" I slam the door.

"What's bothering you?"

"About the world in general?"

She throws a wet sock at me. "You don't feel the greatest," she says. "What's wrong with you? Are you and Banks having problems?" It's a serious question that has my heart squeezing.

Because it shows how much she cares.

"No," I say. "We're doing great." I nibble at my bottom lip. "As you well know—or else I wouldn't have agreed to move in with him."

I toss her the sock back and she shoves it in the dryer, slams the door. "Then you're working too hard."

"I *am* working long hours," I agree. "But not as long as before," I add before she can chastise me. "Atlas and Briar hired an assistant manager so I'm not there every day and when she's fully trained, I'll only be on three nights a week. The other hours I'll be able to work from home for the most part, or just a few hours during the day to meet with vendors and such."

Mrs. X starts up her clothes then turns to me and pats my hand. "That's great, honey. You need balance." A wink. "And plenty of hot, sweaty time with your man."

"You're incorrigible."

"Nope." Another wink. "I'm just old enough to know what's really important."

"And that is?"

"Love."

I still.

"And lots and lots of orgasms."

I laugh, shaking my head. "Priorities."

She grins but sobers. "Yeah, honey. Priorities, and yes, I

know I like to tease you about how hot Banks is, but I'm truly glad that you've found someone who loves you like he does."

My heart thuds against my rib cage because…

Yes, he loves me.

He's told me.

But even before he gave voice to that, I knew it.

I *felt* it.

In his care and kind words, in the way he paid attention and protected me and how he included me in Family Time. In his smile, his touch, the way he kisses me so thoroughly.

He sees me. Likes me. *Loves* me.

And…I love him right back.

Now, I just have to find the courage to tell him.

I throw in a laundry sheet, slam the door, and even as I'm starting up my clothes, I yawn again. Ugh. I know there's no real reason for me to be as exhausted as I am, but I can't lie. Even doing laundry is wearing me out. I guess I'm getting soft in my one-job days.

"Maybe it's the mental load," I tell Mrs. X when her brows flick up, concern clearly evident on her face. "It's been a long time since I've dealt with inventory and ordering and employee scheduling. Not to mention training Vanessa."

Mrs. X tilts her head back toward the chairs. "Well, Ms. Manager," she teases. "Let's park our butts back in those chairs and gossip about all the people you're going to miss when you move into Banks's house."

My mouth ticks up. "The only person who I'm going to miss is you."

Her face gentles. "Turning into a softie now, are you?"

"Apparently." I sink down into the seat, lean my head against the wall.

"Chocolate chip pumpkin bread?" she asks, pulling a container from somewhere and popping off the lid.

I love her baked goods—especially her strudel.

But today, the moment I get a whiff of the sugary, pumpkin concoction my stomach churns.

"Oh!" I jump up to my feet, run across the room, and throw up the piece of toast and cup of coffee I had for breakfast. "Ugh," I mutter a minute later. "I guess the milk was bad." I shake my head as I walk over to my stuff, taking a sip of water from my bottle to erase the awful taste in the back of my throat.

I haven't bothered to go grocery shopping, not when I'm moving out as soon as Banks gets home.

"God," Mrs. X says as I slump into the chair next to her. "You're not pregnant, are you?"

"I'm on birth control," I tell her.

"Well, birth control fails," she says frankly.

My stomach twists, but I shake my head. "Not this one. I have the implant. It's literally the definition of set it and forget it. There's no user error."

Her lips press flat.

I reach over and squeeze her hand. "Tell you what," I say, "if you're so worried, I'll take a test when I go to the doctor this afternoon."

Because I have health insurance now.

And I'm going in for a checkup and an STI test and…

No more condoms for my hot hockey player.

"I'm not worried." Mrs. X tosses the container of pumpkin bread back into her bag.

I glance over at her, lift an eyebrow. "No?"

"Nope," she says. "Because mark my words—"

My pulse speeds up.

"—that boy will always take care of you."

———

A FEW HOURS LATER, I'm tromping up the stairs, my head

spinning with all the things I now need to take care of before I go into work when I see who's standing outside my door.

"The fuck?" I whisper.

Because…

My father is in the hall.

He's tapping his foot, gaze on his cell phone—at least until I reach the final step.

Then his gaze comes to mine and I have the urge to immediately turn on my heel and get the fuck out of here.

But—I lift my chin, straighten my shoulders—I'm not a little girl anymore. This is *my* home. Where I've survived.

No, where I've fucking flourished.

"Well?" my dad asks, exuding pure Rockwell arrogance.

"Well, what?" I mutter, starting forward again, shoving past him and unlocking my door.

"You're working with Atlas Delarosa."

"I'm managing a bar—*one* bar," I counter.

"For Delarosa."

I roll my eyes, push open the door, step inside and start to close the wooden panel, but —surprise of surprises—he catches it before it latches and shoves it inward, moving into my apartment uninvited.

"I'm proud of you," he says, closing it behind him.

Laughter bubbles up in my chest, and—fuck it—I let it out, laughing so hard that I have to bend at the waist, have to catch myself on my knees. "You're…fucking…kidding…me."

"What's wrong with you?"

I straighten, laughter cutting off abruptly. "What's *wrong* with me?" I ask, and maybe it's a little hysterical, but I've already had a shock today. "You're *here*. In my apartment. It's been years since I've heard from you, and you've only come now because I happen to have a connection with someone you deem as beneficial. Am I right? No, don't answer that." I toss my purse on the counter and go to the fridge, pull out a bottle of water. "I know that you're only here because of Atlas." I take a long sip then glare over at him. "Just like I know that your *job offer* is fucking bullshit —a way to get me close enough to manipulate and control again."

"You're my daughter—"

"No," I say. "I'm not a Rockwell in anything more than name, and I haven't been one, not my whole life."

"You sure benefited from being a Rockwell growing up— the money, the clothes, the lavish vacations."

"The isolation. The cruelty. The being married off to a business partner so I can be made small? Or worse, be put away on a shelf, only to be taken down and played with when it suits him, suits *you*."

"That's not what I'm proposing."

"Oh? So, what? I'll be a partner in your businesses? Have the same position as my brothers?"

He rocks back on his heels, and I have the pleasure of seeing the asshole at a loss for words.

"Exactly," I mutter, walking to the door, reaching for the handle. "I'm not coming back. Not now. Not ever. Not when I'm finally happy."

The facade falls away. "And *this*"—he waves a hand around my apartment which is smaller than his linen closet— "is where you're *happy?*"

The disdain.

God, it's familiar.

And…

It's the final straw.

"Yeah, *Dad*," I sneer. "I'm happier in a small apartment than I ever was in a mansion. Happier here working with my hands, putting in long hours, finding out that I'm stronger than I ever thought possible. And"—I open the door—"I'm happier here with a man who I know loves me for *me*, not for my bank account—and no," I add before that glee can spread any further across his face, "that man is *not* Atlas Delarosa. He's my boss and nothing more."

My dad opens his mouth.

I gesture at the open door. "Just like *you're* someone from my past—"

His brows lift, but he walks out into the hall.

"—and nothing more."

And I slam the door on that part of my life.

Forever.

CHAPTER THIRTY-TWO

Banks

I'D GOTTEN in late last night from my road trip, and hadn't wanted to wake Aspen, so I slept at my place.

But first thing this morning I grabbed the guys, picked up breakfast, and headed straight to her apartment. I can't wait for her to move in, and if that means spending my day off doing physical labor, I'm in.

However, how one apartment the size of my bedroom can have so much stuff is beyond me. The boxes piling up in the living room that need to be taken down to Dash's waiting SUV look like we're packing up a mansion, and when Aspen comes out of the bedroom with two more, I can't help but laugh.

"What?" She demands, wrinkling her nose.

"Where was it all?" I ask. "I mean, how can you possibly have so much stuff? This place can't be more than five hundred square feet!"

"Five forty-seven," she says haughtily.

I chuckle. "Again—where do you put it all?"

"Lots of shelves and storage bins," she replies, handing me

the boxes she's carrying. "Plus some of the boxes were already packed. I'm a sucker for a good estate sale, so whenever I find a deal on something I want or need, I grab it, wash it, and pack it for the day I have a bigger place." She grins. "Which apparently, is now."

"Babe, these are heavy," I say, putting them down. "Let me get them."

"I realized that too late." She sinks onto the couch and lays her head back.

She's adorably disheveled today, her hair up in a messy ponytail, no makeup, and wearing yoga pants and an oversized T-shirt. And yet, I want to rip off her clothes and lick her from head to toe.

"I'm going to take these down to Dash, and then he and Atlas are going to take off and drop them off at my house. Then we're taking a break."

"Okay."

I get the next load of boxes loaded into the SUV, thank Dash and Atlas for their help, and then head back upstairs.

Aspen hasn't moved, and I sink down next to her, reaching for her hand.

"You look exhausted," I say. "How about you let me handle the rest of this?"

She shakes her head. "I can help. I just need a minute to get my second wind."

That sounds so completely unlike her, I stare for a beat, wondering if she's okay.

"I'm hungry," she murmurs. "You want eggs? I think I have eggs, some cheese, and bacon left in the fridge."

I frown. It's only ten-thirty. We had breakfast two hours ago, and while, yes, we've been working pretty hard, it's not like we've run a marathon.

But she's already up, heading for the kitchen.

I pad in behind her, watching curiously as she pulls out

eggs, cheese, bacon, and butter, expertly whisking the eggs while warming the frying pan and simultaneously putting the bacon in the microwave.

It's a little mesmerizing, seeing her so efficient in the kitchen, and it makes me smile.

This is what my life is going to look like going forward.

Us waking up together.

Making breakfast.

Watching her cook, hopefully wearing nothing but a smile.

Seeing her lounging around my house.

Skinny-dipping in the hot tub.

The scent of something amazing hits my nostrils and I focus, see she's stirring the eggs when she suddenly gags. The spoon hits the stove, and she rushes to the trash can and heaves.

"Fuck." She's breathing heavily and I walk up behind her worriedly.

"You okay?" I ask, handing her a napkin as I gently stroke her back.

"I will be." She takes a slow, deep breath, and then turns to me.

For the first time, I realize she's a little pale.

How have I missed this?

Guilt washes over me.

Did I encourage Atlas to push her too hard? Did I keep her up too late on the phone while I was on the road? The phone sex was off-the-charts hot, but she needed to rest, not screw around with me.

Dammit, I'm a selfish prick.

"Are you sick?" I ask and then immediately re-think the question. She's puking. Of course she's sick. "Is this because of Atlas? Is he putting too much pressure on you too soon? He's like that, you know? He doesn't realize that not everyone is like him, that not everyone can jump in headfirst and grab a

264 ELISE FABER & KAT MIZERA

task by the balls." I shake my head. "I'm going to talk to him. This isn't fair to you and next road trip I won't keep you up—"

"Banks." She cuts me off, putting a soft hand on my forearm. "Babe. I'm fine. Really." She clears her throat. "I do need to talk to you about something, though."

"If you've changed your mind about moving in after packing all these boxes, I'm not helping you put everything away," I huff. "And"—I nod to the stove—"your second breakfast is burning."

She giggles, but hurries to turn off the burner.

There's that sound again.

I love it.

I love *her*.

"I love a Lord of the Rings reference."

"I know." I reach for her once she takes the pan off the burner and turns off the stove, stops the microwave. "Listen, if Atlas is working you too hard, there's no reason to suffer. I'm trying to make your life better, not worse. In fact, you don't have to work at all unless you want to. Maybe we can find something else to—"

"Stop." She's shaking her head and for the first time I notice a hint of nervousness.

What's going on with her?

She's got nervous energy, fidgeting now that she isn't busy with cooking.

"What's wrong?" I ask, suddenly a little nervous myself.

"I…" She's staring up at me intently, and I would give anything in this moment to be a mind reader. To spare her having to say whatever it is that's making her so anxious.

"A couple of things happened while you were gone."

"Uh oh."

"My dad showed up."

"What?" That's the last thing I expected to hear, and dread fills me. Is he going to cause trouble? I don't know the man, but I've heard he's an ass. "What did he want?"

"To offer me a job." She smiles wryly.

"A job?" I gape. "Doing what?"

"Oh, you know, a low-level version of what my brothers do. No real power or anything, but once he heard I was working for the infamous Atlas Delarosa, that changed everything." She rolls her eyes.

"What did you say?"

She lifts one shoulder. "That I'm good right where I am, and I don't need him or his stupid little job offer."

I lean over and press my lips to her forehead. "Good for you. I'm proud of you."

"It felt good."

"I'll bet." I pause because she said a *couple of things* happened. Her dad offering her a job is just one.

"Anyway." She straightens her spine and lifts her chin. "The other thing is…well…I'm pregnant."

For a moment, her words don't register.

Then I feel a little light-headed.

My stomach knots and my chest gets tight, a combination of fear and fury whipping through me.

"Are you…sure?" I rasp, gripping the edge of the counter.

"I went to the doctor while you were gone." Her eyes are wary again, but I can't help that right now. "Apparently, my implant expired and when the condom broke…I guess I wasn't protected—" She breaks off, nibbling at her bottom lip.

Kids are not on my radar.

I love Frankie, and maybe someday I'll consider adopting, but I don't want biological children. I never have. Not after what happened to my mother.

"No," is all I can manage to say.

"No?" Her brows knit together in confusion. "What does that mean? *No* what?"

"No…baby." I shake my head. "We can't have kids."

She rocks back on her heels. "Why not?"

"Because…I don't want to."

I realize I sound like a petulant child but it's hard to be more articulate than that when I feel like puking.

"You don't want kids? *Ever?* Because the night the condom broke you said you weren't ready, not that you didn't want them at all." She looks annoyed now.

And hurt.

But I can't stop to process that. "If I was to ever have any, it wouldn't be for a long time. Like ten years. Maybe more."

She blinks.

"In ten years, I'll be thirty-eight and potentially at an age where pregnancy could be dangerous," she says. "Yes, women are having babies later and later these days, but I don't want to wait that long."

I gape at her. "So you did this on purpose?"

She takes a step back and puts her hands on her hips. "What the hell are you talking about? We were both there when that condom broke. What's wrong with you?"

"I just told you—I don't want kids. You need to get rid of it."

She blinks again, but this time instead of confusion, there's a storm gathering in her eyes. "Excuse me?"

"You heard me." I'm trying not to be a dick, but I can't help it.

She's *pregnant.*

Fuck me.

I got the woman I love pregnant. That can't happen. *I can't—*

I have to make her understand.

We can't do this.

I can't do this.

"I'm not having an abortion," she says, hurt in her hazel eyes, her chest rising and falling a little faster now. "It's okay for other women, but...I can't do that"—she settles a hand over her belly—"I won't."

"You have to."

"No." A thread of steel in her words. "Actually, I *don't*."

"Aspen, this isn't negotiable." How can I make her understand how bad this is?

The silence stretches for long enough, those hurt eyes on mine, that I open my mouth, desperate to explain.

But the words don't come.

So, I just stand there, staring back at her.

"You're serious." Eyes glassy, she swallows hard, voice quiet when she asks, "What happened to being here for me?"

I don't answer because I don't know how to.

"Wow," she whispers, but then her shoulders straighten and her chin lifts. "Well, if this is your definition of love then it's better I found out now." A sharp shake of her head. "You're no better than my father."

"Little spitfire—"

She jabs a finger in my direction. "*Don't*." And then she turns on her heel and stalks out of the kitchen.

Fuck.

I follow her, snag her arm. "Dammit, Aspen, you have to listen."

"I'm done listening," she snaps. "Apparently, your love and attention and protectiveness is only if I do what *you* want. And I spent way too many years doing what other people want because it was comfortable, because it meant they wanted me." She yanks out of my hold. "Well, you know what? *Fuck that.* I already know what it's like to be uncomfortable, and I was doing just fine before you came along. I didn't need you then and I don't need you now. So if this baby is some kind of deal breaker for you, that's fine. You're welcome to go."

I stare at her.

She stares back.

I want to throw my arms around her and tell her I love her, that I'll make things right.

But I can't.

The idea of her being pregnant terrifies me like nothing else in the world.

Pregnancy, childbirth, the whole thing gives me hives.

My mother died in childbirth. I'm the reason she's dead and there's no universe where I want that for Aspen. Or for any kid of mine. I live with that guilt every day and I can't pass it on to another innocent child.

Frankly, I'm a little pissed that she won't even discuss options. Like it's a foregone conclusion that we're having a baby.

"I don't want to fight," I say, "but we can't just—"

"We're not going to fight," she says in a steely voice. "And you're going to get out of my apartment so that we don't."

When I don't move, she points to the door.

The door that's surrounded by the dozen boxes I'm supposed to be moving to my place. Today. Right now.

"You need to think about this," I say, snatching my keys off the coffee table.

"I don't *need* to think about anything," she replies. "But it sounds like you do."

She lifts her chin a notch, her jaw working with irritation, and I don't miss the fact that her eyes are a little wet.

Motherfucker.

I don't want her to cry.

I don't want to leave.

I don't want any of this to be happening.

But my brain and my mouth are apparently not on speaking terms.

"If you do this, you'll be on your own," I point out.

She laughs derisively. "I've been on my own a long fucking time. I've never needed a man to take care of me, and I never will. Have a good life, Banks." She turns on her heel and walks into the bathroom, quietly closing the door behind her.

Frustrated, I stalk out the front door, slamming it for good measure even though I'm not sure why I do it.

"Hey, Banks!" Mrs. X calls out to me, but I don't respond, taking the stairs two at a time down to the ground floor. I really need to get away from here.

What the fuck just happened?

Not only am I no longer moving my girlfriend into my place, I'm pretty sure I no longer even have a girlfriend.

CHAPTER THIRTY-THREE

Aspen

I'M MISERABLE.

And nauseous.

And looking at papers I keep promising myself I'll throw away.

But, because I'm a glutton for punishment, I keep flipping through them anyway, dissecting the compensation package.

I'll need health insurance benefits.

I'll need my own money.

I'll need—

Groaning, I toss the papers aside.

I'm torturing myself. My father will probably rescind the offer the moment he finds out I'm pregnant anyway. And Atlas isn't going to fire me. I'm doing a good job. I'm valuable to the business. Even if things happen and I end up on my own again, I'll be okay.

I'll survive.

I'll be smart and save and...Banks maybe be acting in a way that is completely inexplicable to the man I love—

"Fuck," I whisper as that settles over me. Because that's

why this hurts so much. Why I'm scrambling to make sense of it.

I love Banks.

I know him, and maybe he and I won't work out, maybe we can't come back from this. I flatten my hand over my belly, over where that tiny acorn-sized baby is growing inside me. He didn't see that on the ultrasound, didn't hear the heartbeat, didn't immediately love that tiny spark of life, but he's got that soft center.

He'll take care of his kid.

I have a safety net.

I may have to do it on my own, but this baby will be loved and cared for and allowed to flourish.

This baby will be as bright and smart and comfortable in her own skin as Frankie is. This baby will be as strong and hardworking in all of his actions as Banks is, as I am.

So…we'll be okay.

Still, I'm not floating with my head in the clouds. I know I need to make arrangements, to sort out childcare and a different apartment and custody and a college fund and—

I sigh.

Yes, I need to do all of that.

But also, no. Because I'm only weeks along. If Banks really —well, if he really doesn't want this baby, then I have months yet to get organized.

There's still time.

Time enough to let my eyes slide closed because this is exhausting—being pregnant; watching the door at The Sapphire Room, hoping that Banks will show up with an apology and an explanation; waiting for my phone to ring, to buzz with a text, with that apology.

Wanting—him to show up at my door, to make sense of his reaction, to make it all better.

But I haven't heard from him.

Not for seven whole days.

And…I'm starting to give up hope.

The hurt has faded. The anger is dulled. The resignation that this wasn't ever going to work out, that I was right to have focused on myself, on my life, on trying to carve out an existence where I'm safe and protected and have the means to take care of myself, has settled deep.

I'm alone.

But that's okay.

I'm used to it.

Exhaling, I settle back into the cushions, pushing away the memories of the first time I sat here with Banks—the memory of how we did so much more than just sitting.

I'll take a little nap, and then I'll get up and finish unpacking.

But just as my eyes slide closed, there's a knock at the door.

I sit up in a rush, heart in my throat, and then I'm on my feet, heart pulsing with hope. Maybe it's Banks. Maybe he's come to apologize. Maybe he'll explain what the hell he was thinking, will make it all make sense.

Hurrying to the door, I whip it open, and—

"Oh," I whisper.

"Such a warm greeting," Briar says dryly, pushing by me and into the apartment. She stops a few feet in, spinning in a circle, likely taking in the mix of boxes that are both packed and opened, the contents rifled through as I've taken out what I've needed throughout the week. "Want to clue me in on this?"

I go to the fridge, pull out a bottle of water and toss it to her before grabbing one for myself. "This is water," I say, twisting the top off. "You drink it when you're thirsty."

She rolls her eyes. "Hilarious." Then she leans against the counter, takes a drink from her own bottle. "Want to clue me in to why the last time we talked, you and Banks were moving in together and now you seem to be doing your best to imper-sonate The Sapphire Room's storage closet?

"I organized that closet," I mutter.

"And it looks a hell of a lot better than this place."

I scowl. "Thanks a lot."

"Aspen," she murmurs, setting the bottle down. "You missed Family Time. You didn't come watch Frankie in her preschool recital like you promised." She reaches across the counter and squeezes my hand. "And Banks looks even more miserable than you do. What's going on with you two?"

That has my heart twisting in my chest.

I promised Frankie I would be there.

And…I hadn't shown.

"I didn't mean to miss her recital." She was so excited to show off the songs she was learning how to sing in class. "How did she do?"

"I know." Briar squeezes my hand and then lets it go again. "And she killed it." Her smile is laced with pride. "She and Royal worked all week on Old MacDonald and she didn't miss a note."

"That's amazing."

"I was particularly fond of the Shaky Egg song."

My lips twitch. "I don't know that one."

"Just wait until she sings you 1, 2, 3, 4, 5…Once I Caught a Fish Alive," Briar says. "You won't ever get it out of your head."

I chuckle, but I'm not all that amused. Not really. Instead, guilt is slicing through my belly. I let Frankie down. "I'm sorry," I say. "I'll make it up to her."

Briar's expression gentles. "I didn't come here to make you feel bad about missing it—"

I snort.

"Or not *that* bad," she amends. Then sighs. "I know something's up. Will you talk to me about it?"

"I'm fine."

She rolls her eyes and spins, walks away from the counter, meandering through the boxes, trailing her fingers over the taped-up ones, peering unabashedly into the open ones. "This is cute," she says, holding up a pitcher I found in one of the secondhand stores not long ago. My heart convulses with hurt.

I imagined filling it with flowers then setting it in the middle of the kitchen island at Banks's house.

Bright yellow sunflowers to highlight the golden specks in the counter, in the glass of the ceramic pitcher.

"Yes," I whisper, blinking down at my bottle. "It'd look really cute at your house."

So I won't have to look at it anymore.

"Hmm."

I glance up, watch Briar carefully place the pitcher back in the box. Then she's moving on to the next one, and the next.

I need to put everything away, need to stop holding on to this hope that this is all just a sick misunderstanding.

"What the *fuck?*"

Blinking, I allow my gaze to focus back on Briar.

Her eyes whip toward mine. "What the actual fuck, Aspen?"

"What—?" I begin.

She's holding up a familiar folder of papers. "Tell me you're not seriously considering this bullshit."

The job offer.

I smother a groan. "Briar—"

"Don't *Briar* me," she snaps. "Your family is awful. You told me that yourself. You can't go and work with them, no fucking way—"

"Briar—"

"Do you know how many TikToks I've seen about them lately? You do know that they've been hit with several lawsuits and that—"

Sighing, I move to her, snagging the papers and tossing them back onto the coffee table. "I'm not going to work for my father," I say. "He came to try to convince me, but I"—I nod at the papers—"can't do it. Even if the money was enough to tempt me away from The Sapphire Room, I can't go back there."

Her shoulders sag in relief. "Oh."

Unbidden, my mouth ticks up. "Yeah," I say. "*Oh.*"

"You're not going back to them?"

I shake my head. "But...you're right," I admit. "Things aren't going well with Banks and I don't think I'll be at Family Time or at Frankie's preschool stuff, at least not for a while."

"But we're your family," she whispers.

"No," I say. "Your *Banks's* family. Not mine."

"That's not true."

"It's okay. I get it. You guys have history. I'm just the new girl and I don't expect—"

"You *should* expect," she snaps, taking my hands, holding them tightly. "You're wonderful and funny and smart and I adore you. We all do."

My eyes burn. "That's nice of you to say—"

"I'm not being nice." Her gaze holds mine, as though willing me to believe. "You're my friend and you're my family."

"Dammit," I whisper.

"Having those big feelings, are you?"

Big. *Huge.* All-encompassing.

And made worse by pregnancy hormones.

It's a wonder I'm not a sopping pile of tears right now.

"Talk to me," she presses. "Just...believe in me, Aspen. Trust me."

Old me wouldn't.

I would lock it down, push her away.

Do this alone.

But...I don't want to.

Or maybe...

I *can't* do it alone any longer.

"I'm pregnant," I whisper.

Her inhale is so sharp that she chokes. "Wh-what?" she asks through her coughing. "Wh-what d-did you say?"

"I'm pregnant."

Her eyes go wide, and she takes a long glug of water. "I—" She bites her bottom lip. "I…are you sure? Banks is usually so careful."

My eyebrows drag together. "I'm sure," I say carefully. "I—well, I didn't have health insurance for a while, and I didn't realize my implant had expired. We've been using condoms and one time…well, they're not always effective."

"Yeah," she murmurs dryly. "Tell *that* to the choir."

"Oh." I shake my head. "Right. I didn't think you—"

"We took precautions. But…" A shrug. "Now I have Frankie." Her eyes come to mine. "How'd he take it?"

No.

You need to get rid of it.

"Not well," I whisper. "He didn't take it…well."

"That's not a surprise."

Shock ripples down my spine. "What do you mean?"

She frowns. "Do you not know?"

Mutely, I shake my head.

"Aspen, honey. Banks's mom died having him."

CHAPTER THIRTY-FOUR

Banks

THIS HAS BEEN the longest fucking week of my life.

Aspen is pregnant.

A road trip where I took too many penalties and got into more fights than I've been in the last two seasons combined.

She won't have an abortion.

I forced myself to skip Family Time because I didn't want to answer questions.

I'm going to be a dad.

The ever-present pounding behind my eyes seems to be intensifying with each passing day and no amount of ibuprofen touches it.

Aspen and I are having a baby.

The words pound into my subconscious until I'm ready to scream.

Whether I want this or not, it's happening and it's tearing me up inside.

I miss her so much it's hard to breathe, but every time I think about her pregnancy, I want to throw up.

The idea that the woman I've come to love more than life itself being pregnant is enough to send me over the edge.

I went through this with Briar, but it was different then.

First of all, she was already five months pregnant before she told us about the baby, so termination wasn't an option.

Second, at the time, she was living far away so I didn't have to see it every day.

And finally, I love Briar deeply, but I'm not *in love* with her.

The distinction makes a huge difference.

Watching a woman I love go through a pregnancy has always been my greatest fear.

I grew up listening to the stories of my mother's pregnancy.

How she and my father were so excited, ignoring all the signs of trouble by attributing them to 'normal pregnancy stuff.' And then she hemorrhaged during childbirth and a few hours later…she was gone. Something about a detached placenta. The details are a little sketchy, but Dad had never gotten over it. He was in the room, watching her bleed out.

Watching her die.

Sitting there helplessly while the doctors were unable to help her.

A shudder rips through me.

There's no way I can do that.

Except…

Aspen and I are having a baby.

No matter what I want or say or do, the baby already exists.

A tiny piece of me connected with a small part of her—despite all our precautions—and now she has a tiny human being growing inside of her. A cousin for Frankie.

I'm going to be a dad.

A soft groan escapes me, and I start. I must have dozed off.

"Banks." Coach sits down next to me on the plane. "You awake? I meant to come over earlier, but you were sleeping."

"Yeah. Of course." I wipe my hands down my face and sit up straighter.

What the fuck?

Coach never sits with us on the plane unless we're playing cards.

"I wanted to talk to you for a minute."

Oh, fuck.

"All right." I gaze at him, hoping he doesn't see how nervous I am.

This is not the time for me to be traded.

Away from Aspen.

Away from my family.

Away from my child.

Fuck!

"You haven't been yourself this week and I want to make sure you know how valued you are on the team."

I stare at him in confusion.

"I've seen how hard you've been working," he continues. "And we see it on the ice too. Even though it's not manifesting the goals I know you want, it still brings a lot to the table. Your presence out there is why we're winning, even if you're not the one scoring."

"I…" How do I respond to this? This isn't the conversation I was expecting.

He claps me on the shoulder. "So whatever it is that's been on your mind lately, I hope this eases some of the burden. We have no plans to get rid of you, son. You're here for a reason. And it goes beyond the numbers on the board. Trust the process. With everything you're doing, it'll come. We've had a lot of changes on the team, and I updated the whole system this season. It takes time, but you'll settle in."

"Er, thanks, Coach," I manage to rasp out. "I appreciate the confidence."

"You wouldn't be here if I didn't have confidence in you."

He pats my shoulder again and then gets up, moving back to his place at the front of the plane.

This is…well, it's everything I want to hear. It's incredible news.

So why do I feel so empty inside?

Because Aspen told you she was pregnant, and you acted like a stubborn teenager who doesn't want to have to get a job so he can take care of his kid.

Fuck.

I need to fix this.

I just don't know how.

If only Colt was still around.

He was the master of figuring out problems.

Relationships, hockey, personal, or professional—he was the guy to help us reason things out.

But he's not here.

I have to do this on my own.

Ish.

I still have my family.

And it's probably time to clue them in.

————

AFTER ANOTHER SLEEPLESS night and a lackluster practice, I don't know what the hell to do with myself.

I'm not ready to talk to Aspen.

I'm not sure what I can possibly say.

Apologizing seems lame.

And the truth is, I don't know what to do.

I'm still spinning out at the idea of the woman I love going through pregnancy and the inevitable childbirth.

It guts me to even get that far in my thought process, and until I can, I have to put off talking to Aspen.

Without putting any conscious effort into it, I find myself driving to Atlas's house.

Back in college, our group was like the five musketeers. Always together. Always making trouble. Always having each other's backs.

But there were separate friendships too.

Dash and Colt were like two peas in a pod, both in ROTC and planning military careers.

It was the same with Atlas and me. Though I was headed to the NHL, and he was going to fast-track an MBA after graduation, we had a lot in common. Wanted many of the same things. Had the same dreams of getting rich, starting businesses, making our marks in the world.

We didn't leave Royal out, he was welcome with all of us, but he was always the loner, busy with his band and his music. He loved hockey, but music was always his priority. Even over friendship. And we were all okay with the dynamic.

So it makes sense for me to come to Atlas's place for some straight talk.

Except when I pull up, Dash's Escalade is out front, along with Royal's Maserati.

Interesting.

"Dude, what the fuck?" Dash says the minute I walk in.

I blink in surprise. "What did I do?"

"It's what you're *not* doing," Royal mutters.

"What are you talking about?" I grumble, frowning at them.

I came here for sympathy and a little straight talk, not a fucking ambush.

"Did you think we wouldn't find out?" Dash demands, throwing up his hands. "I mean, you brought her in and made her part of the family and then just tossed her aside like yesterday's trash?"

"I didn't toss anyone anywhere," I snap.

"Yeah?" Atlas cocks his head. "She told you she was pregnant, and you ghosted her. What would *you* call it?"

"She told me to leave!" I protest.

"That's a copout," Royal says, shaking his head. "I mean, dude, do you have any idea what this is doing to her?"

I stare at him for a split second because Royal is probably the least empathic of the four of us, especially when it comes to women. Other than Briar. And Frankie, of course, but Briar's family and Frankie's a baby, so it's not the same.

They're all watching me intently and discomfort crawls up my spine.

Fuck.

I've handled this whole situation badly and now my friends are pissed too.

"Some douchebag knocked up my sister and walked away without looking back," Dash growls. "You really want to be like him? Like the guy who—despite what she says—very obviously meant something to her. You think it's a coincidence that Briar rarely dates, hasn't been in a relationship since Frankie was born, and spends all of her time either working or taking care of her kid? That guy, whoever he was, *ruined* her. If I ever find out who he is, I'm going to fucking kill him."

I stare at him in surprise.

We've joked about the fact that Briar doesn't date but I never thought about it like that because…why? Because I think of her as a sister, so her romantic and sexual life isn't something I ever want to think about?

But that isn't fair.

She deserves happiness too.

A family beyond her big brothers and her child.

Love.

Romance.

And suddenly, I hate the guy who knocked her up.

"So, you're cool doing the same thing to Aspen?" Dash presses.

"I'm not like that asshole!" I yell, snapping out of my reverie.

"Then fucking act like it!" Dash yells back, shoving me hard.

I know he's projecting.

He's thinking about his sister, and this is apparently some kind of trigger. I feel another prickle of shame that I haven't given Briar's happiness—beyond the surface level stuff—a second thought.

"You think Briar was seeing someone? That she was in love?" I ask.

Dash shrugs.

"And what? She never told us because she was afraid of how we would react?"

"Almost definitely," Atlas says quietly. "But this isn't about Briar. This is about you and Aspen. What the fuck are you doing, man? You love her." He pauses. "Don't you?"

A groan escapes me, and I scrub my hands over my face. "Well, yeah. Of course, I do."

"So what's wrong with you?" Dash demands.

"This is about your mom," Royal says, narrowing his eyes.

He's not wrong.

"You're afraid for Aspen to go through childbirth."

"I can't do it."

"You're already going to have to," Atlas points out.

Fucking hell.

I stalk into the kitchen and pull a beer from the fridge, twisting off the cap with my hands. I drink deeply, almost chugging the whole thing even though it's only two in the afternoon.

When I get back to the family room, they're still sitting there.

Waiting patiently.

"I don't want to lose her," is all I say.

"You're going to if you keep going like you have," Atlas mutters.

"Exactly," Dash adds. "You need to stop being a pussy and focus on what Aspen needs."

"Let's not discount his feelings about his mom," Royal interjects. "We get it, okay? Yeah, it really sucks that your mom died from complications of childbirth. It happens. Could it happen to Aspen? Sure. She could also get hit by a car, or get shot in a drive-by, or any zillion other things that happen in this world. You can't protect her from everything, and she wants this baby."

"How do you know?" I ask quietly. "Have you talked to her?"

"No, but Briar has."

Shit.

I should have expected that.

In a way I'm glad.

I've hated the idea of her dealing with this alone.

But…she hasn't been.

"I don't know what to do," I blurt out, beginning to pace, waving the bottle of beer around as I walk. "I don't want anything to happen to her because of me. And *I* did this to her."

"Just saying"—Dash holds my gaze—"*you* didn't do anything to her. You guys did it together. There's always a risk of pregnancy when you have sex. Nothing is guaranteed."

"I'm the reason my mother died," I whisper, dropping my head. I've never said those words aloud before and I can tell they're momentarily stunned.

"No." Atlas comes over to me, putting a hand on each shoulder to keep me from walking away. "Your parents decided they wanted a baby. *Together*. They wanted a family. They made a conscious decision to have you. You were wanted and loved. What happened to your mom was tragic. The worst thing ever. But it wasn't your fault. Or your dad's. Or even the doctors. It's a shitty part of life. Just like when a non-smoker gets lung cancer or whatever."

"And if Aspen dies?"

"It *won't* be because of you."

Our eyes meet and I see the sincerity in them.

We don't have these kinds of conversations often.

Almost never.

But I know it's what I need to hear, just as his next words hit hard...and right on target.

"You need to do a little soul-searching, my friend. You're better than this. And Aspen deserves more."

Yeah, she does.

So much more.

So much better.

And I know I'm going to have to dig deep and come up with a plan to win her back, because my little spitfire isn't going to make it easy on me.

CHAPTER THIRTY-FIVE

Aspen

"Are you still going to the Vipers game with us tomorrow?" Briar asks, crossing her arms and leaning her hip against the bar next to where I'm working.

I glance up from the lemon I'm squeezing, hating the look in her eyes.

Like she expects me to disappoint her.

"I—"

"Yo, Aspen!" Mitch calls, and I'm a coward, but I'm thankful for an excuse to look away from Briar's frustrated emerald eyes.

"Refill?" I call back.

He nods. "Thanks, baby girl!"

I roll my eyes, but I'll take his sweet version of *baby girl* over the sleezy *sweethearts* of the weeks before.

At least I know that Mitch is a good guy.

And he tips well.

"Well?"

I swallow hard as I fill a chilled glass with his beer then delay in answering as I bring it down the bar to Mitch.

"Thanks, Aspen," he says, passing me a twenty. "Beer on my tab, but that's for you."

See?

A good guy.

Murmuring my thanks, I pocket the cash then know there's no way around it.

I head back to Briar.

"You're going to disappoint Frankie again," she says by way of answering. "Aren't you?"

"I want to spend time with you and Frankie," I tell her, going back to mixing up the lemon drop, pouring it in the shaker and going to town. "I love hanging with you guys," I say as I strain it into the martini glass. "But I don't think it will be good for Banks to see me there." I sigh. "He's struggling already, and I don't want to do anything to mess up his game."

Her face gentles. "I think him seeing you there might be the wake-up call he needs."

"I don't want to be someone's wake-up call," I say, suddenly furious. "I want to be his first choice. I want him to want me more than fear, more than anything else in this world. And"—I settle my hand on my belly—"I want him to want this little person too."

His reaction makes sense. I understand now that Briar clued me in.

But…it doesn't make it any better.

Instead of talking to me, he pushed me away.

You asked him to leave.

I press my lips flat then release them, exhaling heavily.

How many times have I pushed *him* away?

Abruptly, my anger fades.

Because I've pushed him away over and over again. And he kept coming back, continued working his careful way through my protective shields, scaling ten-foot concrete walls, picking his way across barbed wire—and he did all that while gaining my trust and showing me his love.

I love him back.

That's why this hurts so much, why it's so hard to just cut him off and let him go.

Even putting aside the baby, he's shown me what it's like to be loved, to be protected, to be safe.

And…he's given me a family.

"He'll love that baby," Briar says softly. "As much as he loves you."

I swallow the lump in my throat, know that my words are raspy. "I know."

Briar sighs, expression going gentle. "Damn hormones, huh?"

"That and understanding why he freaked out, how scared he must be, and how much it must hurt to feel like he's to blame for his mom's death."

"Yeah," she whispers. "There's that."

I sniff.

And then she's wrapping me in her arms, hugging me tightly. "It'll be okay, you know that, right?"

I sniff again and then blow out a breath, pulling back and forcing my mouth into an approximation of a smile. "I'm always okay."

She tugs a strand of my hair. "Liar." A beat. "But in this case, it's true. I'm here. The guys are here, and Banks will come to his senses."

"Yeah—"

"Yo!"

Briar gives me a rueful smile. "Your adoring audience calls, and I need to rescue Royal from Frankie. But"—her eyes sharpen—"I'll see you tomorrow?"

Phrased as a question.

But it's an order. Definitely.

And, for once, it's an order I'm going to heed.

I love Banks.

I know he feels the same.

So, this time...

I can fight for him.

"Yeah," I agree. "I'll see you tomorrow."

———

I'M nervous as I walk down the long concrete aisle, descend the stairs I've crawled up and down many times before, scrubbing them clean, sweeping up popcorn kernels, wiping off the sticky fingerprints from the metal banister.

Down. Down. *Down* to the glass.

Where the Vipers are warming up.

Frankie swings my hand back and forth, her little fingers laced through mine, grounding me in this moment.

Either that or stopping me from spinning around and running back up the stairs.

Stopping me from escaping.

"Look," she says, all but dragging me down the last couple of steps (or maybe I've slowed, those nerves showing up and trying to take over). "There's Uncle Banks! Hi, Uncle Banks!" she calls, releasing my hand and running up to the glass, banging on the clear plastic, barely tall enough to see above the boards. "Uncle Banks! I'm here! Look! Mom and Auntie Aspen are here too!"

"Sweet baby Jesus," I mutter.

"Subtle she is not," Briar says with a grin, tilting her head toward the ice.

Not so subtle herself.

Case in point?

"Yo, Banks!" she shouts.

Yup. Shouts.

Over Frankie. Over the crunching of skates on the ice and the slaps of sticks meeting pucks and the bang of doors opening and closing.

She shouts loudly enough to be heard by everyone around us.

Including Banks.

My spine goes stiff, nerves eating at my insides. My jaw clenches tightly enough to send a bolt of pain through my face, and I have to physically dig my toes into the soles of my shoes, so I don't turn and sprint back up the long row of stairs.

I can't.

For one, there are people behind me who might get mowed down in my frantic exit.

For another…

I need to do this.

Need to fight for him, for us.

For the baby growing inside of me.

"He loves you," Briar whispers, placing her hand on the small of my back, nudging me down the last couple of steps, prodding me forward until I'm suddenly in front of the small gathering of people gathered at the glass. "You've got this."

And then she shoves something into my hand.

No, not something.

The poster I made with Frankie.

My fingers clench at the thick paper, probably wrinkling the edges, but it's my anchor in this moment, the only thing keeping me from making that quick exit.

Well, that and the fact that Banks is skating toward me, his eyes haunted, his expression riddled with deep lines.

As though this last week has weighed on him as much as it has me.

More, I realize, seeing the dark circles beneath his eyes.

"Hi, Uncle Banks!" Frankie exclaims, breaking the taut connection between our stares. I turn, see her waving excitedly, jumping up and down.

When I turn back to the ice, it's to see Banks smiling.

At least until his gaze comes back to mine.

"Courage," Briar whispers.

And I nod, no longer thinking about sprinting up those stairs.

It's not about escape.

It's not about running.

It's go time.

Exhaling, I step closer to the glass, until my nose is practically pressed flush to it, until I can lift my hand, press my palm to the clear plastic.

And, thank God, Banks moves forward, until he's as close as he can get too, until his gloved palm lifts, resting on mine through the glass. He opens his mouth, but I beat him to it, needing to say the words that have been sitting heavy in my stomach, eating away at my insides.

Because I haven't told him.

Haven't said—

"I love you."

He can't possibly hear me, not over the noise of the rapidly filling arena, the crowd filing in, the cacophony of his team and their opponent tonight, the Sierra, warming up on the ice.

But I know he reads my lips, that he somehow hears or maybe *feels* what I said.

Because his eyes go wide, his mouth drops open, and then—

Something beautiful happens.

His face softens, love filling in all of those hard-etched lines, color creeping into his cheeks, taking away some of the effects of his sleepless nights. His hand flexes on the glass, as though he wishes he could reach through the thick plastic, could lace his fingers through mine.

"I love you," I say again.

And watch him gentle further, watch the beauty those words impart on his face.

He leans forward, his helmet-clad forehead plunking against the glass. "Little spitfire," he mouths. "I'm so—"

But I don't want him thinking about our fight, about the hurdles we still have to overcome.

Not with the game ahead of him.

I want him to not worry for a few hours, to know I'm here, that I love him, that I'm not letting him go.

So, I look away, purposely not watching his apology—

There will be time for that later.

—and I unfold the sign I made.

I know the moment what I wrote on it processes.

The anguish and guilt fade from his face.

They're exchanged for the wicked glint I only see in the bedroom…

Or Cheryl's office.

CHAPTER THIRTY-SIX

Banks

"MEET ME IN CHERYL'S OFFICE?"

The sign simultaneously cracks me up and fills my heart with love.

My little spitfire.

She's here.

With Briar and Frankie.

And all three of them are wearing my jersey.

It's a small, insignificant thing, wearing my jersey, but it means the world to me. I know that Dash, Atlas, and Royal are here, also wearing the damn jersey.

Not because they're huge Vipers fans, even though they do root for the team.

Not because we all played hockey together in college.

But because they know I've been going through a rough time, both personally and professionally.

So they're doing what we do—being there for each other.

I'm so fucking grateful for all I have.

Especially the beautiful woman standing at the glass,

holding up the flimsy sign telling me where she's going to find me after the game.

She sets the sign down and puts her free hand flat back against the glass—her other one now firmly held in Frankie's —and the look in her eyes tells me everything I need to know.

"I love you," she mouths again.

Oh, fuck.

"I'm sorry," I mouth back.

She shakes her head—

"Uncle Banks!" Frankie all but vaults herself at the glass, pounding on it excitedly to get my attention.

"Hey, kiddo." I grab a nearby puck and toss it over the glass to her.

She doesn't need a puck, but I know she loves the attention, and sure enough, everyone around her oohs and aahs.

Aspen hasn't moved, her hand still on the glass, her eyes never leaving mine.

I move closer and pause, flattening my hand over hers again and wishing there wasn't a barrier between us. She's so pretty and vulnerable and fierce, all at once, and I love her so fucking much.

"I love you," I say. I'm not sure if I say the words or if I mouth them, but it doesn't matter. She knows. She hears what my heart is telling her.

Her eyes mist and it's like it's just the two of us.

Standing there with music blaring, my teammates and pucks flying past me, a thousand fans surrounding us, and yet, it's just us.

I want so desperately to touch her. Hold her. Explain why I acted the way I did.

Tell her that I love her and our baby more than anything in the whole world.

"Dude!" West comes by and hip checks me. Lightly.

But it's enough to remind me where I am and that the time on the clock is rapidly running out.

I look up.

Twenty seconds until the buzzer and then I have to go back to the locker room to get ready for the game.

Shit.

I look back at Aspen, but she's moved her hand and picked up Frankie, who blows me kisses.

I blow one back.

There are so many things I need to say and do, and no time in which to do them.

But she understands.

This is my job.

One I haven't been doing very well lately.

It's time to change that.

Tonight, I score for my girls.

Aspen, Frankie, and—for some inexplicable reason, I know what we're going to have—our baby girl.

"I have to go," I say.

Aspen nods.

Then she points to the sign down at her side.

I laugh.

And so does she.

"I love you!" I yell as I skate away, hoping she hears it over the noise.

My teammates certainly do, because they're all laughing their asses off, but I can't care less. Let them laugh. I have my girl back and that's all that matters.

———

SCORING the first goal is me finding my footing, just the way Coach said I would.

The second goal is me getting back to the guy they hired me to be.

My first hat trick in nearly three years is me letting the pieces of my life come together again.

I know it's not solely because of Aspen—but that has to be part of it. It can't be a coincidence that when she's here I do better. I'm a professional. I've been doing this a lot longer than I've known her, but she fulfills parts of me I hadn't realized were empty.

Yeah, it's a stupid cliche, but I'm secure enough in my manhood to know the right person can make your life better.

That's all I'm thinking about as I talk to the press that's determined to get statements from me, let my teammates give me endless shit because they know my girlfriend is here, and desperately try to get clean in the shower.

Because I know what's going to happen in Cheryl's office.

In between apologies and groveling and proclamations of love.

Aspen is most vulnerable when I'm inside of her, and I'm going to be.

I practically skid out of the dressing room, and all but run down the hall to the elevator.

"Banks!" West calls out to me. "Where are you going?"

"I'll be back!" I yell over my shoulder.

I step off the elevator expecting to see her but she's not there, so I keep my head down as I race through the unfamiliar hallways, making a few wrong turns until I find the right place.

And…

There she is.

Leaning against the wall, her dark hair pillowed around her beautiful face.

I slow to a walk, suddenly a little nervous.

She told me she loved me just a couple of hours ago.

She's not still mad, is she?

"Hey, little spitfire."

"Hey, handsome."

"I have so many things to say to you," I say quietly as I approach her.

"Me too." She tilts up her face. "But first, you have to kiss me."

"I can do that." I drop my lips to hers, no longer in a frantic race to touch her.

Because I *am* touching her.

Reclaiming what's mine.

My woman, my baby, my life.

"I'm so sorry, little spitfire," I whisper against her mouth, pressing light kisses there, despite my need to devour her. "I have so much to explain but it wasn't because I don't love you."

"I know." She settles a cool hand against the side of my face. "Briar explained."

Of course she had, but…

"I should have been the one to explain. It was just…in the moment…" My voice trails because I can't quite explain the panic I felt. The fear of losing her the same way my dad lost my mom. The guilt. So many feelings hit me when she told me she was pregnant.

"Here's the thing," she says, searching my face intently. "You don't get to make solo decisions anymore. We're now a *we*, not a you or a me. If you're sad or scared or irritated, you have to talk to me. You can't just say something like, 'get rid of it' and leave."

"I know." I drop my forehead to hers. "I'm so fucking sorry. There are no words to adequately describe how sorry I am. How much I love you." I drop my hand and splay my fingers across her still-flat abdomen. "How excited I am to meet our little girl."

"Little girl?" She cocks her head curiously. "What makes you say that?"

"I don't know," I admit. "It's just a gut feeling."

"It's very early days," she says softly. "Miscarriages happen in about thirty percent of all pregnancies.

"The stats are that high?" I ask in surprise.

"Many pregnancies end before the woman even realizes it happens." She flushes. "I've been doing a little reading."

"I have to catch up," I admit.

"Not tonight." She winds her arms around my neck.

"So, what, exactly, are we doing *tonight*?" I ask playfully, resting my hands on her hips.

She reaches behind her and slowly turns the knob to open the door.

"It's our spot," she whispers, tugging me inside.

I kick the door shut behind us and quickly lock it.

Then she's in my arms and the rush of passion is simultaneous and explosive.

We've had great sex since we've been together, but now she's literally ripping my clothes off me. Buttons fly, her jeans are down around her ankles, my slacks are open but still on, and I scatter a handful of papers and pens as I set her on the desk.

Her tongue is so deep in my mouth I could probably swallow it, but all I'm thinking about is being inside of her.

We fumble around trying to get in position. The desk is low and she's on her back and her skinny jeans aren't coming off. Instead of fighting with them, I push her knees back toward her shoulders and plunge deep. A loud groan escapes her and for a split second, neither of us move. It feels so good being bare inside of her, watching as she wiggles impatiently for me to move.

"Banks, please!" Her voice is a combination of plea and command, and that's all it takes.

I pull out to the tip and then drive deep.

Over and over, listening to her wailing my name.

"That's my girl," I growl. "Tell me you love me, little spitfire."

"I love you!" she cries.

I want to say it back, but I can't because the pleasure

zipping down my spine prevents me from doing anything but thrusting long, hard, and deep. I need to get her there, but it seems to happen all at once. I feel her pussy spasming around me, hear my name on her tongue, and then I'm completely lost in everything that is Aspen.

Her body, her voice, how it feels to be connected, body and soul.

"Fuck!" I drive into her one last time and then we're both completely still.

"Holy shit." She lets out a shaky little laugh long moments later. "Am I still alive?"

"Maybe." I want to stay here like this forever, but we can't.

Eventually, I pull out and grab a handful of tissues before helping her sit up.

"You've never come like that before," I comment with a laugh. "Is that a pregnancy thing?"

"I've never been pregnant before, so I have no idea." She looks around as she cleans up and I do the same, noting the scattered papers, the toppled pencil cup, the desk that's been fucked halfway across the room. "We made a mess."

"Aww." I make a sarcastic sympathy sound. "Poor Cheryl has some cleaning up to do."

"That's gross!" she protests. But she's laughing.

"Tough shit. She's a bitch." I do a little cleaning up of my own before tucking my dick back in then zipping up my pants. "You realize there's no hiding what we just did since"—I gesture down at myself—"I'm now missing four buttons."

She looks at my dress shirt and bites her lip. "Sorry?"

"You are so not sorry," I say, shaking my head.

"I'll make it up to you." She moves against my chest, and I wrap my arms around her.

"I love you, Aspen," I murmur, smoothing down her messy hair. "I hope you know that. Almost since the first time I saw you."

"I love you too." Her mouth kicks up, hazel eyes filled with teasing. "Maybe not quite that long, but almost." She softens. "No one's ever taken care of me the way you do."

I cup her jaw, holding her gaze, needing her to know how much I mean this. "And I give you my word I always will. What happened when you told me you were pregnant will *never* happen again. I swear it on our baby."

"I know."

I flick up my eyebrows in question.

She smirks. "Because Briar will kill you if it does."

I throw back my head and laugh. "Come on, little spitfire. Let's get out of here before we get caught."

She smooths down the jersey and wipes her hands on her jeans. "I need a restroom."

"I have to go back to the dressing room and find another shirt."

We're laughing as I unlock the door and peek out to make sure the coast is clear.

She slides her hand into mine and we've just closed the door behind us when Cheryl comes around the corner. We all freeze but then I smile. Wide.

Cheryl doesn't move, her face a mask of confusion and irritation.

Tough shit, lady.

This is what you get for being a cunt to my girl.

This is *my* arena, not yours.

"Hey, Cheryl." I sling my arm over Aspen's shoulder. "This office is kind of a mess. You might need to clean it up." I draw my woman forward. "Come on, babe."

We walk down the hall and manage not to burst out laughing until we're in the elevators.

"Did you see her face?" Aspen is laughing so hard she's doubled over.

"I did. Karma can be a bitch, you know."

"I guess so." She gazes up at me, her eyes dancing with amusement.

And love.

With a touch of forever.

God, I love this woman.

My woman.

EPILOGUE

Aspen

THERE'S a Christmas explosion at Briar's house—presents have been opened, Frankie's play kitchen has been assembled and all the food and pots and pans and other accouterments are properly placed.

Oh, and the drum set Dash bought her—much to Royal's consternation—is set up in the corner.

Next to the little hockey net and mini-sticks that are my and Banks's contribution to the chaos—along with a promise to pay for any necessary dental work.

Our Connect 4 battle is over, with Banks being the ultimate winner, and Royal's the winning uncle to put Frankie to bed.

Uncle Royal is still the favorite.

Smiling, I sink back into the couch cushions, knowing we've now entered the portion of the evening where food coma is prevalent and naps are creeping in.

Case in point?

Mrs. X is sleeping in a cozy armchair, wearing her luxurious new robe and slippers from Briar and the guys, covered in a blanket printed with Patrick Stewart's face (my contribution).

"You know," I say, sighing in contentment. Briar's at my side, her red hair piled on top of her head, glasses perched on her nose. Her cheeks are pink from the copious amounts of Gamebreakers she and the men have consumed tonight, and she's entered sloth phase too.

"I know?" she prompts, draining her glass and leaning forward to deposit it on the coffee table.

"I know that those"—I nod at the empty cup—"are named after some concoction that Colt came up with—"

A flash of pain washes over her face.

"Sorry," I whisper, squeezing her arm. "We don't have to talk about it," I add. "I just wanted to know where the name Gamebreakers came from."

The pain leaves, and her mouth curves up as she bumps her shoulder against mine. "Now *that's* a fun story."

"What's a fun story?" Dash asks, dropping onto the couch next to me. Not a surprise, but my father hadn't taken my dismissal of him and his job offer well. He spent the weeks after Banks and I got back together making his displeasure known—at least until Dash stepped in. I don't know what kind of magic the bodyguard and security firm owner has—or maybe what kind of blackmail-worthy dirt he was able to dig up on my family—but my dad finally got the message and left me alone.

Dash lifts his hand, his eyes coming to mine for permission, and when I nod, he lightly touches the barely there curve of my belly before he focuses on his sister and lifts an eyebrow in question.

"Where the name Gamebreakers came from," she supplies.

"Now that *is* a good story," he agrees, slinging his arm along the back of the couch.

"With all this build-up," Banks mutters, stepping over Dash's legs and shoving himself between his friend and me, forcing Dash against the arm of the sofa. Smiling even as Dash scowls, he settles his hand over my belly and kisses the side of my cheek. "You'd think it was some sort of legend."

"Come on, now," Atlas says, winking at me as he leans over the coffee table and hands me a mug of hot chocolate—my favorite indulgence these days, "we *were* legends when we played together."

"No other team could stop us when we were on the ice," Royal agrees as he comes into the room. Apparently, Frankie was as tired as we are and went to bed easily. Or it could be speedier than normal because he's been off tonight, quieter than usual. A little surly.

The shadows in his eyes are darker than I've ever seen.

Dash nods. "Yeah, clearly Banks here"—he claps my man on the shoulder—"is the only one of us good enough to go to the show, but there was something special when the five of us were out on the ice together."

"Always the top line," Royal says.

"Crushing our rivals," Dash chimes in.

"Breaking records," Banks murmurs, winking at me.

"National champions," Atlas adds. "Three times over."

"So they were stopped at least once," Briar stage whispers, her smile teasing.

Dash throws a pillow at her.

She giggles as she swats it away. "The truth is they were good, but all five of them together were something special. They could make or *break* a game."

The quiet that follows her words tells me that I'm not the only one thinking that special wasn't just on the ice.

"Well, I think what you've all managed to build since then is pretty special too."

Banks's chest expands on a heavy breath, his fingers flexing on my belly, and his kiss to my temple is gentle. "I think *you're* special, little spitfire."

"That's because he's on his fifth Gamebreaker," Dash teases.

"And also because he gets to sleep with you," Atlas says dryly.

I narrow my eyes at the billionaire. "You're lucky you've bought my adoration with a never-ending supply of hot chocolate."

He grins, holding his glass up in my direction in salute. "And that supply won't end, thus ensuring your endless devotion."

He's not wrong.

He's also a deviously smart businessman.

But if it ensures that I have hot chocolate, I'm in.

Royal just gives me a small smile, as though to say, "You're okay, kid."

I want to hug him. Me, the rabid raccoon with ten-foot concrete walls topped with barbed wire, wants to wrap my arms around him and tell him that everything will be all right.

But…not yet.

I know in my heart that he's not ready.

Briar bumps me with her shoulder again. "You've made it more special."

She means it. I can see it in her eyes, hear it in her voice, feel it in the love coming at me from all sides of this room.

"Dammit!" I snap.

"What?" Banks asks, hand flexing again, worry in his tone.

But Briar gets it in an instant. "Pregnancy hormones," she explains.

I nod, frantically fanning my face with one hand, thankful when she takes the mug from my other and sets it on the coffee table.

And then I'm pulled even closer into the warmth of Banks's big, strong body, his arms wrapping around me, his voice in my ear. "I love you, little spitfire."

I sniff, feel a tear slip down my cheek.

Alone at night, crying in my bed, no hope for a different future…to *this*.

Banks holding me and Briar passing me tissues and Atlas shoving a cookie at me, like the sight of my tears undoes him. Dash cracking a joke, getting me to laugh, and Royal quietly coming over to us, a silent presence perched on the coffee table.

There but separate.

But *there*.

And it means everything.

These people mean everything to me.

"I love you guys," I rasp.

Silence.

A few cleared throats, some eyes coming to mine and then away. Briar squeezes my hand and takes a tissue for herself.

"Dammit!"

Startled, I look up at Banks, who's scowling.

"What's your problem, man?" Dash snaps.

Mischief in his green eyes. "Do you know how long it took for her to tell me that?" He tosses up a hand. "And you guys get it, just like that?"

I giggle and swat at his chest.

Dash blows on his knuckles, buffs them on his shoulder. "That's because we're awesome."

"And we bring her hot chocolate," Atlas says.

"And can sing without sounding like I'm actively murdering kittens," Royal adds. A shrug. "Well, *I* can. These other losers are another story."

"You can't sing?" I ask Banks, loving that I've let him in, that I get to learn these little parts of him as our relationship grows.

Banks glares at Royal. "I can sing perfectly fine!"

Royal smirks and glances at me. "*Fine* is a gross exaggeration."

"Well, then," Mrs. X interjects, apparently having woken from her catnap. "Time to prove him wrong."

"I—uh—" Banks stammers.

A clap of her hands. "Come on now. Don't be a baby. Let's hear it." She winks at me, as though to say, "Gotta keep these boys in check."

"I'll grab the karaoke machine," Briar says gleefully, popping up to her feet and all but running from the room, Banks taking off after her.

"Briar—" he calls.

I push to my feet and cross over to Mrs. X.

"You good, honey?" she asks when I perch on the arm of her chair.

And maybe it's the pregnancy hormones—or maybe it's that I've realized how much I had when I thought I had nothing.

"I love you," I say. "You were the only thing that kept me moving forward."

"No, honey." She takes my hand. "That was all you. I just saw a bright, beautiful girl who was hurt but deserved the world." Her other palm lifts, presses to my cheek. "And I wanted to watch her soar. Because I knew it was only a matter of time, honey. Only a matter of time before you found all of this."

"Dammit," I murmur.

"It's the pregnancy hormones," she says lightly.

But it's not.

Of course it's not.

She wraps her arms around me, hugs me tightly. "And I love you too."

I'm open and vulnerable, exposed and on display…

And I've never *ever* felt safer—

"Here."

I pull out of Mrs. X's hold and see Atlas holding up another mug of hot chocolate.

And I grin.

Tears are the billionaire's kryptonite.

"Better," he mutters, turning away and helping Briar set up the karaoke machine. Royal's pulled a pair of earplugs from somewhere and is hastily shoving them in. Dash is still reclined on the couch, socked feet on the coffee table, smirk in place, clearly ready for the show.

And Banks…

He's grabbing the microphone like the competitive athlete he is.

He's opening his mouth.

And Royal's right—

My man can do a lot of things, almost anything…

But he really can't sing.

———

WE HOPE you loved ICEBREAKER as much as we loved writing Banks and Aspen's happily ever after! If you want to find out who falls next…don't miss HEARTBREAKER! **He's the grumpy, reclusive rock star who's sworn off love who never expects to fall for the sunny, country princess with a heart of gold. But when he does…nothing is going to stop him from keeping her forever.**

Preorder   Icebreaker   here   >
https://geni.us/IcebreakerEFKM

GAMEBREAKERS

Icebreaker
Heartbreaker
Dealbreaker
Rulebreaker

ABOUT THE AUTHORS

USA Today bestselling author, Elise Faber, loves chocolate, Star Wars, Harry Potter, and hockey (the order depending on the day and how well her team — the Sharks! — are playing). She and her husband also play as much hockey as they can squeeze into their schedules, so much so that their typical date night is spent on the ice. Elise is the mom to two exuberant boys and lives in Northern California. Connect with her in her Facebook group, the Fabinators or find more information about her books at www.elisefaber.com.

facebook.com/elisefaberauthor
amazon.com/author/elisefaber
bookbub.com/profile/elise-faber
instagram.com/elisefaber
tiktok.com/@elisefaberauthor
goodreads.com/elisefaber
patreon.com/EliseFaber

ABOUT THE AUTHORS

USA Today Bestselling author Kat Mizera was born in Miami Beach with a healthy dose of wanderlust. She's lived from coast to coast, and everywhere in between, but home is wherever her family is.

A devoted mom and wife to her wonderful and supportive husband (Kevin) and two amazing boys (Nick and Max), Kat loves to travel the globe with her adventurous, hockey loving family. Greece is at the top of that list. She hopes to one day retire there, spending her days writing books on the beach.

Kat is former freelance sports writer who now writes steamy hockey romance about her favorite fictional teams, the Las Vegas Sidewinders and the Alaska Blizzard. The library of novels she's penned also include sexy contemporary stories about baseball stars, alpha sex club owners, special forces heroes, rock stars and royalty. Regardless of genre, her books about bad boys with hearts of gold will steal your breath, rock your world and melt your heart.

WHERE TO FOLLOW KAT:
www.katmizera.com
Kat's Private Facebook Group
https://bit.ly/KatMizeraFBGroup

f facebook.com/authorkatmizera
instagram.com/katmizera